Accidental Fiancé

A Single Dad Fake Engagement Romance

Mia Mara

Copyright © 2024 by Mia Mara
All rights reserved.
No part of this book may be reproduced in any form or by any electronic or mechanical means, including information storage and retrieval systems, without written permission from the author, except for the use of brief quotations in a book review.

**Fake engaged to my best friend by accident?
Oh, this is about to get hot...**

I secretly crushed on Maggie in high school and then lost touch.
Since then I've gone through a messy divorce and earned my stripes as a single dad.

But at our high school reunion, Maggie drops a bombshell:
She blurts out to everyone that we're engaged?!?
She panicked. I get it. Who wouldn't, with those mean girls watching?

So I did what any decent guy would do—I played along.
And damn did we *play*... if you know what I mean.

Now we're fake engaged, and since I'm a single dad with no nanny and she's in need of a little rescue, we figure,
why not?

But moving in together? That's when things get interesting.
Pretending to be madly in love? Easy.
Pretending those sparks between us aren't real? Not so much.

Now, I'm stuck wondering...

Can we pull this off without ruining our friendship?
Or am I about to fall *accidentally* in love with my fake fiancée?

He smelled the best of any boy in our class, but I never had the nerve to ask what cologne he wore. Considering I'd never spoken to him in the thirteen years of school we'd had together, asking about his cologne felt a tad bit awkward.

It was never any one boy who had my complete attention because none of them had the whole package, and if I couldn't get everything I wanted, then what was the point of picking one? I didn't date in high school, and I'd only had a few boyfriends since, but it never went anywhere serious. Thus, my date for the Saturday night reunion was Nora.

Where the hell is she?

The busy hotel lobby had beige, patterned carpet, gleaming dark hardwood, and crystal chandeliers that glowed warm yellow light. It was lovely, and far too high-class for our school. I wasn't sure why the reunion committee selected this hotel when the Rosewood High School's gym would have likely garnered as many attendees. RHS was a lot of things, but classy wasn't one of them.

"Maggie Bryant? Is that you?"

There were voices in the world that could lock up every muscle in my body and send my hair on end.

Chloe Foster had one of them.

It wasn't particularly shrill or cloying, and it wasn't necessarily the voice itself that made me react so viscerally. It was... Chloe herself. Relentless fakeness clung to every syllable that came out of her mouth.

I knew what I would find before I even turned around—a skeletal white woman with long, wavy blonde hair and bright, but somehow lifeless, blue eyes. Her white sleeveless jumpsuit clung to her frame giving her the illusion of curves, her heels offering the only color in her outfit—bright red stilettos that she seemed to be struggling to keep her balance in. Her makeup was perfect; sharp lines and perfect

Chapter 1

Maggie

I had only made it inside of the lobby, but I had come too far to turn back now. It had taken me all day to work up the courage to come to the reunion. Nora agreeing to come with me helped, though it wasn't much of a favor, really. It was her reunion too.

Had it really been fifteen years since high school?

It was hard to believe. It felt like a lifetime ago, yet it also felt like I was in Mr. Wedig's geometry class just yesterday, ignoring him while staring at the freckles on Victor Clyburn's thick neck. It was sun-exposed thanks to his short brown hair and too much time on the football field. He was the kicker. He was cute and a great distraction from isosceles triangles.

No chance in hell he remembered me.

Not that I cared. I had dozens of little crushes like that in high school. They weren't even on the actual person; they were focused more on certain aspects of that person. I wondered what Victor's freckles would taste like, or the feel of Brian Hannigan's pecs, or what it would be like to wake up with my sheets smelling like Austin Graves.

hues applied with precision, from her immaculate eyebrows to her sultry lips. Every inch of her was designer artistry, and while I admired the look, the idea of copying it was laughable. If I wore anything like that, I'd feel like a little girl playing dress up in Mommy's clothes.

I had no patience for intricate makeup, and my clothes, though decent enough, were chosen for comfort over style. My outfit consisted of a simple blue dress with straps wide enough to wear a real bra and cute black ballet flats. My makeup was minimal and in neutral hues. I had, however, treated myself to a new necklace for the event—a silver chain with a blue opal pendant that hung at the top of my cleavage. It was a splurge, but after I'd seen it in the window, I had to have it. When I tried it on, it felt like a talisman, something that could give me the strength to get through the night.

Right now, I might as well have been naked for all the protection it offered me. I was trapped, facing off with the person who had made my public education a nightmare.

Seriously, where the hell was Nora?

I plastered on a fake smile, hoping to make this quick. "Chloe, right?"

She held up her black and diamond clutch with her name tag on it. "In the flesh. It's so good to see you!" She came in for a hug I didn't want but she gave it to me anyway. I nearly gagged on her vanilla perfume. "Can you believe it's been fifteen years?"

I shrugged. "Yeah, I know."

"I was just inside, catching up with some of the girls we used to hang out with. You remember Emma and Harmony, right? And they were talking about how we never see you around town anymore. Why is that?"

Because I have made it an art avoiding the three of you.

"Oh, you know. Big city. Different lives, different circles of friends."

"That makes sense, I guess. I've been positively swamped between volunteering at the historical society and running the reunion. I—"

"You picked the location for the reunion?" I cut her off.

"Well, of course." She smirked. "Did you think we'd be one of those low-rent reunions at our gym? God forbid."

"God forbid," I parroted back, fighting an eye roll.

Her smirk became an annoyed grimace as she glanced around. "This hotel wasn't even the best one on the list, but the committee said I had to reign in the spending. They limited me to only one ice sculpture inside the ballroom, but if I had my way, there'd be three."

"Oh." I had no idea what to say about that.

She sighed before saying, "Some people don't appreciate good taste. I thought you might come with your girlfriend. Did you two break up?" Her face turned bright in almost a mocking way as she said the words.

"Huh?"

"You know, you and that snarky redhead you used to hang out with. We called her Skinny, but I can't remember her real name."

"Nora Skinner." She hated it when people called her Skinny. Not that she wasn't, she was. But to her, it meant they hadn't bothered to learn her real name and they were making fun of her body.

"Right. So, are you two not together anymore?"

"No, we're—"

"Oh, that's too bad. We could have used some diversity here tonight."

"Chloe, we were never together like that. She's my best friend. Not my girlfriend."

4

Those too-blue eyes flickered over my dress before meeting my gaze. "Right. Sure." She leaned forward, her volume dropping. "She said no, huh? That's too bad."

"I'm not into women!"

"No need to get testy about it. People don't care about that kind of thing anymore, Maggie. It's no big deal if you are."

"I'm not!"

Her perfect lips upturned into the very picture of faux understanding and real condescension. "Of course, you're not. But if you were to change your mind, there are a few women here tonight I could introduce you to."

She knew she was irritating me and that ignoring me would be a favor, a gift from her. I saw it all over her face—that sadistic amusement. Her cruel smile gave her away. And if I made a big deal about it, I knew she'd find a way to make me feel like an idiot.

I desperately searched for my patient and calm tone when really all I wanted to do was scream. "I went to school with them, too, Chloe. I don't need you to introduce me to anyone. And that's not even the point. I'm straight."

"Then you must have a boyfriend. Did he come with you tonight?"

"No."

"What kind of a boyfriend doesn't go to his girlfriend's class reunion with her? Are you breaking up with him? You should. That's unacceptable. You deserve better, Maggie."

Oh. My. God. I was quickly losing my patience and it was impossible to not raise my voice at her. I just needed her to listen. "Chloe. I'm here on my own." *Thanks to Nora.* "Any other questions?"

Her lower lip pouted a little while she simultaneously thrust her tits out and slumped her shoulders. It was the same pose she used to give the male teachers to convince them to bump her grade up a letter. Sexy, sad Chloe. They always fell for it and kept her grades up so she could stay on the cheer squad.

"No need to be snippy. I thought we were catching up."

I refused to play into it and changed the topic. "Are you seeing anyone? Married? Anything?"

"You insist that you're straight and then ask me out? Talk about mixed signals—"

"Just making conversation, not a proposal."

"Mm-hmm. I date a few people here and there. Never got married though. I like to keep my options open. Life is too short to be tied down, you know?" Her eyes narrowed ever so slightly when she said the words, and now that they were hanging in the air, I wondered what had gone wrong for her in the romance department.

I'd always thought she'd get married, have kids, get divorced, and become an alimony ex-wife. She was a serial monogamist in high school; she always had a boyfriend, including a backup boyfriend, ready to go. But Chloe Foster, single after thirty? I did not have that on my bingo card.

"Have you—"

"We should go inside so you can get your nametag and catch up with everyone," she said as she looped her arm through mine, forcing me to go in without making a fuss about it. I was trapped by my bully.

Neither option held any appeal, and by everyone I was sure she meant Harmony and Emma. I reluctantly went with her, not wanting to draw any unwanted attention. As much as I loathed Harmony Piedmont, Emma Gonzalez and I had shared a strained friendship back in the day, and admittedly, I was curious about her.

Still, each step toward the convention hall took a Herculean effort. I had hoped to catch up with Emma while having Nora by my side, in case she had gone full mean girl in the years since we'd seen each other. Nora acted as my guard dog—when people were rude she gave it right back to them and more. Nora had better have an amazing excuse for not being here, and that amazing excuse had better not sound like, "I had to work."

Perhaps I had come to rely on her a little too much in the guard dog department. I didn't have time to think about it though, not with Chloe speed walking us into the reunion, leaving me to wonder how she managed it in those heels.

The ballroom had been set up with a DJ, a dance floor, tall tables and a full bar with several bar stools, a sign-up table near the doors. Colored lights pulsed to the music, and a few dozen couples danced while others mingled.

As I signed in and grabbed my nametag, Chloe stood next to me, hands on her hips, staring around the room. Lindsey Panier, the nametag table attendant, bit her bottom lip as she watched her. From what I remembered of Lindsey, she was the nervous sort, always scared about her grades and keeping her clothes clean at recess.

Chloe asked, "Lindsey, what did we agree on about the decorations?"

"Flashy, but classy."

"Then why are the streamers hanging at the wrong angles?"

"Wrong angles? For streamers?" I asked. Was there such a thing?

"I hung them how you told me to."

"Come on, Lindsey, we both know better than that. If you had hung them how I told you to, then I wouldn't be asking about them now," she replied, a predatory smile on her mouth. "Find the ladder and fix them, 'kay?"

"Of course. Right away." Lindsey took off before Chloe could nag her some more.

"The streamers are fine, Chloe. No one cares about that kind of thing."

She took my hand in both of hers, patting the back of it, her fake, syrupy voice cutting through me as she spoke. "It must be nice not to care how things look, but some of us do, and since I'm in charge of the reunion, I want it to be perfect."

If I stayed around her much longer, I might chew through my tongue. "What exactly is that supposed to mean?"

She waved over my shoulder, ignoring me entirely. "Harmony! Over here!"

No, no, no. "I'm going to grab a glass of champagne..."

"Absolutely not! You don't want wrinkles, do you?" Chloe said, whisking me toward Harmony.

Emma stood next to Harmony, and I instantly realized this was going to be a lot to swallow without liquid help. "Wait, you expect me to get through this entire reunion completely sober?"

"You were always so witty."

She thinks I'm kidding. "Yeah. That's me. The funny girl."

"No, that was your girlfriend, Skinny. You're the witty one. It's probably why you two made such a good couple." I jerked my arm free of her grasp, giving her my best forced customer service smile and patient tone. "Chloe, if I have to deal with your condescension and snide comments all night, then I'm going to require a drink. So, bar first, then

Harmony and Emma, 'kay?" I even added a little head tilt to soften my rudeness.

She studied my face for a beat then laughed. "Skinny made you funnier than when you were in high school."

As she ushered me deeper into the reunion, I glanced longingly at the door. *If Nora isn't the next person to walk through that door, I'm running out of here.*

A quick escape was half the reason I wore flats in the first place.

Chapter 2

Julian

I pulled my car up to the valet, gave him my keys, then strolled into The Manchester Hotel. It was one of the nicer hotels in the city, and whenever consultants visited from abroad, my executive assistant often arranged for them to stay there. According to Inga, they had the smoothest sheets on the comfiest beds. I never asked how she knew that. No sense in creating HR drama for my company.

The interior was classy and polished. The front desk staff politely directed me to the location of the reunion after giving me my key card and sending my luggage to my room. So far, I felt good about my out-of-town consultants staying at The Manchester. As soon as I reached the doors to the ballroom, I stopped and pulled my phone out. I had to make a call before I went inside.

I stepped out of the way of a few revelers so I didn't block the door as I waited for her to pick up. Piper's sleepy voice answered, "Hello?"

It made me instantly smile. "Hey, Pip."

"Hi, Pop."

Accidental Fiancé

My daughter had been dealing with night terrors lately, and the doctor's theory was that her circadian rhythm was off. She suggested I allow her to set her own bedtimes at her own pace instead of me setting them for her. Which meant her babysitter had to cooperate with Pip's timetable as well.

Rena was a good babysitter—one of the best we'd had, actually—but she was still a teenager, and she let slip that she was going to study for a test after Piper went to bed. I was calling to check on her as much as Piper. "Rena getting you ready for bed?"

"I'm in bed now."

It was only just after nine. "Did you want to go to bed now?"

"I'm tired."

"Did Rena tell you that you should go to bed?"

She giggled. "I really am tired, Pop."

"Okay, then. I want you to sleep well, have sweet dreams, and remember I love you very much."

She said it back and added, "Dream about cake."

"Why cake?"

"So that you have sweet dreams." She giggled after she said it.

I couldn't help but smile. Piper was only four, but she was smart and witty. "Alright, Pip. Cake dreams for you too then."

The line went dead, and a wave of sadness hit me. It was always that way whenever I hung up with her. But as I heard the beats of old hits from high school pulsing through the wall, I allowed myself to get distracted and threw open the doors to the ballroom.

School colors haunted the massive space, rose and gray dripping from the ceiling, the chairs, the tables and the bar. Confetti stuck to the chilled flutes of cheap champagne and littered the floor. I'd always hated our school colors, but they went with the school's theme since it was Rosewood High School.

Named for the woody stems of the rose farms that were our suburb's lifeblood, RHS was nothing if not a living, breathing theme. Our school mascot was a rose, perhaps the dullest of all school mascots throughout the history of man. The main rivals of our school had a tiger, a devil, and a lightning bolt for their mascots. I had always been embarrassed to be a rose. We were teased often and we never stood a chance.

But it wasn't all bad. The fact we had a historically long losing streak didn't stop us from having school spirit and good times under the Friday night lights for football games. That was the kind of people we were—no matter how many times life kicked us down, we picked ourselves up and tried again.

Tonight, however, wasn't about all the times we fell down. A reunion was about seeing old friends and reconnecting. After the hell I'd been through over the past two years I could use that.

I signed in and took my nametag, affixing it to my suit lapel. Lindsey Panier smiled up at me. "I didn't think you'd show up."

"Why is that?"

"Don't you usually spend your weekends yachting or something?"

I snorted out a laugh. "Not generally, no."

"That's what it says online."

"Life on the internet and real life rarely intersect."

"Well, we're glad you could make it. Have a good time."

"I will, thanks." The line for the bar was mercifully short, and once I had my whiskey in hand, I scanned the crowd for Tim Drake and Victor Clyburn. We'd lost touch over the years, and the older I got, the more I learned the old adage was true—it was harder to make friends as adults.

Tim stood with a woman I didn't recognize and two men I knew from back in the day but couldn't quite remember their names. I was dying to know how things turned out for Tim, and while I could have looked him up, I knew better than to trust the internet for information.

Tim had been a straight-A student, dual-enrolled in college courses as he finished his high school diploma early. Considering he graduated with the class before ours thanks to all that hard work, I was surprised to learn he'd be here, but I was just as glad to see him. "Hey, Tim."

"Julian Black, holy shit, you actually came!" he said, yanking me into a bear hug. Tim's blond hair had gone a little thin on top, but otherwise, he still looked like the guy I knew from back in the day. Taller than me, fit, and smiling. "This is Andra, my wife."

"Nice to meet you." I shook her hand. She was pretty and at least ten years older than the rest of us, with chin-length brown hair and green eyes that crinkled when she smiled. By the depth of those crinkles, she smiled a lot. "Did you two meet in college?"

"You could say that," she said with a shy smirk.

Tim explained, "Andra was my advisor."

"He always had a thing for older women," one of the other guys teased. His nametag read, Will Jones. The second man I didn't recognize was Lewis Penn. Thank God for nametags.

Andra was unfazed by Will's teasing. "That works for me. I've always liked younger men."

We had a laugh, and I asked, "So, Tim, what are you doing these days?"

"Not much."

"Not much?" Andra asked, astounded at his answer. She beamed. "He's the lead researcher on a project that could end world hunger."

"Oh?"

He shook his head, smiling at her. "She's overstating it. We're manipulating the genetic code in certain grains to be able to withstand drought, flood, and high wind conditions to help them survive climate change in order to maintain production while we get our weather back under control."

Lewis tapped Tim on his chest with the back of his hand. "Sounds like ending world hunger to me, man."

"See?" Andra insisted, still grinning at her husband.

"What about you, Lewis?" I asked.

He smiled. "Don't follow sports, do you?"

"Not really. Are you an athlete?" He looked like he wouldn't qualify for a bowling league, but what did I know? I wasn't much of a sports fan outside of high school.

"Nah, I'm an announcer for ESPN."

"That's huge! Congratulations!"

He shrugged. "It's not ending world hunger but it's a fun living."

Andra asked, "And Will, what about you?"

"I'm a vet."

"Thank you for your service."

"Sorry, veterinarian. No thanks needed."

She giggled, then whispered into Tim's ear, turning his cheeks pink. He'd always been too innocent for his own good. I was glad to see he was with someone who clearly appreciated that about him.

He cleared his throat. "Uh, I think I need to take her dancing. Gentlemen, excuse us." He took her hand and led her to the dance floor.

"They make a good couple," I noted. "How come no one asked what I do?"

Will and Lewis exchanged a glance and laughed. Will asked, "Are you kidding?"

"Everyone knows what you do," Lewis added.

"We didn't think you'd be able to come here and make time for us peasants."

"Why wouldn't I come here?"

"You run a multi-billion-dollar medical company," Will said. "I would think that takes up most of your time. Black-Aster is one of the biggest companies in the market, hell, I think you make all of the products in my medicine cabinet."

"And my shower," Lewis mumbled.

I shrugged. "Okay, sure. I'm a busy guy, but that isn't even our best stuff."

"How's that?" Will asked.

"Our best products come from our prosthetics and mobility devices. That's the shit I'm proud of. The products in your bathrooms and medicine cabinets pays the bills for helping to develop all of that, so thanks for keeping us in business."

"What do you mean?"

"Products for the disabled community have a lot of overhead. R&D, customization, training, materials—all of that is pricy and the backend cost of those products runs high. Since we try to provide them at the lowest cost possible, those costs are offset by the shampoo, the body wash, the boner pills, and everything else we make. The more of that stuff you buy, the cheaper we can make custom prosthetic legs for veterans."

"I'm a humanitarian and even I didn't know that," Lewis joked.

Beyond the crowd I spotted Victor Clyburn. As I

started to wave him over, a flash of teal blue caught the corner of my eye before the rest of the package, and I couldn't look away.

Long, curly brown hair draped down her back, and the dress clung to her round ass. My breath caught in my chest. I would have known that ass and that hair anywhere. She pivoted to her left, and there stood Maggie Bryant, stuck in a sea of awful, a forced fake smile on her face. It wasn't the kind of smile the others wore. This one was made out of uncomfortable desperation.

Hell hadn't frozen over so there was no possible way she had become friends with Chloe Foster, Emma Gonzalez, or Harmony Piedmont, no matter how many years had passed since they used to torment her. There were forgivable things in the world, and then there were the things they had done to Maggie.

She was trapped, and just like in high school, I had to help her. "Excuse me. I see someone I need to catch up with." I left before they could say a word.

Chapter 3

Maggie

"Emma, Harmony. Hi." I knew the walls weren't actually closing in on me, but that did nothing to stop the feeling.

Emma Gonzalez was still one of the prettiest people I'd ever met in person. Jet black curly hair that sat perfectly at her shoulders the way I wished my curls would. Whenever my hair was cut short like hers, it just frizzed out instead of laying tame. A long time ago, I might have asked her for the secret to well-managed curls, but those days were long gone.

When she first came to Rosewood, we were friends for about two weeks. But then she figured out I was not on the top tier of the social hierarchy when Chloe came around to make fun of my discount store notebook. Emma and I drifted apart after that, but she was always kinder to me than any of the so-called cool kids. Not kind enough to stand up for me, but she never piled on like the others did.

Her smile was genuine when she spoke. "Hey, Maggie."

"Maggie, hi," Harmony said, brown eyes glowing with malice. "Heard about your little bakery. That's too bad, honey. I'm sure it would have been a big success."

All thoughts dried up in my head. My voice went hoarse. "What?"

She shrugged, smirking at Chloe. "No secrets among friends."

Chloe smiled. "That's right, Maggie. No secrets. So, was it for the insurance money? You can tell us."

My head swirled. I wasn't even sure what she was asking. "I don't... huh?"

"Well, I mean, come on. Fires don't start by accident."

Emma said nothing. She just sipped her champagne and looked uncomfortable.

The fire had been one of the worst days of my life. All that work. All that hope. The freedom my bakery had offered was gone. Every drop of my sweat and tears couldn't put out that raging fire, no matter how hard I tried to stop it. I stood there, crying with a garden hose, hoping that somehow it would be enough after the extinguishers had been exhausted.

The firefighters said they were lucky to put it out before it spread to the buildings next door. Even now, I could still smell the smoke. Flour had a distinct smell when burning. Kind of flat and sour. Not quite like bread, but almost. These days, burnt toast smells like cremated dreams.

It had only been a few months since I'd lost my bakery, and I had been struggling financially ever since. But I couldn't tell them that. Why give them more ammunition? I was already the butt of their jokes.

Still, I tried to find my voice again. "Flour is... it's flammable. And combustible. When you see flour puffing around a bakery at three in the morning during deliveries, that's the most vulnerable time. When the bags are being dragged in it's almost impossible to keep the flour from leaking out. It's too fine. So, it ends up hanging in the air.

And when it's suspended in the air like that, all it takes is the wrong spark at the wrong moment, and there goes your dreams."

Chloe's wild stare darted over my face. "And I'm sure the fat insurance payment made up for that, right?"

"No," I rasped. "It didn't."

She clicked her tongue at me. "You were always so dramatic, Maggie."

"I need a drink," I said, starting for the bar.

But she draped her arm around my shoulders, stopping me. "You don't need any more wrinkles. Stay here. You'll thank me later. Anyway, I've already told you about my selfless volunteering. Emma is also giving back, in her own little way."

Maybe talking to Emma would take some of the attention off of me. "What are you doing?"

"Teaching English. At RHS, actually."

"Oh. Um, congratulations." *Great. Just what the school needs. Mean girl teachers.*

"I love it. Seeing kids improving their critical thinking skills through literary analysis..." A dreamy look appeared in her eyes, and suddenly the ache in my chest doubled.

I remembered the way professional pride felt, and I missed it so badly that I could have bawled right then and there.

"It's the best feeling," she went on. "Shaping young minds, knowing I'm making my mark on the next generation of thinkers—"

"I'd hardly say you're shaping minds," Chloe cut in, chuckling. "You're a high school English teacher, Emma. Calm down. You're not curing cancer."

Emma gave a tight smile to Chloe, and I wondered whether she thought sitting at the popular kids' table in high school was worth this. As much as I had envied her back in the day, I was grateful for my outcast status. I couldn't imagine putting up with Chloe by choice as an adult.

Wait. Isn't that exactly what I'm doing right now? Screw this. What would Nora do? Think. I was done being steamrolled by Chloe, and I hated seeing her do it to anyone else, even if we weren't friends. "Emma, you look like you could use another glass of champagne."

"I just got this one—"

I snatched it from her hand and downed the thing in one shot, before handing it back. "Nope, you need another. Let's go to the bar."

She laughed. "Oh. Okay."

Once I took the lead, Harmony and Chloe followed, Chloe whining about calories and wrinkles the whole time. How had she made it this far in life without someone teaching her to be better? I could never understand that. Maybe her parents tried, or maybe they were worse.

From the urge to demonstrate good manners for Chloe, I asked Harmony, "What are you doing these days?"

"I'm working in pharmaceuticals."

Chloe laughed. "You're an office manager, Harm."

"And a part-time pharma rep," she insisted. "It counts."

We ordered drinks, and even Chloe got a white wine spritzer, much to my surprise. The four of us strolled back to where we'd been standing before—a table against the middle of the far wall. I asked Emma and Harmony, "So, are you two seeing any—"

"Enough about them," Chloe interrupted me. "Who wants to dance?"

I hated dancing. "Yeah, no, I think I'm gonna go—"

"You can't go yet," Emma cut me off. "You just got here."

"Sunk-cost fallacy," I countered. "Leaving a situation is always valid, no matter how much time you've spent in it."

"Come on, stay. They haven't even done trivia yet and I know you'll be great at it. Did you check out the memory wall?" She pointed to a display I hadn't even noticed.

"No, Chloe pretty much wrangled me the minute I arrived."

"Speaking of wrangled," Chloe cackled. "Do you remember when we left a cowbell in your locker?"

Harmony joined her. "Oh my God, I forgot all about that! It was right after the farm field trip, right?"

I gritted my teeth, leaving my tone flat and unamused. "You mean the field trip when Robbie Pachinko said they should have strapped me to one of the milking machines because, according to him, with boobs like mine, I must have plenty of milk? Yeah. I remember. So funny."

Emma winced while the other two laughed harder. "Let's go look at the memory wall."

"Sounds good." I followed her, but to my dismay Chloe and Harmony joined us. There was enough noise that I was certain they couldn't hear me. "What are you doing with them, Emma? You obviously don't like their brand of humor. I don't think you ever have."

She sighed, and we stopped in front of the wall. "You know how it is. You make friends and you just kind of stick with them. Thick and thin."

"Out of habit?"

"Something like that."

"Like I said before, sunk-cost fallacy. You could leave them anytime you—"

Chloe thrust her arm between us and over our shoulders to point at a picture. "There I am! Top of the pyramid. I can still do the splits, you know."

Sure enough, there she was, on top of everyone else. A visual metaphor if there ever was one. And Harmony was right beneath her. Shocker.

If Nora was here, she would be vicious, talking about how many guys had seen Chloe do the splits in private or something equally harsh. Hell, she would have already gotten me out of here by now. Sadly, I was not Nora, being mean was not my thing, and I had no idea how to get out of uncomfortable situations.

It was my curse, thanks to a midwestern mom who didn't have a mean bone in her body and a Southern father who raised me to believe good manners were more important than life itself. One time, at a church picnic, a bee stung his nose during the prayer, and he didn't say anything because he didn't want to interrupt the preacher. Dad was allergic to bees. He nearly died from good manners.

Assertiveness was a sin in our household.

"Where are you, Maggie?" Harmony asked, scanning the pictures on the wall. "I don't see you... oh wait. There you are. Eating."

I was in the background of a cafeteria picture, devouring lunch and sitting with Nora. The central focus of the picture was the football team and all their friends, but we were just inside the frame.

Chloe continued to hunt for anything that was about herself. "Oh, look. There I am at the pep rally."

Harmony, ever the breath of stale air, asked, "Was anyone hurt in the fire?"

Slowly, I twisted to face her. I had no desire to continue speaking to her after that question, but my upbringing yanked an answer out of me. "No."

"Too bad, right? I bet the payout would have been huge if you had gotten hurt."

"What kind of a ghoul are you?" *I'm sorry, Mom, the question just popped out before I could stop it.*

She folded her arms over her chest and scowled. "What's the big deal? You weren't even hurt."

Chloe laid her hand on Harmony's shoulder as she looked at me. "No, she's right, Harm. We should be supportive. I mean, she's single. She worked hard to put herself through culinary school, and then her cute little shop went up in flames. She has nothing. Isn't that right? You're probably destitute at this point. That would explain the dress. I'm shocked you came at all."

Emma quietly said, "Chloe, that's enough."

But she continued, "You're so courageous for showing your face among your much more successful classmates. It's inspiring, Maggie. Like one of those sad human-interest stories on the news. Brave, despite reality. Cheers to you." She lifted her glass in a mock toast and drank.

High school was over, but somehow, Chloe Foster still came out on top.

Except something in me steeled. I was not going to let her ruin my night. Not if I could help it. My high school reunion was not going to be another time she made me feel bad with no repercussions.

I passed a business card to Emma. "If you ever want to get a cup of coffee with someone who will listen to you, someone who is a decent human being, I'd be happy to meet up."

Her smile lit up. "I'd like that."

"No card for me?" Chloe snapped.

"No."

"Why not?"

"I don't spend time with petty, selfish women who haven't changed since high school. Excuse me."

Before I could even turn heel and leave, she stepped in my way. "Where do you think you're going? I'm not done talking to you."

I sidestepped, but she moved to block me again. "Chloe, that's enough."

"I think you owe me an apology for—"

Instead of answering, I spun in the other direction to flee. Just my luck, I smacked face first into some guy's hard chest. It was like headbutting a wall. I blinked in shock. "Oh God, I'm so sorry, I wasn't watching where I was going. Jules? Is that you?"

"Yes, I've been looking for you."

I threw my arms around him, nearly squeezing him to death. Julian Black had been one of my dearest friends in school, and I had never been so relieved to see anyone in my whole life. I quietly squeaked, "I'm so happy to see you!"

He murmured into my hair, "Same here."

Chapter 4

Julian

Chloe and Harmony frowned, but Emma was curious. So I lingered in the hug for a few seconds longer than convention dictated. *Let them wonder about us. It would serve them right.*

Maggie, the former drama student that she was, played into it and leaned against me. I put my arm around her and breathed in her scent. No need to act when it came to sniffing her hair—she still smelled like sweet, rich vanilla, just like she did in high school. It blended well with the whiskey in my other hand.

We had a few classes together, and I was grateful for every teacher who lazily assigned seats in alphabetical order. Black and Bryant always ended up close together. There were certain things that stuck out about those years, and her scent was one of them.

These days, on the rare occasion I have a sweet craving, I always go for sugar cookies. I blame Maggie Bryant for that.

Though I had surpassed even my own aspirations at an early age, I was uncomfortable being surrounded by the high school mean girl squad even now. Strange how emotional scars never really heal. But I wasn't a kid anymore, and I had enough money to cover up at least one murder, maybe three, so I stood tall, daring them to start shit.

In fact, I kept smiling at Chloe Foster despite what I wanted to say to her. "Evening, ladies."

Chloe, for once, kept her mouth shut. She looked good, considering she was at least fifty percent evil by volume. It was a pity my company couldn't figure out how to bottle it as an anti-aging cream. We'd make an even bigger fortune.

Harmony, on the other hand, had never struggled to say what she was thinking. "I'm surprised you came, Julian. You—"

"Yes, I know. I run a big company, and no one thought I'd make it. But you have to make time for what's important, right?" I gave Maggie's waist a squeeze.

"I was going to say I'm surprised you were even invited after what you did to Grant Worthington."

That name clanged through me, and Maggie must have felt it, too, because she stiffened up in my grip. But tonight was not the night to rehash old fights, and I refused to be bated into it. What was done was done, and there was no need for Maggie to learn about what happened that night.

Chloe took that as her cue to jump in. "High school was a long time ago, Harm. I'm sure Julian has no plans to dig up old memories. Right, Julian?" Evidently, she had as little desire as I did to dredge up the past. Tension simmered behind those cold blue eyes.

I smiled. "I believe in letting bygones be bygones, and I'm sure Grant does, too, wherever he is tonight. How are you three this evening? Reminiscing about old times?" I jerked my chin at the memory wall.

Terrible name for the display. The memories weren't for the whole class. They were for the popular kids. The ones who were asked to pose back then. Not the rest of us. We were mere background characters in a world that focused on them and them alone.

I wasn't anyone special in high school. I kept my head down and tried to get grades good enough that my parents wouldn't give me a hard time, and that was it. Ambition didn't strike me until the second half of my senior year, and then, I went balls to the wall on everything. Without a lot of luck, I would have been nothing more than a footnote in the yearbook.

But since I'd become successful, whoever put the memory wall together had cropped some pictures to make it look like I was the focus. Amazing what could be done with some editing and effort, but I knew better. The memory of being ignored doesn't simply disappear because someone altered the pictures.

Emma spoke up, "It's amazing how much has changed since then."

"And yet some things remain the same," Chloe said. She hadn't turned her attention to the memory wall, instead glancing from me to Maggie. "I don't suppose there's a story here..."

"I—"

"We're engaged," Maggie blurted.

I nearly dropped my whiskey when Chloe shouted, "What?" Hell, I'd almost shouted the same thing myself.

But Maggie went on, "I would have said something earlier, but you love to hear yourself talk, Chloe, and I didn't want to interrupt."

"Oh my God, congratulations!" Emma said, taking

Maggie in for a hug. "I had no idea! I'm so happy for you! How did this happen?"

"Yeah," Chloe said, seething. "I'd love to know how this happened."

Maggie's warm brown eyes silently begged me to play along as she played the role of the happy fiancée. "Um, well, it was pretty sudden, right, sweetie?"

"Right," I said, trying to be smooth. My heart drummed in my chest, and my mouth went dry. Another swig of whiskey whetted my whistle. "But when you know, you know."

Chloe's tone went skeptical. "So, the two of you have been dating this whole time? Since high school?"

"No." Maggie clung to my side, no doubt hoping we could make this lie work. I wasn't sure how far we would have to take it, but I could roll with the punches. She explained, "Actually, we lost contact right after high school."

"Then how did you two reconnect?"

Maggie blanched, so I dug into the memories of what I knew of her life now. As much as I didn't rely on the internet for biographical answers, some details were readily available, and Maggie was one of the few people I cared to look up.

"Recently, I was at a fundraiser for an animal shelter, I think that's what—"

"You don't remember where you met up again with the love of your life?" Chloe interrupted me.

"I go to a lot of fundraisers. After a while, they start to blur together. Anyway, Maggie was one of the caterers. We recognized each other and started talking, and we couldn't stop. Even as the lights went down, I couldn't get enough of hearing her beautiful voice." I hoped Chloe took that for the slight it was. "After that night, I knew I wanted to marry her. I don't want to wake up without her by my side ever again."

"Aw," Emma cooed, smiling dreamily at my co-liar.

"We've been together ever since," Maggie said. The way she beamed up at me, I would have believed us too. She was a hell of an actress, but it was something genuine in her smile that thrilled me. Her full cheeks lifted, those sexy lips curled at the ends, and her eyes lit up in a way that made me feel like everything would be alright in the world. Maggie Bryant smiled with her whole being as if that was the thing she was created to do.

I had missed that smile more than I realized.

In truth, I had no idea who Maggie was these days. She was a baker, and her shop had suffered a fire, but that was all I knew. Maybe she wasn't the girl I had a little crush on anymore. Maybe she had become someone else entirely, I certainly had. I imagined she was single by the way she practically jumped at the chance to use me to play defense. Whoever she was now felt like a favor to the girl she once was.

The girl who had helped me get through drama class because I needed an elective to graduate, and she had promised to help me. The girl who had reassured me I wasn't a loser just because my girlfriend had cheated on me. The girl who let me down easy after I stole a kiss.

I was happy to help her now. Outside of it being the right thing to do, I knew playing along would annoy Chloe, and that was more than enough reason. Maggie's bully sneered as she said, "When were you going to tell us? You're not even wearing a ring. How were we supposed to know?"

"Relax, Chloe," I said, smiling. "Didn't anyone tell you this is a party?"

Maggie laughed. "I forgot it at home. I'm still not used to wearing such a big ring when I bake, so I keep leaving it on the nightstand."

"So this 'engagement' is new?" She said engagement in a mocking manner, as if the word itself was in doubt.

"What's it been, sweetheart? Two months?" I casually asked. "Three?"

"Nine weeks, I think? Maybe more. I'm not sure."

"You don't even remember?" Chloe laughed wickedly. "When I get engaged, it'll be a story worth telling."

Maggie just shrugged and wrapped her arms around me, head on my shoulder. "It's funny. I don't remember exactly when he popped the question, actually. In a lot of ways, it feels like we've been together forever. We were at dinner, and he pulled out that ring, and everything else sort of faded away."

I nodded knowingly. "You lose track of time when you're having fun. Isn't that the cliché?"

"Yes, but—"

"That's why you'll remember the exact moment when you get engaged, Chloe," I cut her off. "You don't know how to have fun. It must suck to be you. Now if you'll excuse me, I'd like to dance with my future bride." I set my drink down, took her hand, and led her into the middle of a different kind of chaos.

Chapter 5

Maggie

Julian Black was my knight in shining armor on a white horse. I couldn't believe he did that for me. It was something out of a fairy tale. But when we reached the dance floor, I knew I couldn't keep up the ruse.

I let go of his hand. He turned around, a question forming in those haunted eyes. I explained, "What you did back there, that was amazing. I appreciate it so much. But I'm letting you off the hook here. You don't need to dance with me."

He replied by pulling me into his arms and assuming a dancing position. "They're still watching. I'm willing to keep going if you are."

"I can't ask you to keep this up. I mean, are you even single?"

"Yes. You?"

"I am, but—"

"But nothing. Why not have a little fun tonight? What's the harm? Besides, did you see Chloe's face? I haven't seen her that angry in a long time."

I laughed. He was right. "She was pretty pissed that she didn't already know."

"So, are we dancing or not?"

"Yeah, I like that. Let's do it, we can catch up."

Julian started to sway to the music, and I followed his lead. "So tell me, Maggie Bryant. How has life treated you over the past fifteen years?"

A nervous laugh escaped me. "Not as good as you."

He shrugged. "I had a leg up. Not exactly a fair comparison."

"If I remember right, your dad was wealthy, but nothing like you are now."

"We were comfortable."

"That's what wealthy people say."

He laughed easily, shaking his head. "The truth is often a lot uglier than people realize."

"What does that mean?"

He took a deep breath and smiled as though debating whether or not to tell me the whole story. "The truth of the matter is my family had started to struggle right around the time I was going off to college. If I hadn't had my trust fund from my grandparents, there was no way I would have been able to go."

"But you grew up in a mansion."

"A mansion that was falling apart because we didn't have the money to maintain it. The roof in the east wing had caved in right before my freshman year of high school. There was mold in the walls. We even had bats in the attic and bees building an enormous colony in the chimney in my bedroom fireplace."

I couldn't believe it. "You're kidding. Tell me you're kidding."

He shook his head. "It was my grandparents' mansion.

Accidental Fiancé

Not ours. We inherited it, but my father made some bad investments when I was young, and things fell into disrepair. Really, that's all it takes for generational wealth to fall apart. A few bad choices, and boom, you're just like everybody else."

We were friends back then. I was shocked he hadn't mentioned any of this before. "You never told me."

"I was a proud teenage boy. What was I going to say? Especially after you told me about how you and your mom were living in a one-bedroom apartment after your dad left. Hell, I wanted to offer for you two to move in with us, but I knew that we didn't have a safe space for you. With the amount of mold in the mansion, we were moving from wing to wing for years, trying not to get sick."

"Is that why we always studied at my place or the library?"

He smiled and nodded. "I was too embarrassed to say anything. I felt awful that we couldn't help you."

"That wasn't your fault."

"No. But it was a reminder of how helpless I was at the time. For a while there I sunk into a bit of a depression. But by senior year, I decided that I was not going to let myself fall into my father's footsteps. He had dragged our family down, and I was determined to be the one to pick us up. So I did."

"Your mother must be proud."

He chuckled. "Oh, she is. Especially after I bought her the Country Club that we were kicked out of. Now she gets to make the rules, and one of the first things she did was kick out all of the people who laughed at her when we couldn't afford the dues."

"Turnabout is fair play."

He spun me, then dipped me, making me lightheaded for a breath before he stood me back up. "Turnabout."

I laughed. "How was that turnabout or fair play?"

"We're engaged?"

My cheeks heated. "I'm sorry for putting you on the spot. I just didn't know what to say and I panicked. You were so sweet in high school, and I guess I just... again, thank you for helping me with that."

"I'll be honest, it took the wind out of me for a second. But there are worse things to be called than Maggie Bryant's fiancé."

"You're not mad?"

"How could I be? I was able to be a part of upsetting Chloe and Harmony. I got to make Emma do that little aw thing that she did. That was adorable. I'm not sure how to feel about that since I always thought she was one of the bad ones, and now I'm dancing with you. This is nothing but winning for me."

I didn't know what to say but I couldn't stop smiling at him. It made no sense for him to be so cooperative. Last month, the man was seen smoking cigars on some celebrity's yacht. Now, he was doing this huge favor for me. It didn't add up. "You are a really good sport."

"I hope you are too."

"What do you mean?"

I hadn't noticed that the DJ started to play a slow song until he said something. Julian's hands slid from the middle of my back to just above my ass as he pulled me closer. Being pressed up against him was not something I had expected, but it wasn't exactly unwelcome, either.

Julian Black had grown into a very handsome man.

His dark hair was casually styled. It glinted in the swirling lights, offsetting his tan skin and emerald-green eyes. In the middle of his left eyebrow, a faint, jagged scar bolted through, ending just above his eyelid. It had happened during our senior year, right after his father had died. He refused to tell me what caused it, but later I found out he had picked a fight with Grant Worthington and put him in the hospital with a broken arm.

Grant and Chloe had been dating at the time, so it wasn't hard to put the pieces of the fight together. I imagined she said something rude, and he responded in front of Grant. Teenage boys weren't that hard to set off, and since it had not yet been a week since Julian's father had died, he had an understandable hair trigger. But when I asked him about it after the dust settled, he refused to talk about it so I let it go.

Tonight, I didn't want to let anything go. I was too busy drinking in the sight of him. His suit was dark, and at first I thought it matched his black hair, but when the lights hit it, a navy blue color came through. It was hard not to stare at his full, sensuous lips, so I cast my gaze downward.

His white button-down had been left unbuttoned at his throat, exposing a thick column of muscle that spoke to his diligent work ethic. No one had a body like that without working hard for it. Despite the muscles, he was light on his feet and a far better dancer than me.

I didn't mind when his fingertips began to draw circles on the top of my ass. I laced my fingers at the back of his neck to bring him closer. His cologne made me think of fresh spring rain. Clean and crisp. New, but somehow familiar.

I didn't know how far he would take this, but I was game for anything. He seemed set on selling the charade, and I didn't mind.

It had been a long time since anyone held me like that.

We were strangers now, but that didn't matter. It felt right, my body being close to his. Or maybe that was just a symptom of loneliness. Who could say? The song selection turned sentimental, and somehow, I felt closer to him dancing to it in his arms. Nostalgia was a funny thing.

"Maggie?" His deep voice rumbled through me to my core.

"Yes?"

His large hand cupped my ass, and his warmth penetrated me there. "I hope this isn't too forward."

My brain stuttered. Thoughts evaporated like steam. "We're selling a story, right?"

"Mm-hmm."

"It's fine. It's good. Good salesmanship. Believable." *Stop talking, oh my God, stop talking.*

His jaw grazed my temple as he whispered, "We can't leave any room for doubt with those three. Their eyes are on us, so I'll do my best to sell this. But you have more sales experience than I do. What should we do next to drive this home?" He gave my ass a squeeze when he said drive, and I thought I might melt.

Slow dancing should not cause my body to become this hot.

"Um, I think I need a drink."

"Right now?"

I bobbed my head, too entranced to trust my voice.

He drew back and I couldn't read him anymore. "Then let's get you a drink." We worked our way through the crowd and stood silently in line for the bar. I had no clue what he was thinking, but my thoughts grew lascivious.

It's the loneliness, Maggie. Get your mind out of the gutter.

His warm hand on the small of my back did not help to clean up my dirty mind. We ordered cocktails and found a table on the edge of the dance floor still well within the sight of the Evil Three. They remained near the memory wall, gossiping with or about whomever came along. I wondered whether we were still the topic of conversation or if they'd moved on yet.

Julian smiled, drawing my attention back to him. "They really got to you, didn't they?"

"You witnessed the last five minutes of the conversation but it felt like I was there for an eternity."

"I'm surprised you're here alone."

"Nora Skinner was supposed to come with me. Actually, let me check on her. One sec." I pulled out my phone to see a text from her.

Got stuck at work. I'm so sorry. Be there soon.

I grimaced. I shouldn't be surprised, her work causes her to miss out on things often. "She must have another big case. I don't think she's coming."

"She's a lawyer, right?"

"Yeah, how'd you know?"

"She was involved in a class-action suit that Black-Aster brought against Novonly last year. A rival company," he explained. "I didn't have much to do with it, but I recognized her name on some documents. I meant to give her a call but as usual, life got in the way." He shrugged but then turned pointedly casual. "I understand you had a professional setback not too long ago."

"If you don't mind, I don't want to talk about that right now."

"We can talk about whatever you'd like, Maggie."

I thought it might be weird to make small talk with Julian. But tapping into the memories of our shared history felt natural. "How is your mother doing these days? She was always so sweet to me."

"Aside from running the country club like her own private revenge empire, she's doing great. Your folks?"

"We finally figured out what happened with Dad. Remember how we all said that he was crazy for leaving my mom?"

"Definitely. Your mom's great."

I lifted a shoulder. "Turned out he actually went crazy."

Julian choked on his whiskey and I patted his back for a moment. "He did?"

"Well, he had a stroke. A mini stroke. It happened in the part of the brain that controls personality changes."

"The frontal lobe?"

"Yes. It didn't cause much other disability other than a little aphasia. But we didn't notice right away because he had moved out. It took about nine months for us to find out that there was actually something medically wrong with him, and by that point, the divorce had gone through."

Julian's eyes widened. "I am so sorry, that's terrible."

"It is, and it isn't."

"How's that?"

"Once we figured out what happened and that he didn't mean any of his bullshit, Mom and Dad actually rekindled their romance. He took it upon himself to woo her and make up for his awful behavior.. They got remarried on their anniversary."

He laughed. "Wow. That's... wow. I thought he had an affair. She forgave him for that?"

"Actually, he didn't. He made a deal with his dental hygienist to go on a few fake dates to make Mom jealous."

"You're kidding me."

Accidental Fiancé

"Nope. He thought she was having an affair with her tennis instructor."

"Your mom would never!"

I loved how sure he was of her, even after all these years. "I know, right? Anyway, he wanted to make her jealous, and Diane felt bad for him, so she went along with it. Paranoia is one of the things that the stroke caused, and a mini-stroke is often a precursor to a massive stroke. The doctors said the signs resemble a midlife crisis, so most people never find out until they have the big one, and by then, it's too late. But Dad hit his head on the job site and had to get checked out. That's how they found it."

"That's crazy," he muttered into his drink. "Your mom is a saint."

"She made Dad build her a house to make up for it, but yeah, she pretty much is."

"I'd say she more than earned it."

I drained my negroni cocktail that was too strong yet not strong enough. Liquid courage. "Why play along with me tonight, Jules?"

He paused. "Why wouldn't I?"

"You could be spending your night doing anything with anyone right now. Everyone knows your reputation these days. But you're here, at our high school reunion, pretending to be my fiancé. How come?" I said it, repercussions be damned.

Julian ran his fingertip along the rim of his glass, staring at it intently. "I could be doing anything with anyone right now. And yet I choose to be here, doing this with you."

"But why?"

He peered at me as if he could see right through to my soul. "Because I remember the kind-hearted girl you were, and kindness is something I have missed for a long, long time. I'm curious to see whether it's still in you or if time stole it from you." He covered my hand with his. "I don't think it did."

My mouth went dry from his touch. Lust rolled in like a fog set to blanket my insides. "Jules—"

"They're watching again."

Oh. That. "Think we're still selling it?"

"Not sure. But I know what will do it."

"What's that?"

He cupped my cheek and stared into my eyes. I knew what was coming. It wasn't real, but not one part of me cared it was fake. My brain checked out as my pulse ticked up, and I became dizzy when his mouth slanted over mine.

Chapter 6

Julian

This time, the kiss wasn't stolen. I wasn't some jerk teenager, and Maggie wasn't an innocent girl. When I kissed her, she tipped her mouth up to meet mine, synchronicity and intent wrapped in her lips, in the heat of doing what we wanted. She clutched at my collar, her nails grazing my skin when her fingers curled in at the edge.

She let go of my shirt a moment later—much too soon—and backed away. She blinked as if she couldn't believe what she had done. "I'm sorry."

Not the response I was used to getting after I kissed a woman. "What's wrong?"

"I... I shouldn't have done that."

I laughed. "Maggie, *I* kissed *you*."

"But—"

"So don't spoil it. Maybe you get kissed all the time, but it's been a little while for me, and that was nice."

Her cheeks flushed a dark pink. "Oh. No, I don't get kissed all the time. It's been a while for me, too."

"Hard to believe."

She glanced away, smirking to herself. "It's true, I don't." She was so damn nervous. I had to do something.

"Hey, Maggie?"

"Hmm?"

I stuck my tongue out and crossed my eyes, and she laughed so hard that tears streamed down her cheeks.

Once she caught her breath, she asked, "What was that for?"

"You looked nervous. I had to fix that."

She shook her head, a smile remaining on her face though her tone was a little too defensive. "I'm not nervous."

"Liar."

"I'm not. I'm just... I don't know what I am tonight."

I had a feeling I knew. Every time I touched her, she leaned into it. When I kissed her, she moaned in my mouth. It was hard not to feel something, even if we were only faking. She was so damn responsive, and I fucking loved that. The crush I'd harbored in high school had gone from ember to flame in an hour, and I didn't like pretending otherwise.

But. I still needed to slow this down. Tonight was not about me or my crush. I was trying to be a friend to someone who needed one. A protector to a hen surrounded by wolves. It was nothing more than that for her, and I needed to behave.

The trouble was, I didn't want to. I wanted Maggie, and I hated bullshitting. I changed course and took her hand again. "Dance with me."

She followed my lead and once we were close, I let the music carry us and did what came naturally. Holding her.

Enjoying the softness of her. *Not real, not real, not real.* Maybe if I reminded myself this wasn't a date, and we weren't a couple, I'd be a better man. Chivalrous. Good.

It was pointless to argue with my basic instincts, though.

There wasn't a chivalrous bone in my body when it came to Maggie. Not tonight, not after kissing her. That kiss broke my restraint. When a dirty beat came on, she wriggled and ground against me. If there was a God, this had to be a sign, right? This was meant to happen. She wanted this, too. She didn't have to dance on me like I was her personal stripper pole.

She chose to.

She chose me.

The friction of her body on mine, our chemistry. It was all too much. I held a hand on her stomach to keep her tight against me, and her ample ass coaxed my body out of its slumber.

How long has it been?

I couldn't remember the last time I was with someone, but there was no faking my erection. She must have noticed, too, because she stopped for a moment before starting up again. This time, she rocked against my hard-on ever so slightly as she danced. Not enough to be indecent, but just enough to tell me she knew. The tease.

We weren't the only pair grinding on the dance floor, the song was made for it. But I barely noticed the others. Not with Maggie backing up to me like this. I lifted her hair from her neck and licked her there, relishing the candy sweat on her skin. She shuddered against me in response and caused my cock to throb for more. I didn't want to stop, but distant laughter reminded me we were not alone.

Right. The reunion.

I released her hair and turned her to face me. Those pouty lips were made for biting, and her pupils were blown, eyes wide as she stared up at me. Her large chest heaved with every breath. If I were a lesser man, I might have brought up the fact we were in a great hotel, and I had a room.

But I was trying to be decent for some stupid reason. "Another drink?"

"Yeah."

We practically raced to the bar, both in need of cooling down. Rushing there helped me lose my erection. We each ordered a bottle of water and headed for the same table as before. Water was exactly what she needed, not some guy panting all over her. She'd had a hard night and I needed to respect that and give her some space.

I took off my suit coat and tried to make conversation again as I rolled up my shirt sleeves. "So, have you seen any—"

"My bakery burned down," she muttered as her gaze moved to my newly exposed forearms. Apparently, she was ready to talk about it. It was the last thing on my mind after what happened on the dance floor, but I liked that she was willing to tell me what happened. Maybe after tonight, we could rekindle our friendship.

"I know. I'm so sorry that happened. Do you want to—"

"It was so random..." She sighed and sat back on her bar stool. "The firefighters said it was a one-in-a-million accident. The front door's kickplate hit the doorstop at the wrong moment during the flour delivery. Metal on metal caused a spark and boom. Small explosion, big fire."

"Wow, that's crazy. What are the chances?"

She fiddled with the cap of her bottle. "Yeah, I know. Bad luck, I guess. I keep thinking Dad must have used up all of our family's good luck by having his mini stroke detected early. He's on a bunch of medication to keep the big one from happening. But if the cost of my father's good health is losing my bakery I'm willing to pay it."

I understood the feeling. She had to tell herself a story that made her loss meaningful somehow. But that also meant she felt responsibility for things that were out of her control, and I couldn't let that stand. It was an accident.

"I don't think that's how it works, Maggie."

She rolled her eyes. "I know but it makes it easier to swallow the idea that I lost everything I worked for… that it was for something good and not all for nothing." She got choked up and guzzled most of her water. "I'm sorry, Jules. I'm not normally this emotional."

I reached for her hand. "I'm glad I can be here for you then."

"Are you gunning for sainthood or something?"

"What?"

"You're being so nice to me." The way she looked at me felt like hero worship, and I couldn't let her do that. I was no one's hero.

But I wasn't sure how to respond, either. The truth or something subtle. Maybe shoot down the middle. "Well, to be honest, I'm not being entirely altruistic. I'm getting something out of this too."

"What do you mean?"

I felt like the parent about to tell their kid the truth about Santa Claus. If I told her the truth about me, would she be angry? "You're a beautiful woman, Maggie. I'd be lying if I said I didn't enjoy your company. This is more than reminiscing over high school and lost time. There's a connection here, at least for me."

Her plump lips parted in the slightest gasp, and I took

that for an opportunity knocking. A burning rush came over me as I crushed my mouth to hers, taking charge of the moment. I laced my fingers through her hair to angle her head, deepening the kiss. Her mouth tasted like the orange in her cocktail, and I craved more.

I wanted to be a good friend, but I was just as much of an animal as the next man, entranced and intoxicated by a beautiful woman's seductive kisses. This was undeniable—two stars colliding, sparks flying. We hadn't gotten together when we were kids because I never got the courage to ask her out.

I'm thinking she might've said yes.

It may not have worked out anyway because we were teenagers but it didn't matter now. I wanted to enjoy the present moment. Her moan shot straight to my cock, making me ache for her, and I stopped asking questions.

I broke the kiss, pressing my forehead to hers. "This is wrong."

"It is?" Her voice was barely a whisper. I had to strain to hear her over the music.

I leaned back, and she leaned forward, following me. I stole a deeper view of her cleavage before sitting up straight. "It is. You're vulnerable, Maggie. You went through a huge financial and career loss recently, and then tonight, you had to deal with Chloe and the others... I'm just trying to do a solid for an old friend, so we should probably wait until we see them watching us before we start kissing again. Shouldn't we?" *Say no.*

She shook off the haze. "I guess so."

I took a deep breath of disappointment to clear my head. "Fine. Right. We can do this. We're adults, not horny teenagers—"

"But what sells the engagement story better than a happy couple caught up in each other?"

"I can't fault the logic in that." I hooked my hand around the back of her head and kissed her again—longer, deeper—until we were full-blown making out.

"Get a room!" someone hollered from a distance.

Another brilliant idea. I backed off, but only a fraction of an inch. Her brows lifted in concern, a silent question of why I stopped kissing her. Hoarsely, I asked, "What sells the story better than the two of us running up to my room right now?"

"We should do that," she said, gulping. "To sell the story, I mean."

"Right. For the story." I led her to the lobby's elevators where I kissed her again and again. I couldn't get enough of her mouth, couldn't stop touching her. The elevator dinged at us and once inside, I hit the button for the penthouse suite. Doubt grew loud in the silence. What if she was only doing this for the story and wasn't into me at all?

I might be reading this all wrong so I offered, "We don't have to—"

Maggie launched at me, her fingers clasping at my collar again. She pulled me down for another kiss. I was definitely *not* reading this wrong.

I spun her around and pushed her to the wall, a hand on either side of her head to cage her in as we kissed. The doors opened just in time otherwise I would have stopped the elevator and taken her right then and there.

The hallway was a fever dream of kissing and groping one another. I pressed her to the wall with my body, my hand sliding under her dress while I bit her neck. She groaned and arched herself into my palm.

God, I couldn't get enough of her.

But at this rate, we were going to get arrested, so I dragged myself from her and went down the hall, searching for my suite. Maggie came up behind me and grabbed my ass as I tried to unlock the door. It finally unlatched, and I led us inside the dark penthouse.

Chapter 7

Maggie

I'd never done anything like this before. Not that I was a virgin by any means but going to a man's hotel room was one of those things that should have set off alarm bells in my brain. Every woman knows better. My instincts should have told me to run, that no good could come from being trapped with a strange man.

Except this was no stranger. This was Julian Black, an old friend. An old friend who just happened to have his tongue in my mouth and told me I was beautiful.

He didn't have to say that to me. It wasn't as if Chloe and the others could hear him say it—we were too far away from them, and the music was loud. It wasn't so much that he said it—guys say that kind of thing all the time to get in your pants—but it wasn't like that. The dead serious tone and the look in his eyes told me he meant it.

Julian wanted me, and there was no more addictive feeling in the world than being wanted.

The lights from the city below illuminated his handsome face. He backed me against the wall next to the suite's door and guided my leg around his to grind on me as we kissed. The seam of his pants drove against my clit. The moment I'd felt his erection when we danced, my mind shorted out. I knew then that he wasn't putting on a show. And now I couldn't think straight.

Everything went hazy as he pulled my dress up my thigh, baring my skin to his touch. He pulled back just enough to say, "This dress should be illegal."

I panted and tried to make sense of his words. "Huh?"

"I can't keep my hands off of you." He pressed his lips to mine, his heat burning through me like a wildfire. When his mouth traveled down my throat to my cleavage, I arched into him, silently begging for more. But he moved down further, releasing my leg to kneel in front of me. Without another word, he lifted my dress over his head, placing that same leg over his shoulder.

My breaths became quick and ragged as his fingers slid my underwear out of the way of his mouth. His thumb tortured me with slow circles around my clit, and I pulled my dress up and out of the way to dig my fingers into his hair. But he paid me no mind, intent on his target as he dove forward. I was so wet already that I thought he might drown. He nipped at my swollen clit before sucking me into his mouth long enough to make my back bow.

He dragged his tongue over me, savoring the taste as if I was his personal ice cream cone. My nails dug into his scalp as I arched my back. That spurred him on, his tongue rolling over me again and again at my tempo. I rocked against his face as my core pulsed.

I hissed, "I'm close!"

He redoubled his efforts, and I lost myself in my climax, moaning curses and his name at the same time. When it began to subside, he set my leg back on the ground then

Accidental Fiancé

stood for another kiss, sending jolts of electricity through me. My flavor on his tongue made me lose all capacity for thought or reason.

"You taste better than I could have dreamed," Julian rasped. "If I don't get you splayed out on my bed soon, I'm going to lose my fucking mind."

"Then we'd better get to it."

A chuckle came from his throat before guiding me to the bedroom. The penthouse was lovely—gleaming wood, gold accents, ivory encased furniture, plush rugs—much like the rest of the hotel. But the bedroom was what set it apart. The massive, four-poster king bed sat on a platform in the middle of the space, inviting and imposing. But what caught my eye was an enormous sunken tub next to the floor-to-ceiling windows that overlooked the city.

Julian pulled me into his arms then turned me to face the window and the tub. "Would you let me fuck you pressed up against that window, in front of the whole city? I know how much you like putting on a show."

My center clenched at the thought as I whispered, "Yes."

To my dismay, he left me standing on weak knees to close the automated blind. A panel slid across the windows, making it look like a solid wall as Julian shook his head. "I'm done putting on a show. I'd rather see one instead. Take off your clothes."

I shimmied free of my dress and enjoyed hearing him hold his breath as he looked me up and down. My black bra and panties weren't meant for more than comfort, but he seemed to appreciate them.

"More." A quiet demand.

My heart kicked up as I pulled them off. Would he still think I was beautiful after he saw me completely naked?

He strode over, unbuttoning his shirt as he cut through the room. The more skin he revealed, the more my mind went blank. He pulled his shirt off, standing before me in only his pants, his muscles rippling with every breath. His lips curled into a mischievous grin. "On the bed."

The last firing brain cell I had took control of my mouth. "Condom?"

He pulled a few from his pocket and tossed them on the bed. "Pick one."

I laughed and began to crawl onto the mattress, but his strong hands clasped around my ankles and pulled my legs out from under me, flattening me onto my stomach. He turned me over and stood between my legs, his erection straining against his pants.

He rubbed himself up and down my slit before resting the base of his cock on my clit. It was torture. Pure, delicious torture. The lack of friction set my teeth on edge, and I tried to work myself against him.

"Hold still."

I whimpered, fussy and desperate. I didn't care how it made me look. I needed this.

He leaned down, taking my mouth for his own and brutally grinding against me. Blindly, I reached for one of the condoms while he damn near mounted me. I grabbed his pants, and he swatted my hand away to take them off himself. "That's my job."

"No more teasing, Jules. I can't take it."

He half-smiled before taking the condom from my hand and pulling his trousers off. He slowly began to unroll the rubber down his thick shaft. A little *too* slowly.

Watching him, I started to shake. "You lied."

"Hmm?"

"You're putting on one more show. For me, this time."

He laughed and pulled me just off the edge of the bed before teasing at my entrance. "Tell me what you want."

"I want you to fuck me, Julian. Now."

With a grunt, he thrust hard and sheathed himself halfway. He paused, allowing me to adjust to him, and when I nodded, he filled me to the hilt. It was almost too much.

Almost.

My legs belted his waist, and he reached beneath me, picking me up. Julian drove us up the bed until my head hit the pillows, his cock buried inside of me the whole time. As he moved over me, two thoughts blinked in and out before returning in flashes glimmering at the edges.

One, Julian Black was inside of me.

Two, I was going to come again. Soon.

Whatever he was doing was different from what any of my previous partners had done. His pubic bone mashed against my clit in time with his thrusts, while inside he dragged along my G-spot, turning every prod into fireworks. I writhed beneath him to enhance my own pleasure; there was no way I could simply just lay there. How could anyone hold still when faced with this?

Julian thrust his body into mine faster and harder while he wrapped his fingers around my throat. Not squeezing, but grounding. Like he knew I was about to leave my body, and he had me secure. Steady. My back arced off the bed as my orgasm closed in on me, and just as I came, he kissed me, swallowing my sounds of pleasure while he forced more of them out of my mouth.

Abruptly, he pulled out and flipped me onto my stomach. He picked my hips up and spread my legs, licking me from my clit up before hammering back into me. But then he slowed down and laid on my back, still buried deep. His stubble-covered cheek grazed my ear.

I couldn't move—he was too heavy. Jules reached around and played with my clit as he slowly fucked me. I gripped the edge of the bed beneath the pillows. I had to hold onto something or I'd float away.

His low voice rumbled, "You were always such a good girl, Maggie. Too good for someone like me. But you're being so bad right now, squeezing on my cock like that. Hovering next to your orgasm, shaking like a leaf. You wanted to be bad back then, didn't you?"

"Yes," I whispered.

He thrust as deep as he could and I cried out. "You love it when I pound this little pussy, don't you?"

"Yes, please don't stop!"

"Never," he promised, and his thrusts resumed. "God, you're so fucking wet you're making a mess on these sheets."

I shuddered, so close I could taste it. "That's your fault."

A deep laugh escaped him. "Yeah. It is." He didn't let up on my clit as he fucked me in long strokes. "I'm starting to think you were a dirty girl in hiding." He leaned back, taking my hips with him. Our bodies smacked together as he rode me, one hand on my hip, the other still working my clit. "Show me what a dirty girl you are and come for me."

I lost it right then and there, screaming my fool head off as I came, throbbing on him. He didn't let up. He only worked me harder until I saw stars when I came again. But it was too much. My body couldn't contain this kind of pleasure.

Julian didn't back off, even when I tried to crawl away. The playful growl in his voice set me on edge. "Where do you think you're going?" He yanked me to him and rolled me onto my back again. He kneeled and pulled me onto his lap. Before he entered me again, he asked, "Need to stop?"

I'd barely started to shake my head when he pulled me

onto his cock, his hands bracing my low back so all I had to do was loop my arms around his neck. I was a little sore but I wasn't about to stop. Not when it felt this good.

He bounced me on his length and rearranged us until I was riding him in earnest while he laid back. Thunder rumbled in his chest as he studied me. He reached up, flicking his thumb over my tight nipple. "I love watching your tits bounce like that."

He popped his hips up, almost knocking me off balance. I laughed nervously as he grinned and sat up. Jules cupped my jaw, and that same naughty thumb rubbed over my bottom lip before he bit me there. The slight pain drove me closer to another orgasm as I rode him harder. His other hand found my low back and pressed down as he cocked himself up, the added pressure sending my body raging. My moans became sobs as my body spasmed, and I climaxed again.

He growled and I felt his cock thicken inside of me. "That's it, dirty girl. You're gonna make me come." I fell apart at his warning, another orgasm taking over. Something animalistic thundered out of him as he came inside of me.

Julian devoured my mouth until we had to catch our breath. We held still, bound together like that. Sweat poured down my back. I should have been exhausted, but I wanted more. We pride ourselves apart, both of us collapsing on the bed.

It should have been awkward but it wasn't. Julian spooned me like it was the most natural thing in the world, we fit together perfectly. One arm rested on my waist while the other was my headrest. He planted kisses along my bare shoulder.

I broke the silence. "This is weird, right?"

He stiffened up. "How so?"

"Weird because it isn't weird. Me and you, I mean. Like it should be weird but it's not. I don't get it."

He relaxed again. "Do you always look for problems?"

"We're not a couple, Jules. It's been years, we don't know each other as adults. Yet I still feel comfortable with you. Even after all this time, after what we just did."

"That's unusual for you?"

I bobbed my head. "Sex can be awkward, even for a couple. But there's nothing awkward here. It feels... strange."

He laughed. "It feels strange because it's *not* awkward? Do you always look for problems?"

"Okay, maybe, but how else am I supposed to anticipate things? When you let your guard down, life disappoints you." *And by life, I mean people.*

"Then let's make tonight a one-time thing. This doesn't need to be something with expectations. It's one night of fun, and by the sound of things, we both need something without pressure attached to it."

"That's such a guy thing to suggest."

Another chuckle. "Well, I am a guy, so..."

I rolled over to face him. "You're sure that's what you want? A one-night stand?"

He went quiet for a beat. "That's the standard operating procedure for reunion hook-ups, isn't it?"

"Right." It was good we were being straight with each other. I'd never had a true one-night stand before, and it always sounded better than a relationship. Less pressure, like he said. I know a one-night stand can be seen as being used but as long as it's mutual, which, in this case, it is, I don't see anything wrong with it. Honesty is best for most things, especially in this case. "No promises to call, no future plans. Just fun."

Again, he took a moment to answer. "Exactly."

"You know, there are all kinds of things we can do in one night."

He smiled wryly. "Show me."

So, I did.

Chapter 8
Julian

In the morning, I needed more of her.

Hints of sunlight crept in at the edges of the window panels and I didn't want to open them. We'd stayed up too late, exploring each other for hours before we finally dozed off. I woke breathing her in, having buried my face in her vanilla-scented hair.

I clutched at her hip and dragged my hard cock against the soft skin on her ass, leaving a trail of precum. She gasped and tensed for just a moment. I was rewarded with a faint, "Oh. Good morning to you too."

"I know we said one night, but how about one night and one morning?"

She giggled and pulled my hand between her legs. My dirty girl was wet already. "I had some incredibly good dreams, thanks to you, so yes. Morning is just an extended late night, isn't it?"

"Flawless logic once again." I groped for a condom and slid it on before lining up behind her. Her tight heat swallowed me whole, and a growl built in my core. She inhaled, thrusting back to meet me with every stroke. Her body tensed and released over and over. "Fucking hell, dirty girl, you're so tight."

"That's because you're so big," she panted.

I caught her rhythm, and when her body went taut, I went harder to make her come. She shook all over, and I hung on while she rode it out, although it was more like her orgasm rode her. Her body went choppy against mine. When she began to catch her breath, I flattened her against the bed on her stomach and pounded her into the bed, chasing my own pleasure until I found it.

I rolled off of her, both of us panting. What she said last night rang in my ears. *Tonight is just for fun. This should be weird. No promises to call.* All things no one should ever say out loud after sex. I wasn't going to be another thing in her life that disappointed her. I refused to put pressure on her about any of this.

I had been the one with a crush when we were kids. Not her. And she had been through too much already. She didn't need expectations put on her. This was for release, nothing more. That crushing reality was hard to swallow last night, but it was made easier by the fact that right after she said all that, the girl showed me she could suck the soul out of an angel.

I stretched and yawned, feeling a bit grungy. "I'm going to shower. Do you want to order room service for us? Get whatever you want."

"Oh. Okay, that sounds good. What do you want?"

I turned on the nightstand light and perused the menu. "Egg white omelet, spinach and tomato, side of dry whole wheat toast. Thanks. Just use the iPad by the phone. You don't even need to speak to anyone."

She cringed. "That's all you want? Pretty sure you

earned more than the old man special. You've been a busy boy."

"I like a boring breakfast, but thanks." I sauntered to the shower and cranked up the heat to scalding. It was impossible not to get up in my head about where things stood with Maggie. Last night had been the culmination of so many years of fantasies that it was impossible not to take certain aspects personally.

Watching her ride me... *fuck*. That had been ninety percent of my dreams back in my teenage years. The rest of the night and this morning was pure wish fulfillment. I didn't want it to end. Selfish, but true.

Maggie was unlike any woman I had ever known. Funny, silly, and hot as hell. She was willing to show me those sides of her, to let me in, even just a little. And for once in my adult life, I allowed myself to be open too. Maybe we were both looking for a friend we could do that with. She had said she wanted one night of fun, but that didn't mean we couldn't be friends going forward.

That's a lie, and you know it.

It wouldn't matter what type of friends we chose to be, I'd still be thinking of how she tasted on my tongue, the feel of her mouth on my cock. The way she gagged on me and kept at it. The look on her face when I first entered her.

Friendship was impossible, who was I kidding. I'd done this, and now, I had to live with the consequences. Such was life.

I stepped out of the shower and dried off, my cock going hard whenever I thought about Maggie. I glared down at myself. "Stop it."

But my cock was never good at listening.

Just then, I heard Maggie's voice in the bedroom. Only,

she wasn't talking to me through the door. She must have been on the phone.

She giggled, and I found my ear glued to the door. She couldn't have wanted privacy or she would have gone to the living room to have her conversation, right? At least that was my justification for spying on her.

Thin reasoning and I knew it, but I didn't give a shit.

"...I know, I know. But you left me all alone at the reunion. What else was I supposed to do?"

I soon realized she was talking to Nora. I still couldn't believe Nora didn't show up to her own reunion, leaving Maggie hanging.

"Well, you've been busy and," she paused then, her laugh slicing through the door. "I'm kidding, I'm kidding. No, I'm not engaged to Julian Black. That was just a cover story I came up with, and he was kind enough to play along. He hates Chloe as much as we do, and I think he knew how much it would annoy her to see us happy."

She was right about that. Chloe was a menace, a mean girl who clearly hadn't changed a bit since high school.

"I think they bought it. And I'm sure seeing us making out helped to sell the story." Her girlish giggles should not have turned me on but they did. "Nor, he's a really good kisser. I mean... wow."

Who doesn't want to hear that?

But then her voice turned sour. "The sex? Mmm, I'm not sure I should say anything."

Say it. I need to know. My stomach flipped. What did I do wrong?

"I know you don't like hearing about straight sex."

Nora's gay?

"Alright, alright. I have never come so many times in a night. Ever." More of those infectious giggles. "Seriously, if you ever decide to try men again, I strongly recommend giving Julian a try."

I am not a piece of meat. But... flattering. Kind of.

"His tongue should be insured. His fingers, his dick, the way he moves, it's unreal. But there was this one thing... you know what? I shouldn't say anything. He'd probably be weirded out if he knew I was telling you any of this, and besides, criticizing someone's bedroom performance feels wrong."

Again, my stomach flipped. *Just say it!*

"If you say so. I mean, most guys have something strange they do during sex, right?"

We do?

"When he was on top of me, I noticed he made the oddest face. And the sounds that came out of him, it was like he was a runaway train, like in the old black and white films. I half expected him to shout, "Choo, choo!" when he came."

I wanted to die.

"And when he finally did, it got weird. Like everything between us suddenly became awkward, and..."

Wait—didn't she say the opposite last night?

The door flew open, and there she stood, phone in hand. "When I caught him listening to my private conversation, I knew I had to get him back for spying on me by saying terrible things about his performance." She held out her phone, showing me no one was on the line. Her smart-ass grin made me want to kiss the taste out of her mouth.

"You brat!"

She giggled hard. "You totally had that coming."

"How did you know?"

"The lights are off in here. You blocked the light from under the bathroom door when you stood there."

I sighed at myself. "Sorry."

She shrugged. "I could have gone to the other room but screwing with you was too much fun. Breakfast is here." As she turned to walk away I smacked her ass, making her whoop and dart for the living room.

We ate at the dining table near the windows. "So, how did Nora know about last night?"

"After you got in the shower, I checked my phone and had a dozen texts from her, demanding details. I knew I had to call her first thing—apparently, she showed up right as we were making our escape and she asked around. According to her, when Chloe said something about us being engaged, she played it off and told Chloe she thought everyone knew about our engagement."

"Smooth."

Maggie bit into a slice of crispy bacon and savored it, making me wish I'd ordered some too. "I think she was more surprised than I was about last night."

"How so?"

"I've never done the one-night stand thing before. That's more Nora's territory than mine, so she was shocked to hear about it."

"Yeah, I overheard you say something about her not wanting details about straight sex. She's gay?"

"No," she said with a shake of her head. "She's a fetishist with a preference for women."

"Come again?"

"As she puts it, she gets more out of dominating people than she does out of having sex. But on the rare occasion she has sex, it's almost always with a woman or two."

"Huh. That explains why she's such a good litigator."

She laughed. "Yeah, you could say that."

We fell into a companionable silence for a few bites

while my mind wandered dangerously close to reality and what the future held. If my body was still, my mind was not.

"So, what's in the near future for you, Maggie Bryant?"

"That piece of toast."

I snorted. "You know what I mean."

"I do, but the future is a dark and scary thing. I've been successfully avoiding thinking about it for a while now and I plan to keep doing that. You?"

Given her circumstances, that was as fair an answer as I could ask for. "Truth is, I'm not a big fan of thinking about my immediate future, either. But we all have to face our demons, right?"

Her brow lined in a frown. "Demons? Is everything okay?"

I shrugged. "It will be." *I sure hope so.*

"You don't sound so convinced about that." She reached over the table, taking my hand. "If you want to talk about it, I'm here for you."

She would never understand how much that meant to hear that from her. The weight of my crush threatened to live up to its name. Strange how old feelings could be reincarnated into something new yet strikingly the same.

I patted her hand and took mine back to keep eating. "It's not your problem but thank you for offering."

"It's none of my business, but are you healthy, Jules?"

She was not going to let this go, was she? "It's nothing like that. Don't worry about it. I'm fine. It's just family stuff."

"Oh. Okay." She returned to her meal, distracted by the mystery I'd failed to lay out.

Now, it's weird.

Chapter 9

Maggie

I wasn't sure how to get him to open up. He'd been so forthcoming about everything before, shutting me out now felt personal. What else could it be? I must have screwed up somewhere along the line. "Did I say something wrong?"

Julian leaned back in his chair and closed his eyes, running his fingers through his hair. When he sat up again, a lock of it dangled over his forehead the way it had last night when he was on top of me, and I flashed back to that moment. I had to squeeze my thighs together to stop from moaning out loud. He cleared his throat. "I promise, this has nothing to do with you."

"So much so that you can't tell me about it? I thought we were, well, not friends exactly, but we used to be. We used to talk about everything. Maybe I can help. It's not like I have any place to be or a job to get to."

"You're right," he said with sudden interest.

"Well, you don't have to rub it in."

"No, no, I don't mean about the job thing. Actually, I do." He tapped his fingers together in thought as he took a deep breath that spread open his hotel robe just enough to show off the defined midline between his pecs. When he licked his lip I wanted to climb across the table and take over for him.

If I spent any more time with Julian, I was going to want to pounce on him again, and I was already wrecked from last night and this morning.

He admitted, "I'm going to ask something very, very stupid, and you're going to tell me no, and that will be the end of it, okay? But I'll only say it on the condition that you agree you're going to tell me no."

"This is about the problem you alluded to?"

"Yes."

Whatever was on his mind felt like a trap. "But if you're about to ask me a favor, why would I agree to say no?"

"Because otherwise, I won't be foolish enough to ask."

"Your logic is unlike our earth logic." We had binged Buffy the Vampire Slayer when we were kids, and I hoped he remembered the quote.

He laughed. "Nice. But I still need you to agree, okay?"

I shrugged. "Sure."

He took a breath and began. "In about two weeks, my grandmother will be turning eighty. Her birthdays are always a big celebration since she's the oldest person in the family. Everyone will be there, their spouses, kids, all of us. It doubles as an annual family reunion because we're too busy to get together otherwise. Yaya is the only person we'd go through the trouble for."

"Yaya? That's so cute. But I'm not hearing a problem yet."

"I was getting to that."

He pulled out his phone and showed me a picture of a

precious little girl. Which seemed like an odd thing for him to have on his phone.

"Um, who is that?"

"This is Piper. My daughter."

I blinked at him, my heart stumbling. "You have a daughter? Are you married?"

"Not anymore. We're divorced."

"Oh. I'm sorry." *But only a little.* "Do you want to talk about it?"

"Not much to say, really. My wife—ex-wife—had an affair with one of my former business associates. She moved to Beijing to be with him and left Piper with me."

How could she leave her own daughter like that? I couldn't picture my mother doing that in a million years. "That's... what do you mean, she left her with you? She still sees her, right?"

He shook his head. "According to Britney, we're in her past."

"Wow."

"Piper is four. She was one when the affair started and two by the time the divorce was finalized. She barely remembers her mom, and I doubt she will when she's older. It was shitty of Britney, but at least she left instead of dragging things out. Small favors."

I couldn't wrap my head around it. "Why would she have a kid only to abandon her?"

"It's funny, most people say something similar when they hear about it. Men do it all the time and no one bats an eye. But when a woman does it, people have all sorts of questions." He chuckled sadly to himself. "I believe she didn't want to be a mom in the first place, but she did it because that's what was expected of her. I'm not trying to analyze my ex-wife any more than I already have, and that's not why I brought her up."

I swallowed. "Okay. Why then?"

"Since the day she left, my family has been on me about getting a new wife to take care of Piper. At first, I was understanding about it. But it's been over two years, and they hound me even more now every time we talk. Honestly, it's insulting."

"Insulting?"

"Yes. I'm a single father with a busy schedule, but I am capable of hiring nannies and babysitters and ensuring she has all the things she needs. I want her to have a feminine influence, but they act like I'm some feeble man who doesn't understand women. And it's not like they even want me to get married for *me*, for *my* companionship. They only ever bring it up as something to help Piper."

I shrugged and smiled. "I can see both sides of it, to be honest. Not the feeble man part. Just that it's good for a kid to have a variety of influences around."

"I get that too. But they are really brutal about it. So that's where you come in."

"What do you mean?"

"If I show up to another family function with no one on my arm, I'll never hear the end of it."

"Oh. Oh! You want me to come with you?"

"Yes, and pretend to be my fiancée. Again. Like we did last night." He paused. "Stop thinking about it and say no."

I laughed. "Why do you want me to say no?"

"Because doing it for one night is one thing and doing it for a whole week is another."

"Her birthday party lasts a week?"

He nodded. "Which is why it's a terrible idea and I shouldn't have mentioned it at all."

Accidental Fiancé

"No, I—"

"Thank you for saying no because that takes the pressure off of you." He thought for a moment. "It adds pressure to me and the birthday party, but that's fine. I'll just tell them to shut up or I'll leave. That should give me at least five minutes of relief before they start up again."

"I wasn't saying no, Jules. It's not a terrible idea. I mean, last night we were convincing enough that the rumor mill was so strong my best friend thought I was secretly engaged. Clearly, we can pull off being a fake couple."

"Sure, but again, that was one night. This isn't being in a hotel where we can hide from everyone else. Yaya's birthday party is a week of staying in the mansion with the rest of my family, and that's why it's a bad idea and I never should have brought it up."

I sighed, scraping my fork on my plate. "Show me your daughter again."

He grinned instantly and I felt it in my bones. He was so proud of her. "See there? That's one of her art pieces."

It was a crayon scribble that might have been a duck.

"Oh. That's a...?"

He looked at me like I was dumb. "That's a palm tree."

"Of course it is."

He scrolled through some more pictures, bragging about each featured achievement. The man glowed when he talked about her, and it was so endearing I could have died on the spot. There was also video. "...this is actually her second cartwheel. When she did the first one I didn't get it on camera."

The girl's legs barely got off the ground. But when she stood up, she shouted, "Daddy, did you see?" and ran to him. She had olive skin like her father, long, straight black hair, and giant blue eyes that shone with adoration upon seeking his approval.

He picked her up. "I did, Pip. That was the best cartwheel ever." The video turned off.

"You two are precious together."

"She's my everything." He sighed. "I'm sorry I even asked about the party—"

"I'll do it."

"What? No. You agreed you wouldn't say that."

I shrugged. "I lied."

"Maggie—"

"You need help. You helped me out last night so it's the least I can do. We'll call it even."

"This isn't some tit-for-tat thing."

"I know that. But it obviously bothers you and I want to help. Besides, it's not like I have anything else going on. I'm happy to do it."

He steepled his fingers together while he thought about it. "This has the potential to blow up in our faces."

"It does. But that's why we'll be careful, right?"

He drummed his fingertips. "I have another bad idea."

"I'm all ears."

Chapter 10

Julian

Maggie waited with bated breath for my next bad idea. I had practically choked to get the first one out so saying this one out loud just might end me.

I chugged the last of my coffee to buy time. No going back now. She already agreed to be my fake fiancée for the party. My chest tightened from the war going on inside. A part of me knew this was a big mistake, that lying was never the right way to do things. But the other part of me—the part that hated the disappointed looks on my family's faces—knew this was the only way to get past their nonsense. A week ago, I had considered hiring an actress for the party to pretend to be my girlfriend. At least with Maggie, we had a shared history. I was hopeful that would make things easier and more believable.

I knew this was an absurd idea, but ever since I saw Maggie again, doing absurd things had become the norm. What was one more?

"The thing is, Piper is a very astute little girl. She notices things other people her age don't, always watching, always thinking. She pays too much attention at times, and if I show up with someone she's never even met, that could ruin the—"

"What are you saying, Jules? Just spit it out."

"Move in with us."

She coughed on her orange juice. "What?"

"I have a few spare bedrooms, so I'm not asking anything inappropriate. I'm not asking you to sleep in my bed with me. I know we agreed to one night."

"That's not why I choked."

"If you stay with us, it'll give you and Piper time to get to know each other, so when you're at the party, we can pass for a real couple, and Piper won't think anything of it."

Maggie sat back. "That's a lot to ask, Jules."

"I know. I told you—stupid ideas aplenty over here. But that's why I'm good at business."

"I don't see the connection."

"I have a lot of ideas, some good, some bad. Part of my success comes from saying the stupid shit out loud to get to the good stuff."

She smirked. "I can see how that would be helpful."

"Think of it as an all-expenses-paid vacation, only you'll be spending time with a kid, getting to know her."

Her smirk fell. "Truth is, I could use one of those. A vacation, that is. I'm about to lose my apartment and I am going to have to move back in with my parents."

"Oh shit, Maggie, I didn't know. I'm sorry." I could not imagine moving back in with my mom at this age. The woman was a treasure, but fully grown children living with their parents was a great way to destroy families. Between her gossipy friends driving me up the wall and her utter lack of common sense, I doubted our relationship would survive such a thing.

"The only people who know are Nora and my parents. It's not exactly my finest hour, so I don't talk about it much. Nora was kind enough to offer me a job at her law firm but I don't know anything about law. Besides, I don't want to be a burden on her like that."

"What did she plan to have you do?"

She rolled her eyes. "She wanted to hire me as a food and beverage consultant."

I thought about that for a moment. "Pretty sure that's not a standard job at a law firm."

"No, it is not. It was a bullshit title so she'd have an excuse to pay me way too much money for making cupcakes and pastries for her office."

That made me smile. "Sounds like you've got an excellent best friend."

"She puts the *best* in best friend. But still, I couldn't do it. Pride may be stupid but it's all I have left right now."

"Then it sounds like you can come to spend the next three-ish weeks with my family."

Maggie took a deep breath, and when she did, her cleavage threatened the integrity of her robe's belt, tugging on it as she inhaled. "Yeah. It makes sense. I don't want Piper to let the cat out of the bag. The week with your family will be stressful enough without that added to it."

"I'm asking too much, aren't I?"

"No, I didn't mean it that way."

"If you don't want to—"

She grabbed my hand and smiled. "Stop trying to talk me out of this, Jules. You're stuck with me, remember? You fake-proposed and everything."

I laughed, giving her hand a squeeze. "Guess I did, huh?"

"Yes, and we have to talk about how we're going to sell this to your family. I'll need a ring."

"That's easy enough. What else?"

She thought for a moment. "What kind of women do you normally date? I'm going to have to transform into one of them."

A laugh escaped me. "Please don't."

"I should confess something." She sat up fully and locked eyes with me. "I've googled you, and it sounds like you're a bit of a man-whore."

I chuckled. "What?"

"Look, I know you date actresses and the like so just tell me about them, so I'll know how to dress and act around your family. If I'm out of character they might suspect something."

I didn't know where to begin. "Uh, okay. My ex-wife, Claudia, was a model when she was younger, but she became a fitness instructor a few years before we met, and—"

"Are you joking? Tell me you're joking."

"I'm not. Why do you sound upset?"

A nervous laugh puffed out of her. "Last night... what did you think of when you saw me naked?"

"Yippee."

"What?"

"You asked what I thought of. My mind went blank, but that's what the teenager in my head shouted."

"No, I mean, it sounds like your ex-wife was this toned goddess and I am not that."

I shrugged. "No, you're soft and beautiful and warm, and you have these curves that make me want to..." I took a breath and blew it out hard, ignoring the tightness in my

Accidental Fiancé

balls. "Okay, I'm getting sidetracked. Let's stay on topic. My point is that Claudia was a high-strung person who was way too into her body and how she looked."

"Yeah, but the actresses..."

"Are fodder for tabloids and nothing more."

"I don't understand."

Once again, I was the parent ruining Christmas by revealing too much. "Publicity is a funny thing. If I have the latest starlet on my arm at a media-covered event, she gets good press for being involved with a rich man, and my company gets good press because I snagged the newest hot girl. It's shallow but it works. Most of the time when you see that kind of combination in a tabloid, that's why you're seeing it. Publicity. Nothing more."

"Oh. Wow."

"Don't get me started on pay closets."

"What's that?"

"One of the more tasteless things I've learned about since fake dating celebrities." I stared out the window, looking at the mountains and the city that sat below them. "Some celebrities, those with significant followings, have what are called pay closets. You ever notice how they tend to go around town wearing way too many clothes for the weather? Too many pieces of jewelry, far too many layers, scarves, sunglasses, hats, that kind of thing?"

She shrugged. "I figured it was to hide from paparazzi or to feel less exposed."

"I'm sure it is, in some cases. But for a lot of them, each piece they wear garners them a payout from the company that sent them that piece. Assuming the picture goes viral, of course."

"You're serious about this."

I nodded. "If they do it right, they can make enough to buy a car with one picture."

Her lips parted as if she wanted to say something but she only laughed. "I'm about to be kicked out of my apartment because my bakery burned down, yet they can buy a car with money they make simply from wearing clothes and getting their picture published. Clearly, I got into the wrong damn business."

Just hearing that made me want to give her money but I knew I couldn't. She'd never take it, and she'd be insulted the same way she was by Nora's well-meaning job offer. Her pride would never allow it.

"It's not all glitz and glamor for them if that makes you feel any better."

"How so?"

"I'm sure it sounds like nothing to you given your circumstances but imagine being beholden to that kind of pressure. Not being able to age or change your physical appearance. Choosing what you wear based on who will pay the most for you to wear it, not because it's something you want to wear. Being stalked, getting chased by the paparazzi, and having your picture taken everywhere you go. Never a true moment of rest or privacy. Not knowing if your kids will be kidnapped and/or bullied because of some decision you made or whether their accomplishments will ever be considered to be their own, not due to you and the connections you afford them."

She bounced her head from side to side, considering what I said. "Since I ate ramen for most of the past week, I'll happily trade their problems for mine right now."

"Great. I'm an insensitive jerk."

She giggled. "You're not too bad."

Accidental Fiancé

"I didn't mean anything by it."

"I know that, Jules. But what was your point in all of that?"

Time to come clean. "I don't date, Maggie."

"You just said—"

"Those aren't dates. They're publicity stunts. Nothing more. Since Claudia left, I've gone out a few times but none of it meant anything. Before she and I started dating, I had a couple of girlfriends, but it was never serious."

There was no sense in making her feel bad by telling the truth. Maggie had given me unrealistic expectations of what women were like. She had set the bar too high without even meaning to, and by the time I figured out that was the reason why I was disappointed in the girls I dated, I'd papered over my crush and moved on. Or at least, I tried to.

I finished college and built my business. By the time Claudia came along, she heard my family name and clamped onto me as hard as she could, thinking we were still wealthy. I did my level best to keep her thinking that because money was all I could bring to the table. I thought love would come eventually. I was wrong.

I admitted, "If I'm being honest, I don't think I had a realistic idea of what marriage should be. I'm not saying that to excuse Claudia's affair. But I'd be lying if I put it all on her."

"How is her affair your fault?"

"I don't mean it like that." I wasn't sure how to explain it. "I was in my late twenties when we got married, and I'd never seen what a good marriage was supposed to look like. My parents, well, you saw how they were before Dad died."

She swallowed. "They were… loud."

I huffed at that. "I think part of it is a Greek thing. But

yeah, the shouting, the plates breaking... loud is a good word for it. My grandparents were loud, too. I actually thought your parents had the perfect marriage until your dad's thing. Point is, I never saw what a good marriage was so I tried to make one out of what I thought it should be. I was working all the time and so was Claudia. But she was pretty and knew which fork to use at family dinners; I guess I thought that would be enough to build on."

Her tone was sweet but her words were harsh. "Young and stupid, huh?"

"Naïve might be a nicer way to put it, but yeah. Definitely."

"So you don't date at all?"

"I'm the CEO of a multibillion-dollar company and a single father. Dating is a time suck. So, no, I don't date. Not in any real capacity. Which means my family has little to no expectations of the woman I bring with me to the party."

"Hm." She sipped her juice. "Okay, but it'll cost you a wardrobe suitable for the week."

"Wait—is that why you asked what my exes dressed like?"

She smiled and nodded. "If we're selling me as your fiancée, they won't believe you'd downgrade to someone whose wardrobe staple is yoga pants and old tee shirts. That's not the kinda girl you'd marry."

"That's exactly the kind of girl I'd marry. But if you want a new wardrobe in payment for doing this for me, by all means, let's get out of here and go shopping."

"Now?"

"Sure, why not? Piper's babysitter is paid through today, and we need to get you moved in quickly."

Maggie bit her bottom lip. "Fine. Shower first, then shopping."

"As long as I get to watch."

She laughed and rolled her eyes, throwing her napkin at me, her tits bouncing when she did so. She teased, "Pervert."

"What can I say? You bring out the best in me."

Chapter 11

Maggie

I never knew a man who could shop like Jules. His first suggestion was a series of boutiques, but I opted for a mall. I couldn't stand the idea of him dropping boutique money on me. It felt like taking advantage. But once I got him into the mall, I realized my mistake.

The way his eyes lit up when we looked at the directory should have been my first clue. I should have gotten worried when he insisted the first store we hit should be the sneaker store. His explanation was innocuous enough. "That way we have comfortable shoes for walking around."

Which made sense so I didn't see the marathon coming.

Six hours later, he had made half a dozen trips to unload our bags at his SUV. He insisted we grab a bite to eat before heading to his place, so we stopped at a little diner close by. When we sat in the booth, my back creaked like I was a hundred years old.

"You're sure you're not going to make me do more shopping after this? Because I'll need more espresso if that's the case."

Accidental Fiancé

He smiled and shook his head as he perused the menu. "Unless there's something else you need."

"Oh my God, no. I didn't even need the last three handbags you bought, Jules. Why all the stuff?"

"You looked at them like you wanted them."

I cocked my head and frowned. "Huh?"

"You looked at them the same way you looked at me last night."

My cheeks heated. What the hell was I supposed to say to that? "I was just... it was acting when I looked at you like that last night."

"Acting. I see." His sly smile made me tingle in places I should not have been tingling. We were friends, nothing more. He lowered his voice, his tone cocky as he teased, "Then should I return them?"

He wasn't wrong about the purses. I wanted them. I just didn't realize how easily he could read me. I tried to sound casual. "No, we can keep them. I like them."

His damn smirk said he knew I wasn't acting last night. So I dodged his gaze by ducking behind my menu. It was safer back there.

Once our food arrived, I said, "Tell me more about Piper."

Again, he lit up. "She goes to a private day school for kids her age. It's at a semi-retired nanny's house, Etta Pence. Etta is amazing. She takes eight kids a year, maximum, and she has them during the day from ten to three, Monday through Friday. She teaches them all kinds of things—Piper can already read at a fifth-grade level, thanks to Etta."

"That's great." *What am I going to do during the five hours she's gone?*

"You have a car, right?"

"Yeah. She's older than I am, but she runs."

A single vertical line formed right between his brows as he frowned. "No safety features?"

I laughed flatly. "Outside of seatbelts? No."

"We'll have to rent you a car since you'll be taking Piper to Etta's." He must have noticed my expression because he quickly added, "If you don't mind."

I shrugged. "I'll kind of be nannying for her, right? While we get to know each other, I mean."

His mouth tightened. "If you're okay with it, yes."

"Then, sure. I don't want to cart her around in something you're not comfortable with."

Jules paused, smiling slightly. "Sorry, I assumed you'd be alright with taking care of Piper. Not everyone is a kid person, and I shouldn't have assumed that."

"Not a big deal."

"It is a big deal. But I appreciate that you're giving me some leeway on it. I'll try not to assume things like that going forward."

"It's going to be an adjustment for all of us. We're both bound to say and do some out-of-pocket things, right?"

He nodded. "Agreed. After we eat we'll stop by a rental place and get a safer car squared away."

"More shopping?" I whined.

"Is picking out a car really that much of a burden?"

"Stop having a good point."

It was after dark by the time I followed him in my rental car to his house. Even still, I could see how beautiful his home was. I parked and stared up, muttering to myself, "A mansion. Of course."

I shouldn't have been surprised, but the place was huge, especially for only two people. The building was three stories of white brick surrounded by sharply manicured foliage. Even the front walkway was white brick, illumi-

Accidental Fiancé

nated by subtle lighting. Everything was neat and tidy, and as much as I appreciated the look, it somehow made me feel out of place. Like I'd come in and mess everything up.

Jules stood at my door with a questioning smile on his handsome face, and suddenly, I wanted to go inside with him. He asked, "Do you like the car so much that you're going to sleep in it?"

I rolled my eyes and got out. "No, smart ass. I'm coming in."

"Good. I can't wait for you to meet Piper."

"Me too."

He drove into the four-car garage and emerged with a trolley to transport the bags from our shopping trip. As we loaded it up, he said, "Grocery day is easier when you have a trolley."

"How much food are you buying that you need a trolley? There's only two of you."

"It comes in handy when my cousin comes to visit or when I'm hosting friends or clients, having a party, that kind of stuff. Ready?"

"Sure."

The truth was, I was nervous. What if Piper didn't like me? What if all of this went wrong before we even got to Yaya's birthday party? When the reunion came up, I believed Nora would be by my side, weathering it with me. With her by my side, I could handle anything.

She wouldn't be by my side these next three weeks.

Wait. Last night, I handled it. Sure, Julian came along and helped—a lot—but I was handling Chloe just fine. I can handle this, too. A four-year-old can't be any worse than a pack of adult mean girls, right?

"Worried?" Julian asked as we wrangled the trolley to the side door. Tightly packed rose bushes lined the side walkway, illuminated by solar lights. No one was getting through those bushes without losing skin.

"Hmm?"

"You're drumming your nails on the trolley, Maggie."

I chuckled at myself and stretched my fingers out. "Sorry."

He stopped the trolley, the hanging bags swinging silently back and forth for a moment. "It's okay to be nervous about all of this. I am too. But I'm here for you. If this is too much, just tell me."

I shook my head. "It's not. I'm just overthinking things. It'll be fine once I meet her."

"Ok, good. Then let's go." He opened the French doors to the pristine white kitchen, and my breath caught. I wanted to live there. It was decked out in the latest top-of-the-line professional gear and stainless steel appliances. There was a large section of stainless steel countertop beneath a window, perfect for rolling out dough. The rest of the counters were white and gray marble, matching the floor. A large island sat in the middle, several gorgeous pots and pans hanging above it. There was a walk-in pantry next to the industrial-sized fridge. A large gas stove top, double ovens... a fantasy home kitchen if ever there was one.

Julian called out, "Rena? Pip? Where are you guys?"

The pitter-patter of tiny feet slapping against the marble floors drew my attention. "Pop!" An enthusiastic black-haired blur ran past me to hug his leg. He scooped her up, swinging her onto his hip. Only then did I realize she was also holding a purple stuffed squid-monster. It matched her pajamas.

Every time Julian had spoken of his daughter, he glowed. But now, his smile was almost blinding.

"Piper Black, I'd like you to meet Maggie Bryant."

Instead of shaking my hand, she held out her monster. "This is Cooloo."

I shook one of the monster's stuffed tentacles. "Pleasure to meet you, Cooloo."

Jules laughed. "It's Cthulhu, but she can't pronounce it, so—"

"Coo...loo...," Piper proudly said, as if she was showing off her pronunciation skills.

"Sounds like Cooloo to me, Jules."

She stuck her tongue out at her father, who sighed at me. "Already ganging up on me, huh? I knew this was a bad idea."

"Hey, Mr. Black." A twenty-something girl with long red hair and bright green eyes walked into the kitchen. She had the kind of looks that belonged painted on the side of a World War II bomber plane. A walking, breathing fantasy straight out of a men's magazine. She gave me a cautious smile and stuck out her hand. "I'm Rena."

"The weekend babysitter?" I asked her as I shook her hand.

Julian nodded as he set Piper down. "Rena, this is Maggie. She's moving in."

That statement earned wide eyes from Rena but they quickly vanished in a slight smile. "Okay, well, since you're home, I'm going to head out unless you need me for anything else."

"Dinner?"

"She's one peanut butter and jelly in."

"Alright, thanks Rena."

"See you later, munchkin." Rena brushed her hand against Piper's cheek and said goodnight.

Julian set his daughter onto the trolley then ran it down the hallway with her squealing all the way. As much as I hated her mom for leaving her behind, I enjoyed seeing them together like this. I followed, half-paying attention to them while the other half took in my surroundings.

Sandy beige walls complemented the light wood floors, and every space we passed had warm lighting and enormous windows showcasing the views of the ocean landscape. Family pictures and Piper's drawings lined the walls. Not much in the way of decor other than a few plants here and there. Despite the enormity of the mansion, it felt like a home.

Julian stopped the trolley at the end of the long hallway. "Okay, Pip, this is where Maggie will be sleeping. Grab some bags and—"

"No!" she shouted with glee, giggling as she ran into the bedroom.

He turned to me. "One of these days, I'll train her to be a good bellhop. Alas, today is not that day."

"Terrible service at this hotel. Two stars," I teased as I brushed past him into the bedroom.

The large canopy bed begged for me to jump on it next to Piper, who was busy tucking Cooloo into the crisp sheets. There was a large set of windows offering a beautiful view of the ocean. I walked over and cracked one open to allow the breeze to fill up the space and so I could listen to the waves all night long. I'd always wanted that but had never lived anywhere I could hear the waves crashing on the cliffs below.

The rest of the bedroom was as lovely as the house, with the same wood floors and sandy beige walls. The rich oak furniture was modern with fine detailing, copper handles, and smooth lines. A few watercolor paintings hung on the walls, each one an herb in the style of a scientific drawing. I spotted a quaint ensuite bathroom off to the left. Simple and cozy, yet elegant.

"What do you think?" Julian asked from behind.

"It's perfect," I breathed.

"Are you sure? There are three others available if you want to switch."

"I love it. I might explore the house some more tomorrow, but for tonight, I want this room."

Wonder lingered in his eyes. He didn't say what he was thinking, but I wasn't going to drag it out of him in front of Piper. His smile faltered. "Then this is your room for the night. You can unpack or wait until after you've toured the other bedrooms tomorrow. Entirely your choice. Pip, how about we leave Maggie to it?"

"To what?" she asked innocently.

"She needs to get settled in, change into her pajamas, that kind of thing. Come on."

"But I just put Cooloo to bed. He needs his beauty sleep."

"I don't think he's going to get any prettier, sweetie." He swiped Cooloo from my bed and picked Piper up. "You carry him, and I'll carry you, and we'll go eat leftover Thai food. Deal?"

"I get the noodles."

"Of course." At the doorway, he said, "Welcome home. If you want to join us for leftover Thai or order something else, feel free."

"Thanks, Jules. For everything."

"Same here."

Chapter 12

Julian

One thing I was adamant about was saying goodnight to my daughter. On the nights I was home, I made sure I was the one to help her get ready for bed and to tuck her in. With Maggie in the house, I worried Pip might feel a little weird about it.

As I pulled the sheets and blanket up for her and Cooloo, Piper huffed. I knew that huff all too well. It wasn't good. I sat on the edge of the bed. "What is it, Pip?"

"Nothing."

"Are you mad Rena didn't stay longer?"

"No."

Dread crept in. "Are you mad Maggie is here?"

She screwed her little face up in confusion and matter-of-factly said, "No."

"Then what's bugging you?"

She huffed again and flopped her arms over the blankets. "I want pretty hair like Maggie. She has princess hair."

"Princess hair?"

"You know, like..." she drew circles in the air with her fingertips. "Like that."

Accidental Fiancé

"You mean curls?"

She nodded. "I want curls. You have to have curls to be a princess."

"Who made up that rule?"

She shrugged and yawned. "I dunno. But all of them have it. Moana and Tiana—"

"What about Rapunzel? I remember her hair being pretty and straight."

"Yeah, but that's magic hair. It doesn't count. And then she gets it all cut off. I like my hair long."

"Well, maybe in the morning, we can try to get you curls." Not that I knew anything about long hair or curling it though I figured I could find her a wig that would make her happy.

"Okay," she said as she yawned again and scooted beneath the blanket. "Goodnight, Pop."

I bent and kissed her forehead. "Goodnight, Pip." She held up Cthulhu, so I kissed him, too. "Goodnight, Cooloo."

In as gruff a voice as she could manage, Piper said, "Goodnight, Juloo."

I snort-laughed. "Is that what he calls me?"

She grinned and nodded, curling him to her chest. "Unless you're mean. Then he calls you Mean Daddy."

"When am I mean?"

"I don't think you are but Cooloo says you're mean when I can't get the spicy noodles."

"The spicy noodles hurt your tummy."

"That's what I told him but he doesn't listen."

I rolled my eyes and smiled at the two of them. "Goodnight, troublemakers." I turned out the lights and gently closed the door.

Now, onto my other troublemaker.

I found Maggie in the first floor living room sipping a

cup of cocoa with her legs tucked under her on the couch. Her purple satin pajamas reflected the flickering light from the fireplace, and I could have stared at her all night long. Piper was right—she did have princess hair. Those long brown curls trailed over her shoulders and down her back in an enchanting, silky fall.

It was a challenge to pull myself away from staring. I cleared my throat, so I didn't startle her. "Hey, how about some wine instead?"

"That sounds nice. But I've committed to the cocoa. Would you happen to have peppermint schnapps?"

"I happen to have a game room slash man cave which also has a fully stocked bar. You can pick out whatever flavor of schnapps you'd like."

She was on her feet quickly. "Lead the way."

The stairs to the game room were located off the kitchen from the living room, so she didn't get much of a tour of the house, but I could make that up to her in the morning. "Pinball, poker table, ping pong, darts, billiards, arcades, a shuffleboard table. The bar is in the corner. Go nuts."

"Seriously, Jules, why do you ever leave the house?" she asked on her way to the bar.

I sighed. "I find myself asking that more and more lately, truth be told. But I haven't found anyone I'd be comfortable letting take the reins of my company just yet. When I do, I have a feeling I'll be spending a lot more time here."

She took a moment to examine her options and poured butterscotch schnapps instead of peppermint while I upgraded from wine to whiskey. "Cheers," she said, clinking her mug to my rocks glass. "The only thing this room needs is that comfortable couch from the living room."

"Back to it, then?"

Accidental Fiancé

"Yes, please. I want to be buried in that couch."

I chuckled and followed her back up the stairs. It was almost impossible not to take a bite of her ass, especially in those pajamas. So round and right in my face. It wasn't fair. But we were friends. Friends who didn't make moves on each other. Friends who didn't bite each other's asses.

Back at the couch, I took an arm seat, and she sat next to me, leaning on me. Was that what she did with her friends? I wasn't about to ask, I didn't want her to move away from me. Her vanilla scent filled the room, intoxicating my senses. Maggie was soon becoming my own personal drug.

"...want to disturb you."

I blinked out of the lust haze. "What was that?"

"I heard you tucking Piper in, and I was going to offer to read her a story so we could do a little bonding, but I didn't want to disturb you."

I was relieved to hear that. All day, I'd worried she would feel awkward around Piper, but it was nice to know she wanted to jump right in with her. "Maybe tomorrow night. Say, do you know how to curl a little girl's hair? Piper says she wants princess curls like yours."

She giggled, choking a little on her cocoa. "Oh my God, I would have killed to have her hair when I was her age. Maybe then my mom wouldn't have cut it all off to keep it manageable. Um, I'm not sure how to get my curls onto her head, but maybe if I had a curling iron or some rollers? I'm not sure. When I do my hair, it's usually with the goal of heat damaging it enough to get the curls to be pretty instead of frizzy, which means straightening out a lot of it."

"Don't you dare," I said, only teasing a little. "Your curls are perfect. Back in high school, I used to love to watch them bounce when you walked. Did I say that out loud?"

She shrugged. "I fetishized all kinds of things back then.

Freckle patterns, the way a tee shirt stretched tight over a guy's pecs. I think that's called being a teenager with hormones."

"Maybe."

"About the curls, remember when I disappeared into the hotel bathroom forever?"

"Yes."

"That was mostly to do my hair."

"Oh." Damn.

She nodded and drank heartily, draining her mug. "Maybe before I try to give her curls, I'll let her watch me get mine into line. She'll see they're not all they're cracked up to be."

I ran my fingers through her hair, relishing the texture. "I don't know. I think they're worth a lot."

She sighed and laid her head on my chest as she leaned into my hand. "That feels nice."

I hadn't realized I'd begun massaging her scalp. My hands seemed to have a mind of their own. But it felt right, as if that was what my hands were always supposed to be doing. When I dug my fingertips against her scalp, she moaned like she had during sex. That was all my cock needed to hear.

I tried to be casual about shifting myself away from her but it was impossible. She was already too close not to notice my erection. But she hadn't moved away from me, either. Instead, she leaned against me harder, unwinding tension from every inch of her body. I dug in more, desperate to hear more out of her.

Her breaths picked up, chest heaving enough to disturb the top button on her pajamas and display a lot more cleavage. The more I rubbed, the more she moaned. I worked down from her scalp to her neck, and that earned an appreciative, "Oh God" from her lips.

I gulped, trying to keep my urges out of it. "Too hard?"

"Never."

"Do you want me to go harder?"

Her voice quivered. "Yes."

I dug into her neck, craning my thumbs up either side of her spine to strip away her tension. The primal groan that poured out of her was unreal. Her velvety skin begged for more than my hands, and I pulled her hair over her right shoulder to bare the left one. Against the shell of Maggie's ear, I whispered, "We could stop right now if you wanted."

Her breath hitched in her chest. "Don't you dare."

I snaked my hand down her pajama top to reach her big, soft tits, one after the other. I flicked my thumb over her nipples, but they were already hard for me. She arched herself into my palm, and a low rumble built in my core. "Fuck, Maggie, I love these."

"What if she wakes up?"

"She won't." I didn't want to go into the details of my child's sleep habits at the moment. Saying her name would break the spell Maggie had on me. "But we could go to my bedroom if you're more comfortable there."

She answered by turning over and pressing her lips to mine. She tasted like chocolate and butterscotch. So sweet and so perfect. As she climbed over me, Maggie reached into my lounge pants for my cock, stroking me with her silken hand. It felt like heaven. She jerked me while I pumped against her hand, and if I didn't have other goals in mind, I might have left it at that.

But I pulled from her lips. "I need to be inside you."

She quickly nodded and stood up to scoot her pajamas off while I pulled mine out of the way just enough to expose myself and grabbed a blanket to throw over us. This was crazy enough without having to worry about innocent eyes seeing things they shouldn't.

Maggie kissed her way back up my body until she straddled me. Just before she sat to take me in, she asked, "Condom?"

That single word cleared my head just a little. "Shit." I thought for a moment. "I'll pull out."

She giggled. "I'm on birth control pills, and my last test came back disease-free. You?"

"I'm clean, no worries there."

"Then we don't really need condoms, right?"

"Thank fuck," I muttered as I grabbed her hips and pulled her on top of me. Her wet tightness sent my eyes rolling back in my skull. Too fucking good. I hadn't gone bare in years and worried it might be over too quickly, so I slowed her down by jutting myself up deeper into her.

Which only made things more exquisite.

"Fuck, Maggie, you feel like heaven."

"So do you," she gasped as she rode me, her pajama top still on but unbuttoned.

I sat up and took her nipples into my mouth, left to right and back again. This woman was a feast, and I had been a starving man. I wanted to devour every inch of her. "I love the way you feel."

She shuddered a gasp. "You... too." Her nails planted into my shoulders over my tee shirt, and her body went taut. "I'm... oh fuck, Julian, I'm going to... "

I pulled her down for a kiss as she came screaming into my mouth, writhing on my cock, shaking uncontrollably. Her pussy squeezed on me as she came, and I lost what little control I had left, shooting deep inside of her. We breathed into one another, too wrapped up in each other to remember there was a world beyond that moment. It was all I could do to remember my own name, but then hearing her calling it out as she came brought me back.

"Maggie?"

"Yeah?"

"I'm glad you moved in."

She giggled hard enough to squeeze me again, which was too much on my sensitive cock. Once she realized why I squirmed, she couldn't stop giggling, and I had to lift her off of me.

"Sorry."

"No, you're not," I teased.

"You're right. I'm not." Her sexy smirk was almost enough to get me going again.

Chapter 13

Maggie

I woke up alone in my room. We had agreed it would just be that one night, but I couldn't keep my hands off of him after he started playing with my hair. It was one of my trigger spots, want and desire burning through me like a blaze when he touched me there.

I didn't regret it. There was something about Julian that made me want him, and even though I had never thought of him that way back in high school, things were different now.

Hell, our chemistry alone might sell our story to his family.

I showered and dressed in my new clothes, and it felt like I was playing dress-up. The clothes I had picked out were what I imagined elegant, wealthy people would wear. Since I was trying to sell myself as his fiancée, I had to go big or go home. Some were comfortable, some were not, but I could survive if I picked up some of my own clothes from my place and incorporated them into my new stuff.

As it turned out, I was an early riser compared to Julian and Piper. I was up long before they were. That gave me enough time to bake a batch of fresh blueberry muffins. I also made some Irish soda bread for toast; in case they were savory breakfast people.

I had time left over to get a batch of cupcakes baked and cooling by the time Piper padded into the kitchen, rubbing her eyes. "What smells so good?"

"I made some—"

"What's going on?" Julian asked, looking equally sleepy as he came in. He was already dressed for the day in a light gray button-down and charcoal trousers, his suit jacket over his arm.

"Um, well, when I don't have anything else to do, I bake. Or when I'm stressed out, I bake. Or on a day that ends in y, I bake." I shrugged. "It's what I do."

He smiled. "So what'd you make?"

I smiled back. "Blueberry muffins with streusel, Irish soda bread, and there's a batch of cupcakes cooling that I'll frost later."

"Cupcakes?" Piper asked excitedly.

He winced ever so slightly. "For *after* school, Pip. Cupcakes are not a breakfast food."

"What a terrible thing to say," I countered. "But they're not ready anyway so muffin or soda bread?"

"You put soda in bread?" Piper squeaked. "Eww."

"Do you like toast?"

"Uh-huh."

"Peanut butter? Jelly? Marshmallow crème?"

She frowned. "Marshmallow crème?"

I was aghast. "You have never given her toast with marshmallow crème?"

A low chuckle carried through him as he grabbed a muffin. "I do try to be a responsible parent, you know."

"Well, since you have none here, I know where I'm going after I drop her off at Etta's. First, my place for some tee shirts and leggings. Don't make that face. I know we bought too many clothes yesterday, but sometimes, I need my cozies. And then the grocery store because your baking supplies are sorely lacking, sir."

He passed me a credit card. "Anything you need, put it on there. I'm going to take this muffin to go. I'll text you Etta's address." He kissed my cheek before realizing what he'd done. I could tell by the stunned look on his face and Piper's giggle.

"Pop kissed you."

I froze up.

His green eyes went wide but he forced a smile. "I kiss you before I leave, don't I?" He kissed her on top of her head. "Thanks for the muffin. Gotta run!" He started for the door.

"That muffin has as much sugar as a cupcake by the way," I called out after him. From around the corner, where Piper couldn't see, he playfully flipped me off.

I sighed, wondering what the hell to think about all of it. But instead of having time to dwell, I had Piper on my hands. Just the two of us. Without any clue how to talk to a four-year-old and no one else around, I asked, "So, breakfast?"

"Peanut butter toast, please."

"You got it, kiddo." I set her up with a slice and one for myself. "You go to Etta's for a while, and then what happens?" I probably should have asked Julian that before he left, but after that kiss, he nearly ran out the door. Not that I blamed him.

"Miss Carradine picks me up, and then we go swimming."

A text from Julian lit my phone. The details of Piper's usual day, along with addresses and scanned photo IDs of anyone involved. A good security measure, I supposed, though I had never considered what might be entailed in the daily life of a billionaire's child. Was I part of her security team now?

Once we finished breakfast, Piper took me on a tour of her favorite parts of the mansion. Getting the Piper's eye view of the place, I might have thought the mansion was a life support system for the pool because it was all she wanted to talk about. "...and this is where I do my flips. I can do three in a row. How many can you do?"

"I haven't done flips in the water in a long time. But maybe this afternoon, I can try."

"It's okay if you're scared. I was at first, too. But Miss Carradine will keep you safe. She was a limbic swimmer."

"Do you mean Olympic?"

"That's what I said." She pointed out the slides—as if I couldn't see them—and the hot tub, which she said was Julian's favorite but it was too hot for her. The pool even had its own lazy river and wave maker. The place was her own little water park, so I didn't blame her for wanting to stay there. But I had to insist that we get going, I didn't want to be late the first day I was dropping her off. I wanted Etta to like me.

She didn't.

I got Piper there on time and politely rang the bell to her Victorian-style home. The older woman gave me a stiff look when she answered the door. It might have been the over-starched clothes or the prim high collar on her blouse that caused it, but I doubted that. "And you are?"

"This is Maggie," Piper introduced me. "My dad kisses her. She lives with us now."

I could have died on the spot.

"It's not what you think. Julian was just caught up in

leaving for work. A kiss on the cheek as he's leaving doesn't... I mean, it's not like... we're not a thing. I'm just staying with him for a little while." *Why am I explaining myself to this woman? Stop talking.* I smiled, silently praying to melt into the concrete porch.

A judgmental huff escaped the crone's lips. "Very well, Piper. Come in."

"Okay. Bye Maggie!" she said as she dashed past the old woman.

"Should I come in too?"

"Certainly not. Mr. Black has approved my facilities and my methods. I do not require the presence of his... *friend*." She might as well have said floozy for all the distaste she threw on that word.

"Great. Bye, Piper," I said before jogging to my rental car. There was no one to judge me in there.

With five hours Piper-free, I had time to run errands. I stopped by my place and packed more boxes to drop off at my storage rental. A couple more days like this, and I'd be all moved out before the end of the week, which was good since my landlord had prorated my rent weekly at a much steeper cost.

I had until Friday to get my things out or he'd charge me for another week, and I couldn't afford that. But I also didn't have enough time to box everything up before Piper was out of school, so I had to spread out the work for the next few days. Thankfully, it was going to be much easier with the rented SUV than my old coupe.

The majority of my entire apartment sat in my storage space, looking at me as I shut the door. Things didn't have souls, obviously, but leaving my stuff behind felt oddly like I was abandoning it. I couldn't tell Julian I was nearly living out of my storage unit—I saw the pity in his eyes when I

Accidental Fiancé

mentioned I'd be living with my parents. If I told him the full scope of the situation, he would insist I stay with him until I got back on my feet.

And then where would we be?

After last night, I wasn't sure. In fact, every time I thought about last night, my brain shorted out. It was hot and crazy to do that in the living room, but I couldn't think straight when he touched me like that. Or whenever he was near me. Or whenever I thought about him.

A car blared its horn behind me.

Shit. Green light. I waved and said, "Sorry," as if they could hear me before I hit the gas again. I had to do something about this situation with Julian, and since I was terrible with men, I decided to call in the big guns.

I went back to Julian's, frosted the cupcakes, then drove downtown. It was a busy Monday, full of bustling streets and cool breezes, the most winter we'd likely get. The cacophony of downtown always made me feel claustrophobic as if those voices were pressing in on me. But when I pulled up to Nora's law firm, that sensation disappeared.

Skinner and Associates was known for their brutal tactics, and the building was as harsh as their reputation. Angular and vaguely threatening, the concrete architecture of the Brutalism movement was why Nora wanted this building in particular. No one else liked it, so she bought the ugly thing as a statement. She knew the potential of making the opposition meet her in an ominous space would work to her advantage, and she was right.

That was Nora's gift. She was always right.

The interior was modern, every area boasting personal touches because employees were encouraged to make each of their spaces their own. Nora might be a ballbuster, but she adored her employees and took great care of them.

When I walked in, the receptionist, Brandy, beamed at me. "Hi, Maggie. Do you have an appointment?"

"No, I was just—"

"No problem. I'll buzz you in."

"Thanks." It wasn't two minutes before Nora emerged. "Hey, Nora."

"Maggie!" She pulled me in for a tight hug. I never told her that her hugs hurt because she was a thin and bony beauty. Jerking her chin to my bag, she asked, "You brought cupcakes, didn't you?"

"I did."

"Perfect." She opened the bag and took two, then left the rest on Brandy's desk. "Pass these out for everyone. Maggie, my office." With that, she turned on her heel and plunged deep into the building.

I had to make an effort to keep up. Nora never slowed down for anything. Her blue pantsuit was an electric color that would have suited no one but her, given her fiery red pixie cut and pale white skin. Once we reached her office and she closed the door behind us, I said, "I might have made a mistake."

"Sit. We will cupcake and chat while I wait for my next meeting to arrive. Coffee?"

"Yes, please," I said enthusiastically as I plopped onto her office couch. It always surprised me that she hadn't knocked down the wall between her office and the next one to give herself more space. But as she put it, she didn't need a giant office to tell people she was in charge. They already knew.

The office was painted in varying shades of gray, white décor accents throughout. She kept the thermostat low but physically comfortable. After she delivered coffee and sat on the other end of the couch, she smirked at me as if she already knew about last night. "And what might that mistake be? Sleeping with your high school crush?"

I laughed, shaking my head. "Okay, first of all, Julian is not my high school crush."

"Oh, bullshit, doll. You had it bad for him back then."

"I did not!"

"Really? What was all that hanging out, just you and him about?"

"I hung out with you all the time, too. Does that mean that you were also my high school crush?"

Her smirk sharpened as she lifted a shoulder. "I don't know. You tell me."

I rolled my eyes. "No, you weren't. And neither was Julian. We were just friends."

"Mm-hmm. And the reunion?"

"I owe you a shin kick for not being there. And maybe a tit punch."

Nora snorted a laugh. "That's fair. Chloe was in a foul mood after you two left, so nice work. But what happened after that?"

My whole body heated from the inside. "Stuff."

"Yeah, I figured that out by the morning after call. But you're not the type to just show up without an appointment. It's one of my favorite things about you, not that you're not welcome to do so when needed. Maggie, what else happened?"

I took a deep breath and let it out slowly before explaining everything else that had happened since. "It feels like we've been on a dozen dates because we've spent so much time together in the past two and a half days. But also, because we did know each other back in the day, and now, after last night and this morning's goodbye kiss, I don't know what to think. Give me advice."

"He's a man. Run while you still can." Her usual recommendation.

"Not helping. This isn't a normal situation."

"No, it isn't. It's much worse."

"Why is that?"

"Because you like him."

I started to deny it but I couldn't. "It's too soon for that."

"And yet, here you are."

I sipped my coffee, trying to think of a rebuttal. "Stop being right all the time."

"It's my curse."

Chapter 14

Julian

"You got one more in the tank, I know you do! Come on, Julian, one more!" Dix cheered me on while my arms embarrassingly shook as if this were the first time I'd benched in my life. I could hardly get the bar back up without his assistance but seeing his hands hovering, ready to grab it, was enough for me to lift it over the edge of the hooks. Once the weight settled, I could breathe again.

"Fuck."

"Monday getting you, or is something else hitting?" Dixon Weaver was one of the best personal trainers in the world, and his physique proved it. He was tall and bald, and his muscles had their own muscles. He had been a professional football player until too many concussions caused an early retirement.

His gym was glorious. Every piece was made to his specifications, some having been handcrafted by the man himself. The outer wall of windows overlooked the ocean, but inside, the place was nothing but blood, sweat, and tears. Scuffed plates, wear and tear on the padding, worn knurling. The kind of gym that felt lived-in, the irony being that his apartment was the entire second floor above it.

"It's nothing. Just need to get my head in the game." *And Maggie out of it.* That was what the extra-long workout was for.

I had been distracted all day at work. I'd see a brown-haired woman and lament to myself that her hair wasn't as brown or as curly as Maggie's. When I smelled freshly baked chocolate chip cookies in the cafeteria, the scent overpowered me making me think of her, and I ended up agreeing to some ludicrous suggestion from the HR VP about decreasing vacation time. I fixed it right after but that could have been disastrous.

I could not escape her influence. It was a problem.

Dix knew me too well. "Who is she?"

"What makes you think there's a woman involved? It's Monday. Mondays are tough on everyone."

"Not you, Julian. You come in, you bang out your work, you stay focused, grounded. That's who you are, Monday or not. So...?"

I sat up, wiping my face. "Too soon to say."

"Ah, I knew it." He grinned. "Tell me about her. Didn't you have your class reunion this weekend?"

"Yes and I don't want to get into it."

"Whatever you say. Drop and give me twenty."

I cocked a brow at him. "What?"

"If you don't want to talk, then you want to work. Twenty pushups, and if you don't get on them quickly, I'm adding twenty burpees."

"Her name is Maggie."

He chuckled and put the plates back for me. "And is Maggie a blast from the past?"

I sighed. There was no way to get out of this without

destroying my body or my pride, so I opted for pride and told him everything. "I've had a crush on her since high school and this weekend all of my fantasies came true. But now, in the cold light of day, I'm not sure taking her to Yaya's party is such a good idea."

"You said it's for three weeks, give or take, right?"

"Right, but three weeks of living together suddenly feels longer, you know? We were together most of the weekend, and this morning, I accidentally kissed her in front of Piper. That's not what you do when it's a temporary thing."

"For sure. But you're comfortable with her."

I nodded.

"You like her."

"Yeah."

"So, why not move things to the next level when enough time has passed? What's the big deal?"

"Because she's my fantasy, I'm not hers." The words hung in the air like the scent of rancid garbage. Heavy, oppressive. Horrible. All my insecurities in one sentence. Dix had seen me at my worst during my divorce but this was hitting differently. I felt more vulnerable and I hated it.

He took a beat to recalibrate. "I think you're selling yourself short, man."

"I'm not." I moved to the dumbbells for curls to burn out the last of what I had in the tank. "She never thought of me like this in high school, and I'm not going to make things weird for her. If she brings it up, I'll apologize and play it off. If she never brings it up, even better. But I'm not going to be a creep about it. The kiss this morning was a one-time thing."

"Like the night of the reunion?"

I exhaled my disapproval loudly but kept going at my curls.

"And the following morning? That was a one-time thing too, right?"

"Must you continue?"

He chuckled. "Chin higher. Too much give in your back."

I did as he instructed. "Better?"

"Yes. And another thing—"

"Can we not? I've been overthinking this all day."

"Whatever you say. Shoulders back."

I made the adjustment and got a better burn in the bicep. "What do you mean by that?"

"I mean that if she didn't want to be kissed this morning, she wouldn't have climbed on you last night."

"You don't know Maggie."

"Do you? It's been a minute since you two hung out, so maybe you should get to know one another again instead of pounding each other's brains out for a night. She's your fantasy girl, but reality might pour some cold water down your shorts."

He had a point.

How much did I really know about her as an adult? Not a lot. But that didn't seem to matter when I pulled in at home and saw her rental car parked in front of the garage. Something deep inside of me settled down, knowing she was inside the house with Piper. I might not have known the details of who she was these days, but I knew who Maggie was at her core.

Which was why it was so hard to keep my fucking head about her.

When I walked into the house, the aroma of tomato sauce wafted up my nose and I followed it like a drooling animal to the kitchen. There, I found Piper, wearing a chef hat and an apron, next to Maggie, who wore the same thing.

That feeling that had settled down in my chest now lifted and swooned.

They were too cute together.

"Hey, you two."

They both jumped, and Maggie ended up with tomato sauce dripping onto her apron from the wooden spoon in her hand. "Oh damn it, I mean dang it. Piper, you can't say the other one."

My daughter laughed while Maggie cleaned herself up. She teased, "Dammit!"

"Pip, language. What is all this?"

"Thought we'd make you a proper supper. She says she loves noodles, so we decided on spaghetti and meatballs. Sound good?"

"Sounds incredible. But you could have ordered something." I sat at the kitchen bar and rolled up my sleeves.

"Where's the fun in that? I'll make you a bowl."

Piper came to sit next to me. "Pop, did you know you could make noodles?"

"Yes, I... Maggie, did you make the spaghetti?"

"Mm-hmm," she said as she ladled everything together.

"I don't know how much work that is, but I'm sure it goes way beyond opening a box. Why go to all the trouble?"

She shrugged and set the bowl in front of me. "Taste it first and let me know if it needs anything."

I did, and the supple noodle had edges on it that picked up the sauce in a way I didn't realize spaghetti could. The sauce itself was succulent, yet not overly heavy, and seasoned to perfection. And the meatball was the stuff of meatball dreams, full of flavor with just the right density. I had no words. I just kept eating.

"Does it need anything?"

I shook my head and kept at it.

The three of us slurped pasta together, putting a serious dent in the massive amount Maggie had made. She swore it was impossible to make a small amount, so she had made enough to feed a small army. I was so full by the end of it that I said, "If you keep cooking like this, I'll have to do extra-long sessions with my personal trainer every day."

She smiled at me over her glass of wine. "Salad tomorrow?"

"That'll make up for tonight, but what about the next day when I ask you to make spaghetti again?"

"I'm glad you liked it. But I have other plans for the rest of the week."

"No more spaghetti?" A terrible thought.

"Nope, something else. Hopefully, you'll like it just as much. And there will be more vegetables involved."

"No!" Piper shouted as she climbed down from her chair.

But Maggie insisted, "You remember all the vegetables I put in the sauce and the meatballs? It'll be like that. You won't even notice them. I promise."

"Okay. We can have yucky vegetables."

I couldn't believe she caved so easily to Maggie's demands. Piper never did that. She must really like her.

"How about you start getting ready for bed, so when you get sleepy, you're all set?"

"Only if you get in your pajamas, too."

"Deal."

"Yay!" Piper ran down the hall to her bedroom.

I shook my head in disbelief. "How are you getting her to comply so easily? Non-compliance is sixty percent of her personality."

"It's probably just because I'm new. Once she gets

comfortable around me, I'm sure the honeymoon phase will be over. All set?" she asked, her hand out for my bowl.

I gave it a teasing smack. "No possible way. You made this amazing dinner from scratch. The least I can do is clean up. You sit and have another glass of wine. Tell me about your day." I picked up my bowl and Piper's and carried them to the sink. Maggie had already snuck hers in and rinsed it off. I pointed at a new device in the kitchen. "What's this thing?"

"That's my stand mixer. I used it to make the pasta. It's handwash only."

"Got it." I tackled the kitchen, starting with the mixer first. "So, things with Piper today went well, I take it?"

"She's a fun kid. Loves her swimming pool."

I laughed. "Yes, she does. Her swim lessons went okay?"

"Yes, her lessons with an Olympic gold medalist went just fine." The way she said it made me worry.

"What's that about?"

Maggie laughed to herself, rolling her eyes. "You hired a gold freaking medalist to teach your kid's swim lessons, Jules. That's not exactly normal."

I shrugged and went back to what I was doing. "I want the best for my little girl. Go on."

"Um, Etta does not like me."

"The only people Etta likes are children. She's amazing with them. Adults, not so much."

Maggie went quiet for a moment. "Piper mentioned to her that you kissed me this morning and that I'm living here. She must think I'm the girlfriend of the week by the look she gave me."

"Did she say something snide to you?"

"No. Just a look. Like I was trash."

"I'll have a talk with her."

"Don't you dare! Not until after I'm gone. I don't want you to say something to her that makes things weird when I'm dropping Piper off in the mornings."

That word again. "We certainly wouldn't want anything to be weird."

"What do you mean?"

"Mag-gie! You're not in your pajamas!" Piper shouted from down the hall, my saving grace.

"Right." She scooted off her chair. "Excuse me. Duty calls." She took her wine with her.

Once the kitchen was cleaned and I changed into my loungewear for the night, the three of us gathered in the first floor living room for a movie. Maggie made popcorn—something I never kept in the house—and Piper ate it up as if she had never had popcorn in her life. Which come to think of it, she might not have.

We let her pick the movie, something about fairies battling an evil wizard. But all I could think of was how much I wanted Maggie to sit closer to me. How I wanted to drape my arm around her shoulders and smell her hair while we watched the movie.

Instead, I plunked Piper between us as a buffer. Between her and the giant popcorn bowl, I had a safe distance from temptation. Casually, I snuck a hand into the bowl and snatched some for myself.

"Pop! That's my corn!"

"And we can make more," Maggie said sweetly. "No need to be greedy with it."

"Okay. Sorry, Pop."

I shot Maggie another glance. New or not, I did not understand the spell she had over my daughter. "That's alright, sweetie. I know how you are with food."

"I don't share."

Accidental Fiancé

Maggie laughed. "Isn't sharing a good thing?"

"I like it when other people share with me. But I don't like to share with other people."

I interjected, "We're working on it."

"Hmm," Maggie said, thinking aloud. "Maybe if the adults around Piper asked for popcorn before digging their thieving hand into the bowl, she would be more willing to share."

Piper grinned up at me. "Pop has thief hands."

"She doesn't like to share, and I don't like hearing no. It's a volatile combination." I grabbed another handful out of sheer rebellion.

"Pop!"

"Am I going to have to move the popcorn bowl over here so only Piper and I can reach it?" she teasingly chided.

"I have long arms, and I'm not afraid to use them."

Piper defiantly placed the bowl onto Maggie's lap. "No corn for Pop!"

But Maggie threw a piece at my face and giggled. "Maybe just one piece."

"Oh, it's on!" I reached over, but she held the bowl away, twisting to keep me from it. So I tickled her to make her drop it.

Piper scooted out from between us and shouted, "Tickle fight!" then she went after my feet, knowing how much I hated that.

Maggie, the voice of reason, tried to pull away and stand up, but I yanked her back down onto the couch for more torture until she whooped and squirmed sufficiently enough to satisfy me. I let her up and she stood there, breaths heaving as her smile faded. She chewed her bottom lip as she looked into my eyes.

But Piper was undeterred. "Get him, Maggie!"

113

"No, I-I need more wine. Be right back." She left the bowl on the end table.

"She knew I'd win," Pip said as she climbed back onto the couch next to me. "That's why she stopped."

But I had a feeling that was not the reason. The truth was, all of this was too easy. Maggie fit into our life seamlessly, enhancing it in just a day. The breakfast treats, the meals, the suddenly compliant child. It was as if she took the little things that were mildly bothersome—making dinner, managing Piper's defiant streak—and turned them into pleasantries.

Now I understood what she meant when she said it was weird because things *weren't* weird, especially where they should be. She made this situation too comfortable, and I didn't know what to do about it.

But I had to figure it out and soon. Otherwise, when she left for good, she'd walk out with my heart in her handbag.

Chapter 15

Maggie

I stared at the ceiling all night long. That moment of the three of us tickle-fighting on the couch was too much. I replayed it over and over in my head, and I knew what the problem was, but I didn't want to put a name on it. I didn't want to acknowledge it. I wanted to pretend it didn't happen because I didn't want to be one of those pathetic people who imagined themselves in the perfect life with the perfect family.

Crap.

I was one of those people. I had grown up thinking I had the perfect family until my father's stroke, and even after that, things were hell for a while but we got through it. I wasn't some child with unrealistic expectations of the world. I knew how it worked.

I understood the kind of work that went into keeping a family together, or in our case, gluing it back together. My parents never had an easy time with money, so I understood the value of hard work, too. Life wasn't easy for people like us.

So how in the hell did I end up sleeping in a mansion on

the beach? Throughout the night, I replayed the events of the past few days, trying to figure out the point where I screwed up. This had become more than just a favor for a friend. And the scary part was my heart wanted exactly that, it wanted things with Julian to be more.

He had saved me from Chloe and Harmony. But that was what friends do for each other. The mistake came when I blurted out that we were engaged, when I let him kiss me, when I went up to his penthouse suite...

The guys I dated couldn't bribe their way into a penthouse suite much less afford one. That room, that night, everything that happened in it... it all felt like a dream. That was someone else's fantasy that came true, not mine. Real-life fantasies like that didn't happen to girls like me.

I didn't live in a fantasy world. I didn't even daydream about things like that. My feet were firmly planted on the ground. That was how it had to be otherwise I'd be setting myself up for disappointment. My motto was: keep your nose clean, eyes on the prize, don't deviate from the plan, and you'll be fine.

Dad always said stuff like that and Mom concurred. That was how they paid for their house, how they afforded a vacation every couple of years, how they lived their lives. Simple. Below their means. They firmly believed that was the way to get ahead. They taught me to stand on my own two feet and not depend on anyone but myself.

But then my bakery burned down. No amount of keeping my eyes on the prize or sticking to a plan could have prevented my dreams from going up in smoke. It was a freak accident, according to the investigators. They dragged their feet on the insurance payment, as meager as it was. It would take a long time for me to save up enough money to start over.

Accidental Fiancé

Maybe I was being naïve but the fire shook my worldview. I was so focused on the plan—get my bakery established and popular enough to open a second then a third, eventually branching out into a chain of them. Made-from-scratch delicious pastries bringing smiles to anyone that ate them. I'd build a life out of making other people happy while doing what I loved. It was as close to perfect as I could ever imagine.

And then poof. All gone.

Mom and Dad didn't know how to help get me through it, either. They were just as shocked as I was when the fire happened; all of those years of careful planning and execution going up in smoke, pun intended. Mom simply told me, "Move in with us, and we'll figure out a new game plan together."

That was it. My Plan B was figuring out a new plan. I had never allowed myself to have a Plan B before or to think about failure because as Dad would say, "That's quitter talk. You gotta believe in yourself, kiddo." But no amount of positive thinking would rebuild my bakery.

I hadn't told my parents I was staying with Julian. I wasn't sure how they'd react to me living in a short-term situation, especially one so glamorous. Hell, when I was a kid, they didn't like it when I watched shows with wealth or magic in them because they said it gave me the wrong impression, that life was easy. I grew up on documentaries and the History Channel instead.

Nothing but reality for the Bryant's, they told me.

The reality at Julian's was my sheets were cool and smooth, and felt delicious on my skin. The mattress was firm and comfy. The canopy danced in the ocean breeze. I listened to the sound of the waves echoing through my room as they lapped at the cliffs below, which sat approximately ten feet above a tiny private beach. A wooden stair path led down to it and I loved it.

For a few brief and wonderful moments, I could believe this was my home.

But that wasn't *my* reality. Last night I wanted to buy into the fantasy of slipping into Jules' family, *Jules'* reality, and that hurt more than I realized it could. This was not my world, and I had to remember that, no matter how nice it felt to lose myself in it.

In my world, parents couldn't hire Olympic athletes to teach their kids to swim. People didn't pass out credit cards like candy or rent someone an SUV so they had better safety features. Buying someone an entire wardrobe as payment for a simple favor was something people in my world only saw on TV.

Being in Julian's home was like playing make-believe with an adult-sized dollhouse. None of it was real. But it *felt* real, and that was the problem. Because last night, for just a moment, I let myself believe that it was.

I threw the covers back, got dressed, and headed for the kitchen. I needed to bake some feelings out. Today felt like a bagel day, so I pulled out my trusty stand mixer. Between letting them rise and boiling them before the bake, it took a while to get them right. But a fresh homemade bagel was well worth the effort.

Once the first batch was ready, a pair of curious noses came trudging down the hall. Julian's hair was still rumpled, which made him all the sexier. "You made bagels?"

"Yep. There's cream cheese in the fridge."

"Damn, girl, my trainer is going to love you." He swung the door open and bent at the waist, making his muscular ass stick out just a little. He did not have that ass in high school.

"That's great because I think I love him too. There's lox underneath the cream cheese."

"You're my hero." He grabbed both, and we set up a bagel station on the kitchen island bar.

Piper devoured her breakfast without a word. Moments later, she went back to bed.

"Is she okay?"

He nodded. "She has night terrors. According to her doctor, it's best if I let her work out her own sleep schedule. We tried a strict one before, and that only made them worse."

"Poor thing."

"What do you have on tap for the day?"

I wasn't used to telling someone my plans, and even though it was an innocent question, I still bristled at it. "I think I'm going to hang out here today. Get more acquainted with my surroundings. I haven't been to the third floor yet—"

"It's just old books mostly," he said with a shrug. "Mementos, that kind of thing. But feel free to explore."

"Not worried about me finding your kinky sex dungeon?" The moment the words left my mouth, I knew I shouldn't have said them. It was too flirty. Too suggestive.

A slow smile formed on his lips. "Are you?"

My heart sped up, and my mouth went dry. "Should I be?"

His smile widened a little more. "Get as acquainted as you like." He picked up his bag. "I'll see you later."

When he left, the lack of a kiss this time was felt. "Stupid," I muttered to myself. Julian was not mine. As I scrubbed the counter, I reminded myself that the only things in the house that were mine were my stand mixer and my clothes. Hell, not even the car was mine. I had to keep myself tethered to that reality, no matter what.

When it came time to take Piper to school, I gently knocked on her door. "Piper?"

She opened the door, dressed and ready to go. "You're taking me again?"

"I am. I will be for a few weeks if that's okay."

She bobbed her head and took my hand. Hers was so small, and for some reason, that made my heart wobble. I didn't understand it. I'd never been a kid person, but maybe Piper was a grown-up person.

In the car, I turned on the music and sang along to each song, teaching her the words so she could sing along with me. It was a party until we reached Etta's doorstep. I smiled and kept things pleasant if for no other reason than to be the bigger person.

Back at the house, I ventured up to the third floor to find Julian was right. It consisted of books and an area with boxes full of memorabilia. There, I found his dusty old yearbooks and pictures from childhood. Rosewood High School spared every expense on the quality of such things—I was surprised they hadn't fallen apart. The materials were so shoddy that a stiff breeze could easily have blown them away.

Flipping through the pages, I found a picture of me and Julian sitting outside laughing. He and Nora made high school pleasant for me. Without them, I might have gone into mean girl territory myself just to survive. Kind of like Emma. How easy it would have been to end up like her, had I not had Julian and Nora.

A few pages later, I found a picture that took my breath away. My hand clutched at my throat when I saw it. I'd let Nora braid my hair that morning, something I rarely did. In

Accidental Fiancé

the picture, I was upset, walking down the hallway with Nora. About ten feet behind us was Jules. He looked bereft. That day came to mind so fast that it was like being there all over again.

We had gone behind the cafeteria where no one hung out, so I could rant without getting yelled at for bad language. I was mad about getting a B on a calculus test because I had shown my work, and the teacher still said it wasn't enough, that I had done too much of the math in my head. I was frustrated and distracted so I hadn't noticed when Julian moved in. Not until I had a close-up view of the gray specks in his iris. The next thing I knew, his lips were on mine, a lustful, hungry kiss.

I told him the first thing that came to mind—that a kiss wouldn't fix my grade. He laughed it off and said he was willing to try anything to help. But then the bell rang, and I had to get to class. We didn't have the chance to talk about any of it afterward.

The moment I saw Nora, I knew I couldn't say anything to her about the kiss. I loved her, but she would have teased me about it, and I didn't want to hear it. I just wanted to forget it ever happened. Julian was my friend. Nothing more.

At least that's what I told myself. But maybe he had always been more.

It wasn't hard to believe the narrative she mentioned yesterday. That he and I were always hanging out if she wasn't around. Was it more than a friendship? Had he told himself it was and that's why he had kissed me? Or was he just experimenting with me to see how I'd react?

That was what I had told myself back then, that it was just a harmless kiss to distract me from being upset. Maybe I had told myself what I needed to believe at the time because seeing this picture of him following me in the hall with that look on his face was not the face of a boy who had tried to make his friend feel better. It was the face of a boy who just had his heart broken. I had humiliated him with a casual joke and he had been kind enough to let it go so he didn't upset me any more than I already was.

I flopped onto my back on the rug and told the ceiling, "Ugh, I'm an asshole." I could not believe I didn't see it sooner. Maybe it was because in high school we all had multiple types of pressures we were under, and we were all just trying to survive.

Shortly after the kiss, Julian's father died, and that overshadowed everything that had come before it. He was emotionally distant for a while and I was too young to have the grace to handle it well. Eventually, we came back to each other right before he left for college. It wasn't the same, easy-breezy thing we had before, but we were still us. I worked to put myself through culinary school while he was away and we were both too busy to keep up with old friends.

But things were different now. We were adults with bills, responsibilities, a kid in his case. Every time I thought about Jules a passionate warmth filled me up, making me want his goodbye kiss every morning. I liked him, and I was tired of pretending otherwise. My parents were right—embracing reality was the smart thing to do. Even though we agreed in the beginning things would be short term with us, that didn't mean we couldn't keep this going.

The alarm chime rang loudly, letting me know a door had opened. I ran down the stairs with the yearbook still in hand and found Julian walking into the kitchen. I was still back in high school in my head so I saw the cute boy overlayed with the handsome man he had become. It was dizzying.

"Oh, hey."

"Been on the third floor, I see," he said, jutting his chin at the yearbook.

"Yeah. You're home early. Is everything alright?"

He nodded, looking tense. "I wanted to talk to you without Piper around."

"That sounds serious."

"Not really," he replied, sitting at the kitchen island. "I'd like to pay you as a consultant for your time, Maggie. That being said, we keep things *strictly* professional between us moving forward. No more lines crossed. What do you think?"

Something fractured in my chest, and for a moment, I couldn't speak.

Chapter 16

Julian

"Yeah. Okay. Great."

Her words were clipped. Which was how my manhood felt—clipped. I didn't understand why. This was the perfect solution. Had I said something wrong? "Why are you agreeing but you sound pissed?"

She started cleaning though everything was already clean. "I'm fine, Jules. Staying strictly professional is fine if that's what you want to do. This sounds like a wonderful plan."

Why do women say fine when they mean anything but? I was having flashbacks of my marriage, and if she didn't hold still and listen to me, this conversation would go just as well as that did. "Maggie, put the sponge down. Let's talk about this."

"There's nothing to talk about. You've already decided." She stood before me, sponge poised in her hand. "Lift your forearms for me."

I did as she asked. She wiped beneath them then quickly spun away. "There's no need to be snippy."

"I'm cleaning. Since when is cleaning being snippy? I

Accidental Fiancé

thought you'd appreciate that your *employee* is doing their job."

Fuck. I stood and cleared the distance between us to stand in front of her. But she stepped back, dead coldness in her eyes. That chill made me want to shrivel up and die.

Okay. I clearly had to give her some space. She would soon realize this was the best thing for both of us but she had to figure it out on her own terms. I had never been good at explaining my rationale, but if I left now, she wouldn't understand why I believed this was the only right way to do this.

"I should have had this arrangement in place before you moved in. That was my bad, and I'm amending it with back pay. But first of all, you're not an employee." I snatched the sponge from her hand and threw it into the sink. "You're a consultant. That's a completely different tax form."

Her icy glare didn't budge.

Okay, bad attempt to diffuse the situation.

"Secondly, the only part of this that is a job is when you pretend to be my fiancée at my mother's home. The cooking you've done here, the cleaning, that's entirely up to you whether or not you want to continue. I don't expect it, but I do appreciate it. More than I can say. Maybe I can figure out some kind of bonus for that."

"Whatever you say, boss."

My head dropped back in frustration. "Maggie, I'm trying to keep things above board here, and you're making me feel like I did something wrong when I'm literally trying to do the *right* thing. So how about you tell me what the right thing is, according to you."

"This is great. I need money and this is a legitimate way for me to earn it. Can't think of a better arrangement. Done and dusted, right?"

"Then why do you sound and seem so pissed?"

"Because you threw my sponge into the sink, and I was using it."

I gritted my teeth. "You sounded pissed before I took the sponge."

"Must be your imagination."

I stretched my fingers to stop from cursing. "Fine. If that's how it is—"

"That's how it is." The wrong kind of fire lit her from within, and I hated that I was the one who sparked it.

"Glad we had this talk. I'm going to the gym."

"Oh, that was all? I thought you wanted to talk about something important," she spat as she turned to the sink.

I felt two inches tall. I'd hurt her feelings and that was not my intention. "Maggie," I said as I reached for her shoulder. Her whole body tensed at my touch and not in a good way.

"Just go, Julian. Please."

I left. It felt like I was being kicked out of my own home but I didn't care. I wasn't about to ask her to leave when I was the one who had caused her to be so upset.

As soon as I walked into the gym, Dix read me. "What did you do wrong this time?"

"How the hell do you do that?"

He shrugged his massive shoulders. "It's a gift. Wanna get changed and then we can talk about it?"

"I'd rather lift about it."

"That's the spirit. I'll meet you here."

After I changed and rejoined him on the floor, we warmed up with a run on the treadmills where I explained things. "...so really, it's what's best for everyone."

"Julian Black. Brilliant billionaire yet total idiot when it comes to women."

I hit the stop button on his machine and mine. "How's that?"

"You gave her an out when she wanted an in."

"What are you talking about?"

"Think about it from her point of view."

"That's all I've been doing, Dix. She doesn't want me. She never has. I just made things easier for her."

"I'm gonna make you give me twenty push-ups every time you say something dumb. As of now you owe me sixty."

"You are out of your mind if you think—"

He shook his head. "She doesn't want you? She never has? You're making things easier for her? That's three right there. Three times twenty is sixty. Start now so you can get through them."

He was not going to let up so I gave in. Screw it. Between reps I said, "She doesn't. I tried in high school. I kissed her. She blew me off. I've never been on her radar, Dix. Not once. Making this into a business thing makes it easier for her when she leaves, so she doesn't have to feel bad about leaving me and Piper behind."

"This is my house. We don't lie in my house, Julian."

"I'm not lying!" I rolled onto my ass after number sixty.

He sat beside me and we stared at the ocean through the glass wall. "A man who says he's not lying is either definitely lying, truly not lying, or lying to himself. Only one of those choices makes it a true statement, so there's a two out of three chance that you're lying, and half of that means you're lying to yourself and you don't even know it, which is just sad and unlike you. You're more conscientious than that. So the most likely situation is that you're lying, you know it, and you're still going to do it because that's what's comfortable for you. Am I right?"

"That was too much math and philosophy for me all at once. I needed Maggie to get me through both of those classes back in the day, so…"

He slugged my shoulder. He had one hell of a punch, even when playing around. "Go make up with your girl."

"She's not my girl! None of this is real!"

Dix blew out a breath, a considerate expression on his face, while eighties punk rock played on the speakers. Our usual workout music. "I'm a simple man, Julian. I like my steak rare. My wine red and full-bodied. I like to lift heavy. The steak, the wine, the weights, they're as real as things get. Good steak and good wine, you can't fake those. The weights weigh the same if you lift them here in California or in Timbuktu. That's how I like things, and I'd consider myself somewhat of an expert on what's the genuine article."

"Your point?"

"You ran into your old crush. Found her in trouble and helped her out. Had a night of passion that turned into a morning of it, then proposed a cockamamie idea to her, which she willingly accepted. You had another passionate night with her, and now, you're pulling back. Maybe you got scared, maybe you didn't, but it's pretty typical for guys to withdraw at the start of things."

"So what?" I ran my fingers through my hair. "I swear to God if you don't get to the point soon…"

"What I'm saying is, it might have been on an abbreviated timeline, but all of it sounds fucking real to me."

"It's not that simple."

"Falling in love is the simplest thing in the world, Julian. It's people who make it complicated."

I frowned so hard it hurt my face. "What?"

Accidental Fiancé

"The first time I fell in love it was with a 1973 VW Thing. You know what those are?"

"Some strange-looking old car."

"Bite your tongue. They are gorgeous. Not everyone's cup of tea, but still. That convertible had me from the moment I saw her. Falling for her was simple. Love at first sight. I knew I had to have her." He smoothed his hand over his bare scalp. "Felt the same way about my first girlfriend, too, but she had to go and make it complicated. Eventually, I understood her. Some people like to play hard to get."

"Maggie's not like that."

"I'm not talking about Maggie. Sharon and I dated for two years in college while I was playing ball. Things were great. Until she tried to change me. My point is that people tend to make love complicated when it's not. But if you insist on making things complicated for yourself, we'll work it out of you. Time for the stair climber."

Instead of moving, I laid back. "You're bringing the stair climber into this because you're annoyed I won't go talk to Maggie?"

"Your point?"

"That's not how training works."

He snorted a laugh. "You're gonna tell me how training works now? Should I tell you how the pharmaceutical industry works? Get your ass up, boy. Stair climber or burpees. We're gonna cook some of that attitude out of you."

"Stair climber it is." The grueling march up the fake stairs burned my legs and ass like hell. Even my lungs were smoked in short order. "Feeling cooked."

"Good. Keep going."

I smacked the stop button instead. "What is this really about, Dix? Why are you riding me so hard about Maggie?"

"Who else is going to? You're not going to listen to her for some dumbass reason, and you barely talk to your family. So that leaves me, and it's my job to kick your ass. Professionally speaking, of course."

"Yeah, but I..."

"I had you on the treadmill, push-ups, and now this beast. You wanna know why?"

I shrugged. "Sure."

"Because when your head ain't in the game, you're more likely to hurt yourself on the heavy equipment, and Julian, your head is so far up your own ass that you can't possibly have it in the game."

"Bullshit."

"You almost sounded like you believed yourself, that it's better for her this way."

"It is."

He clapped my shoulder. "What you meant to say is that it's better for *you* this way."

"In what world is this better for me?" I asked a question I already knew the answer to. I was stalling for time until I thought of something to distract him with.

"If this is just a transactional relationship, then once it's over, you don't have to feel bad about it later. Didn't you tell me you planned to hire an actress for your family thing?"

"Yeah. So?"

"Why didn't you go with that original plan? You know it'd be less messy than this. But when opportunity knocked, you went for it with Maggie. So why not hire the actress?"

"Maggie knows me."

"Maggie *knew* you."

"Exactly. That's why it made sense to go with her. We could make it more believable seeing as we had shared history to reminisce about in front of my family."

He laughed, shaking his head. "Maybe you should have been an actor, man. I could have almost believed that line."

"Dix."

"Get over yourself and go get your girl or be complicated and miserable. The choice is up to you. But no more lying in my gym."

"Since when are you my therapist?"

Another laugh. He pointed at the diploma on the wall. "Since you walked through my door six years ago. Remember?"

"You're not playing fair. I forgot you're a therapist."

He grinned. "Never said I played fair. I play to win."

"So do I." I marched off the stair climber past him to the locker room.

"Where are you going?"

"To fix this."

Chapter 17

Maggie

The next time Julian decided to come home early he texted first to make sure I was there. Oh, goody. Just what I needed. More of him.

Piper was in the back with her swim coach so at least she wouldn't hear us fighting. If it even came to that. I didn't know what he was coming home for. Another arrangement? Another fuck? His emotions felt like a moving target. It wasn't fair.

None of this was fair.

Things with Jules had somehow become complicated. I never knew where I stood with him. We talked my first day but since then, there hasn't really been much of a connection. With Piper around, it seems like we can't talk to each other in the way we want to.

I imagined that was how most parents normally felt. Happy to have their kids but also stifled when it came to interacting with their partner. I felt like I owed my parents an apology for existing.

I didn't want to talk to him. Not after he made me an employee. No, wait, not an employee. *That's a different tax*

Accidental Fiancé

form. God, I couldn't believe he said that. I swore sometimes I did not understand what was going through a man's head.

While waiting for Julian to show up, I texted Nora. "Drinks?"

"When and where?"

I suggested a bar to meet at so I could give her the full dish, and she promised she'd show up, but I had my doubts. With her schedule being what it was, I didn't know whether or not I could count on her. All I knew was that I would be there. I needed a freaking drink. And since I still had Julian's credit card, it would be on him.

A fleeting thought hit me. What if she never showed but I met a guy there? I'd be well within my rights to hook up with someone. Not that I had ever done that kind of thing. My first one-night stand was with Julian and look how that turned out.

Maybe I just wasn't cut out for a one-night stand. Whenever I hooked up with somebody, we'd seen each other at least a couple of times. Sex was always something that I considered personal and private. I was careful about my heart. I never wanted to get too attached too soon. Attachment was supposed to grow over time, not in minutes or days.

I wondered if I should bail on the situation entirely. Maybe all of it was just too complicated for me.

But then Julian walked in, and my stupid hormones kicked up, nearly choking the words out of my brain. I blurted, "Glad you're home. Are you staying this time? Because I'm going to go get drinks with Nora."

"Piper in the pool?"

"Yep."

"Good. I was hoping to talk to you."

"Two talks in one day? I'm a lucky girl."

He sighed loudly. "Maggie. We knew from the start what this was. The moment you told Chloe that we were engaged, you knew what this was. The moment you agreed to be my date for the party and stay here you knew what it was. You made the rules. I wanted to come up with a way to pay you for your time. A new wardrobe is not enough for what you're dealing with."

I laughed bitterly. "No shit, Sherlock."

"So this is better, right? Drawing clear lines and solid boundaries? I can't help but think that this is the way to go about all of this. It keeps us on a level playing ground."

"I didn't realize we were playing a game."

"I'm not. Bad metaphor. If you could just hear me out and see things from my perspective maybe we could—"

"No need." I grabbed my keys and headed for the door. "Jules, I'm a big girl. I can handle the truth. I don't need you to make this into anything more than it is. You want things to be cut and dry? Fine. That's what they'll be."

"Maggie, don't leave angry."

"Like you said, I'm your fiancée when we're around your family. Until then, I'm on my own. Like I've always been. So I get to decide how I feel about things, not you. And if I want to leave angry, then I will fucking leave angry." I slammed the door behind me and ran to my car.

I couldn't handle the thought of Piper seeing me like that. I had to get out as fast as I could.

I drove so fast that I passed the bar before I realized it and had to do several illegal turns to get into their parking lot. But once I parked, I didn't want to go inside. The rental car was a safe place. No one was there to tell me what to do or how to feel. No one telling me that they'd pay me to be their girlfriend.

What the hell did he think I was?

I smacked my hands on the steering wheel a few times in an attempt to get the anger out. But it only made it worse. I reached absentmindedly into the glove box for the package of Altoids I always kept in my car. They weren't there. I shouted obscenities as I remembered that I was not in my car. I was in a car that Julian had provided to me. My rental. His rental, really.

I got out and slammed the door. Being in the rental felt like being surrounded by him. And I just couldn't take that right now.

The distance from the rental to the door was short. The place looked like a thousand other dive bars I'd been to in and around LA. Sticky floors, black painted walls, neon lighting, and a fully stocked bar with a grungy-looking bartender behind it waiting to serve me. Exactly what I needed at a time like this.

I ordered a whiskey and coke and found a booth in the back to wait for Nora. If she ever showed up though I wasn't sure how much it mattered. Not until I was flooded with relief when she walked in. She ordered her drink and joined me at the table.

Sometimes I hated that she had a big fancy lawyer job because it meant she was always well-dressed when I looked like crap. "What's the emergency, doll?"

That was all it took before I became a blubbering mess. I told her the whole story, including what had happened on the third floor and the memory that the yearbook had conjured along with how I felt when I saw Julian after that.

I also told her about the consultant title.

She drummed her perfectly polished nails on the gross table. "Get it in writing."

"What?"

"The consultant title and everything that goes along

with it. Not just the money but any perks he's offering as well. Get it all in writing."

I braced my forehead on my fingertips, trying not to scream. "Nora, that's not the problem here."

"Oh, I'm well aware of what the problem is. The problem is that you've found yourself falling for your crush again. But what I'm telling you is to focus on the things you can control. Your tender little heart is gonna do stupid things. You can't control that. But you can get this newfound bullshit in writing. At least walk out of the situation with some serious money in your pocket."

"Take off the big lawyer hat and put on the best friend hat because that's the kind of advice I need right now."

She yanked a napkin out of the dispenser and passed it to me. "Clean yourself up, doll. And for the record, that was the best friend advice. The lawyer in me is screaming right now because there is so much legally wrong here, not the least of which is the fact that you could get one of the most powerful men on the planet brought up on charges for being a john."

That made me laugh. "Sure, that's exactly what I want."

Her lips turned upward at the corners. "Got you to laugh, didn't I?"

In spite of myself, I laughed again. Then I kicked her shin. "I owed you, remember?"

"Yeah, yeah. Seriously, are you going to go through with this?"

"Honestly, I don't know. I don't know what the right call is anymore. I was just starting to realize my feelings for Julian when he came at me with this and now I don't know what to think. Was all of this just some kind of conquest because he wanted me back then?"

She smiled at me with nothing but kindness in her eyes,

and I knew something bad was coming. "Remember how we talked about the two of you hanging out a lot, especially when I wasn't around?"

"Yeah."

"I know you said it was platonic. Maybe you thought it was but I don't think it was that way for him. And I really wonder how much it was for you too."

"I told you I didn't have feelings for him back then."

She held up her hands like she was about to give up. But I knew Nora. That was never going to happen. "Maybe you didn't have conscious feelings for him, but can you leave room for the possibility that you had unconscious feelings for him?"

"What are you talking about?"

"You didn't date back in high school."

"So?"

"Why do you suppose that was? Why do you think you didn't start dating until you were in culinary school? That you never had any interest in any of the boys at our school?"

I shrugged, not sure if I liked where she was headed with this. "I don't know."

"Maggie, he was your boyfriend in everything but the term and the physicality. There may not have been kissing or handholding or any of that kind of intimacy, but you two were tight as hell. You didn't need a boyfriend. You had him. He was your fake boyfriend years before you were ever his fake fiancée."

Her words knocked the wind from me. "Oh. Shit."

She sipped her drink and looked at me with those knowing eyes. "Sorry to be the one to break the news to you. I kind of thought you already knew."

"I never thought of it that way. I just thought that we were friends."

"And I'm pretty sure that he thought that building on that friendship would guarantee a good romantic relationship."

It made sense when she said it but it still hurt. "So you think he was faking a friendship with me that whole time?"

She grabbed my hand and squeezed it. "You know that I am not a fan of the lesser sex, but I will say this for him—he has been a truer friend to you than most people ever have. He has always been there for you in your hour of need. I think you owe it to yourself and to him to work this out. And I cannot believe that I am saying that in favor of a male."

I snort-laughed. "Me either. It's so unlike you."

She shrugged. "It's this new therapist. She's got me thinking that men are humans too. Gross, I know."

"Nora, they're not all bad."

"After everything you've been through you can actually say that with a straight face?"

"Well, I mean, Mr. Rogers was a man."

"How do you know that for sure?"

I opened my mouth to speak but found myself frowning instead. She had a point. "Okay, I don't know that for sure, but probably."

Chapter 18

Julian

"I thought Maggie was gonna read to me," Piper said as I tucked her in.

As if I needed another dagger in the heart. "She had to go help a friend. I'm sorry, sweetie. Do you want me to read to you?"

"No." But her dismayed tone said otherwise.

"I don't mind."

"Being read to at bedtime is kid stuff."

"Well, that's okay because you're a kid."

Still, she shook her head. "I was gonna let Maggie read to me because she wanted to. Not because I needed it."

"I see. Well, do you mind if I want to read to you?" *Please, kid, I need a win today.*

"Okay."

I scanned through her books and picked one of my old favorites—The Cat in the Hat. She was asleep before Thing 1 and Thing 2 arrived. I wasn't sure why I liked the book so much. Looking at it from an adult standpoint, it was kind of ridiculous. But maybe that was why I liked it.

Things had always been so serious when I was a child.

My mother hadn't been able to live her best life until after my father died, and it bothered me to think the same was true for me. Sure, we were a version of upper-crust destitute after his death, but things worked out in the end. My father could be a difficult man. Some days, I worshipped the ground he walked on, and other days, I couldn't stand to look at him. Maybe it was just that way between fathers and sons.

I kissed Piper's forehead and tucked her in a little tighter before leaving the room. I would do whatever it took to make sure that we never had that kind of relationship. It was hard not to spoil her, and I knew I did a bad job of it. But she was silly and fun, an easygoing little girl. I wanted to nurture all of that in her. I wanted her to have the childhood that I wished I'd been able to have.

If that meant reading The Cat in the Hat until she fell asleep so be it. I wanted her to have an active imagination full of whimsical and silly dreams. Everyone needed a little of that in their lives.

When Maggie walked in the door, I knew right away how much I needed it. Though maybe calling it walking was a little generous; she more like stumbled through the door.

"Hey."

"Hey, yourself." She leaned on the kitchen island.

I could smell the cheap whiskey on her from five feet away. "You didn't drive home like that, did you?"

"And what if I did? What's it to you?"

"Maggie, come on—"

"I didn't," she interrupted me. "I don't do that. Nora drove me."

"She didn't want to come in?"

"Pfft." A curly strand fell in front of her eyes, and she

tried to blow it back into place, failing. I leaned in and tucked it behind her ear. She recoiled a full ten seconds later. "Don't do that!"

"Sorry, I was just trying to help."

"You don't get to do that kind of thing. You're not my boyfriend."

Just what I needed to hear. "I never said I was. I was just trying to help you out, Maggie."

"Why?"

"Because when my hair gets a little long and falls in front of my forehead it bothers me."

"No, not that." Her coffee-brown eyes held warmth again, and I felt less left out in the cold. "Why do you help me?"

"Because you're my friend. That's what friends do."

For a long moment she stared at the scar in my eyebrow. I held my breath. What had Nora told her?

Finally she said, "You should have more scars. They suit you. You're too pretty otherwise."

I laughed, both relieved and because what she said was funny. "Sorry, almost all my scars are emotional. Hard to see those."

"Not really." Maggie stepped over to me. I felt her heat through her clothes. She drew a line with her finger down my jaw. "There's a scar here."

Her touch made it impossible to breathe. "I don't have a scar there."

"Yeah, you do. When you get mad, you clinch right here."

"I don't think—"

She placed her palm over my heart. "You have one here, too."

I swallowed hard, certain she could feel how hard my heart was pounding. "More than one."

"Why am I here, Julian?"

A tricky question. "In what capacity do you mean?"

"Why me? Why this?"

"We're just two friends helping each other out." The words sounded as hollow as they felt.

"And this business arrangement makes things easier, right?"

No. "Right."

"I'm sorry about earlier. I know I reacted badly but I'm doing better now. I'd like it if we could put all of that behind us. This is a business arrangement. Basically, we're colleagues."

Why did it gut me to hear her say that, when that was exactly what I wanted? I cleared my throat. "Right. Colleagues."

"We had a little indiscretion. It was fun but it's over. Now we can move on to the business part of things." She poked my chest with her pointer finger then sat down, almost toppling her chair over before sitting properly.

The distance helped me clear my head. "Where are you going with this?"

"Nora says I should get all of this in writing. Our arrangement, that is. And I think she's right. I mean, if we're gonna keep this to a business professional relationship, then we should have some set rules. A written contract."

This was getting worse. "That sounds like a great idea. That way, we can agree on terms."

"Exactly," she said, gesturing emphatically. "I'd like to talk pay."

"Are you sure you don't want your lawyer present?"

She drew her finger down the kitchen island. "Somehow, I don't think you're gonna screw me on this."

And now I wanted to screw her on the kitchen island. I rasped, "What do you have in mind, Maggie?"

"I'd like—"

"What was your take-home pay for a year at the bakery?"

She laughed sharply. "You think my bakery was financially sound? I'm flattered.

"What does that mean?"

"Basically, I took home enough to be able to pay my rent, and that was about it."

"Fine. Let's figure out what the average baker takes home in a year, and that will be your day rate for a month in case things run long with my family. Deal?"

She stared at me for a moment, her voice coming out in a whisper. "That's a lot of money."

"I can afford it."

I tried not to fall into the trap of her giggles again but they were infectious. "Okay. Put that in writing."

So I did, writing it on the nearest piece of paper I could find. A paper towel. I signed it and passed her the pen along with the "contract."

"There you go."

She giggled some more as she signed it. "I don't think this is technically legal."

"I'll have my legal department draw something up in the morning. This is just a preliminary contract, so we're both on the same page."

"If you say so." She stumbled getting off the chair and I had to catch her before she fell. Our faces were startlingly close together as I helped her stand up. "Thanks."

"Don't mention it." *Ever again.*

Her words came out slow and slurred. "I'm going to go to bed now."

I hated myself for what I was about to say. "Can you do that safely?"

"Well, I've been doing it for quite some time so I believe I can."

"Maggie, you can barely stand. Do you need help getting to your bedroom?"

"Maybe."

I shouldn't be doing this. I put my arm out for her to take. "Let me escort you to your room at least."

As she took my arm her scent about killed me. It was as if every part of her was designed to knock down my boundaries. Her softness, her warmth, her very presence. I wanted it all. Each step toward her bedroom felt like hell.

When she walked in drunk, I thought for sure we were headed either for a fight or to the bedroom. A checkmate either way. But this bizarre stalemate didn't sit well with me. I wanted a clear win or a clear loss. Not a tie.

Once I got her to her room I knew things were about to get worse. She didn't let go of my arm as she walked inside. Instead, she pulled me in with her and closed the door.

"Maggie, what are you doing?"

"I think I need more help."

"What is it?"

She sighed and turned around, lifting her hair to expose the button on her shirt. It fastened at the nape of her neck. "I don't think I can unbutton this on my own."

I laughed under my breath and unfastened it for her. "You're all set."

"I'm not though." She lifted her top over her shoulders and threw it onto the floor. My blood pressure shot up like a rocket, among other things. "I need help to get my bra undone, too."

This woman was trying to kill me. Seeing her take off her blouse was enough to give me a hard-on. Something so simple on its own but I had to aim my hips away from her as I reached over and unclasped her bra.

I'd be fucked for sure if she felt me.

I wasn't sure that was a bad thing anymore.

Before I could say another word, she had her hands over her breasts and turned around, keeping the cursed bra in place. "Thank you, Julian. You can go now."

Hoarsely, I asked, "Are you sure?"

"Mm-hmm. Thanks for all your help."

I clicked my tongue when I realized what she was doing. "You're welcome. See you in the morning, Maggie." My pace as I exited was somewhere between a run and a walk. If I didn't escape her, things were going to turn into something that neither one of us could handle.

That wouldn't have been fair to anyone.

As much as I wanted to believe that she was just playing a game, I wasn't sure anymore. Was she flirting with me to punish me? To tempt me? To prove that we couldn't be professional about this? If this was just a game to her, then how did she feel about me?

It didn't matter. I had to do the smart thing for my future, for my daughter, and that was keeping this professional. Nothing more.

I couldn't afford for it to be anything more.

Chapter 19
Maggie

A long unpaved road wound through an orange grove to reach the Black family property. When the trees parted from the roadside, I caught my first glimpse of the mansion. It was grand, its architecture reminding me of pictures I'd seen of Greece. Many of California's older mansions were inspired by Spanish style—red terracotta roofs, stucco walls, arched doorways and windows with decorative wrought iron elements.

The Black family home looked like it belonged in Athens, built for the mythological Greek gods.

Surrounded by several acres of private land, the mansion was a testament to the Black family fortune. It was no wonder that when it fell into disrepair, they needed a lot of money to fix it. I couldn't imagine attempting to repair this place with some glue and duct tape—my father's go-to fix for most household problems.

Everywhere I looked there were columns and arches. The walls gleamed white and the front door was a brilliant blue, similar to the deepest parts of the Mediterranean Sea.

An appreciative whistle came out of me as we pulled up

Accidental Fiancé

to the entryway where a group of uniformed men waited. "Your mom has a valet?"

"Only for special occasions," Julian said. "They'll take the bags for us, too."

There were details of his world that still astonished me and this was one of them. But I brushed past it to keep the peace.

For the past few days, things had been tense between us though not as bad as when he first brought up the idea of keeping things strictly business. I kept myself in check and so did he. There were no inappropriate incidences of groping, grabbing, or anything else, and we both found excuses to avoid being left alone in the same room with each other.

Here, we would get no such reprieve. Here, for all intents and purposes, we were a couple. An engaged couple, which meant we would be sharing the same room. I was fine with that. I could keep my hands off of him. I just hoped that he could do the same.

At least, that was what I told myself. But days of closeness with no real connection had started to wear on me. Though, at this point, I was afraid to ask him what he actually thought of me. It was strange to play the role of an escort for a friend, and I wondered if he even considered us friends anymore. Things had gotten so muddled in the past week that I didn't know what to think. All I knew was I needed to get a job done, get paid, and get the hell out of here.

Things like friendship and romance could wait. I had bills to pay.

We had a contract in place, and it listed very clear boundaries between us. But we were also adults with urges, and that made things a little less than cozy at home. Here, with one fewer boundary between us, I didn't know how I would handle things. Plenty of people would be around us in the mansion most of the time. I hoped that would be enough to distract us and keep things amiable.

A smiling older woman stood in the doorway. She was generously proportioned and elegantly dressed in red. Her silky salt and pepper hair had been pinned into pretty waves near her face to frame it. When she spied Piper, it was as if her whole being came alive. "There's my baby girl!"

"Yaya!" Piper squealed as she ran to her, arms wide.

"Pipsqueak!" she replied lovingly as she crouched and hugged her.

I sensed Julian's anxiety as we joined the two of them at the doorway. I wasn't sure how much of his nervousness was an act but I certainly couldn't blame him for it. One wrong word, and this was all over. Thankfully, Nora had told me to have it written in the contract that if things went tits up with his family, I still got paid for the full month. He hadn't balked at that, adding if things went well, I'd also get a bonus.

He cleared his throat to interrupt their hug. "Hey, Mom."

"There he is," she said, smiling warmly and embracing him. "Nice of you to make time in your day to come see your family."

His lip curled in annoyance at that slight. "We're here for the week. Just like everybody else."

She lowered her sunglasses and looked me over with the same piercing green eyes Julian had. I knew the first meeting would be tense, and considering who she was, I needed her to like me. I'd done what I could to look as presentable as possible, but I had no idea if I'd pass the sniff test.

Accidental Fiancé

I was dressed in a cream blouse with striped navy slacks. Nothing flashy, nothing too trendy. My makeup was minimal, my jewelry simple. I'd even gotten my curls to go in the same direction, so they looked purposefully arranged. It was the best I could do without an army of stylists, which Julian had offered to hire.

But we were here for a week, so unless he wanted all those stylists to tag along, it seemed like overkill.

"Aren't you lovely. Julian, is this your lady friend?"

"Maggie Bryant, this is my mother, Artemis Black."

I shook her hand, and it took her only seconds to clock the ring on my finger. She glanced up at her son. "Is there something you need to tell me?"

He kneeled next to Piper. "Sweetie, go find your cousins and play, okay?"

"Okay!" She ran inside.

Once she was gone, he put his arm around me. "Yes, there is, but we're trying to keep things lowkey for Piper, given the sensitivity of the situation with Britney. So please, no big announcements this week. If people ask about the ring, that's fine, but I don't want this week to become about our engagement. This is still new."

"Far be it from me to want to make a big announcement about my only son's engagement. You must think I'm a monster for wanting to celebrate such an occasion. If you want to break your mother's heart by forcing her to keep all of this happiness bottled up inside, I'm not going to stop you."

I wasn't sure how, but I felt as if we'd fallen into a trap. But Julian merely laughed it off. "Mom, cut the theatrics. I'm hoping Maggie likes our family enough to still want to join it by the end of the week, and you're not helping."

They grinned at each other, and although I wasn't

sure what had just happened, she came in for a hug and said, "Welcome to the family, Maggie. Please, come inside. Julian, show your future bride the house then meet the rest of us in the lounge. Almost everyone is already here." She twirled around and disappeared down a long hall.

In fact, it seemed everything around me was long halls. The whole building was built like a hotel, complete with a grand dual staircase foyer with black banisters accommodating white marble stairs. Along the back, French doors framed a view of the mountains and a large swimming pool enclosed with a retractable tinted canopy.

"This way," Julian said, taking my hand as he led me down the first-floor hall. "We'll be staying on the second floor in my old room—it's where I always stay when I visit. But I wanted to show you this first." He opened a set of double doors, and low and behold, I gasped like a movie heroine ready to faint.

This was the real fantasy.

A kitchen as glorious in the truest sense of the word. Appliances I didn't even recognize lined the walls, both vintage and new. Metal rack after metal rack sat at one end, organized like a library of small appliances. Multiple stainless and marble counters took up most of the open space.

I hardly noticed the staff, and once I realized they were there, I felt terrible about it. "Sorry to gawk," I blurted upon the realization.

A woman with thick forearms and a happy smile shrugged. "No worries. Fresh tiropsomo will be available in ten, so feel free to come back."

"Tiropsomo?"

"It's a Greek bread, similar to focaccia," Julian explained. "But with feta and more herbs."

My stomach growled. "Oh, I'm gonna need some of that."

"We grow our own food here. The olive oil is freshly pressed," she went on. "If you're into food, I'd be happy to tell you more."

"I am. Very much."

"You're welcome to visit anytime, then."

He put his arm around me. "I have a feeling if I don't get you out of here, I'll never see you again."

"Would that be so bad?"

"Come on," he said, grinning.

"I finally find a kindred spirit in your world and I get dragged away."

Once in the hall, he explained, "Eleni will talk your ear off, and we have other business to attend to. Sorry. In your downtime, feel free to seek her out."

"Business. Right." That word still stuck in my craw. "Where to next?"

"Our room. You need to be able to find it even after multiple shots of ouzo."

"My liver is not going to have an easy week, is it?"

"I'm afraid not."

As we ascended the staircase I asked, "So this is where you grew up?"

"Indeed."

"No wonder you didn't want me and Mom moving in. It would have been too crowded."

He rolled his eyes. "I told you—we had to do a ton of repairs back then. Honestly, it's amazing we were able to salvage the place, considering the mold issue among other things."

The second-floor hallway had thick, patterned rugs and potted plants to warm the space, but that didn't change the hotel feel. Doors lined either side, and I half-expected to see room numbers on them.

Julian opened a door at the end of the hall. "Here we are."

"I'm sure I'll be able to find the door at the end of the hall regardless of how inebriated I am. Didn't really need a tour for that."

He cracked a smile. "Is it so wrong that I want to spend time with my fiancée?"

There was no one around, so I didn't know who he was pitching this to. But we had talked about it beforehand, and unless we were behind closed doors, we were going to play our roles as best we could.

"I suppose not." I walked in as he held the door for me.

The bedroom was bigger than my old apartment. A sitting area and bookshelves made up one side while the bed and an enormous fireplace filled the other. Our luggage sat near the books. I glanced outside the window and spotted lemon trees lined up with lush greenery in between. They smelled wonderful.

I faced him. "Was your mom trying to get you laid by giving you this bedroom?"

"I doubt it. This has been my room since I was a boy. I don't think she had that in mind when she decided this would be my space."

"I know you call this place home, but Julian, this isn't a home. It's a hotel."

He laughed and shrugged. "Home is where the heart is, right?"

"That's what they say."

"We should probably catch up to the others in the lounge and see what terror Piper has wreaked on her cousins."

Accidental Fiancé

"She's the troublemaker out of the kids?"

"At times." My body tightened as he came closer. "Before we go, I just wanted to say how much I appreciate you being here, appreciate you doing this for me. I know I'm paying you for your time, but thank you, Maggie, really."

It felt like the perfect kissing moment, but since we weren't doing that, I chucked his shoulder instead. "Anytime, pal. Ready to catch up with your family?"

"Sure."

The lounge was on the first floor in the other wing. As it turned out, the house had three—east, west, and north. The remaining area consisted of the pool. At first glance it did not appear to be anything out of the ordinary. But upon closer inspection, it was enormous. His grandfather had insisted on an Olympic-sized regulation pool for his home, so the house was built around that feature. In addition, there were two jacuzzis, a water slide, and a lazy river. Similar to what Julian had in his home but on a much larger scale.

I was caught up in the grandeur of my surroundings as we walked into the high-ceilinged lounge when a distinct voice cut through the din of people chatting over cocktails. "Oh my God, Maggie, how are you?"

No, no, no.

Talons gripped my shoulder and turned me around. There, smiling like evil incarnate, was Chloe Foster.

My brain shorted out, and I stammered, "Wha-what are you doing here, Chloe?"

"You're such a kidder," she said, hugging me. "I'm sure Artemis is thrilled to have such a funny future daughter-in-law. Oops, did I let the cat out of the bag?"

"Chloe," Julian said sharply. "Why are you here?"

"Don't you ever talk to your cousins? I'm dating

Marcus." She lowered her voice, "It's gotten serious, so he invited me."

I muttered to myself, "What fresh hell is this?"

She laughed. "Come, I'll introduce you."

"No, Chloe, that's my job," Julian said firmly. "Thanks, but no thanks. See you around." He whisked me away to a corner by the bar. "Cocktails, then we figure out a game plan, okay? Don't quit on me now."

But I wasn't quitting. There was a difference between quitting and understanding you were outmaneuvered. "She'll tell. She must know something."

He leaned in close to my ear. "She doesn't know shit other than we pawed each other at the reunion. If anything, this sells the story. Can you handle her, or do we need to create a dying relative of yours as an exit excuse?"

From across the room, Chloe's laughter shot through me. Instantly, I assumed it was about me though chances were probable it wasn't. That was the trouble with bullies, they made it impossible to stop thinking about the next time they'd attack.

I had decided at the reunion that I had ceded enough territory to Chloe over the years and that was over. I wasn't going back.

I drew a quick breath. "I'm good. Get me a cocktail, and I'll be golden."

He smiled slyly. "On it."

I hoped I hadn't lied.

Chapter 20

Julian

What the fuck is Chloe Foster doing here with Marcus?

It was hard not to ask the question aloud. But I had cocktails to order. "Two whiskey and cokes. Thanks." The bartender hustled for our drinks and they were perfect. They were always perfect here. Mom had a thing about hiring good help, and when the family came over, she pulled out all the stops.

Yaya's birthday was the biggest family occasion of the year. Bigger than Easter, Thanksgiving, or Christmas. Mom believed people deserved to be celebrated more than traditions. Even though Yaya wanted her to be more traditional, she wasn't about to turn down celebrating with family.

Ever since coming to the states, Yaya was adamant that she see the family as often as possible. Our Greek relatives weren't able to visit often, so we stepped up to the plate whenever we could. When I was growing up, Sunday dinners were always a big deal. But as me and my cousins got older and created lives of our own, we weren't as available. Eventually, things boiled down to a week to celebrate Yaya, and we were basically off the hook for the rest of the year.

Which begged the question: Why was Chloe here?

This event was for family. Not casual acquaintances, tenuous significant others, or buddies. The only people who brought friends were the kids, and that was rare. So anyone who made it into the house was important, and that could mean only one thing—Chloe Foster's relationship with my cousin Marcus was serious.

I could not let that stand.

But more importantly, I couldn't leave Maggie alone anywhere. Normally, Yaya's birthday week included a variety of events, and that included a spa day for the ladies of the family. I had to figure out how to keep Maggie out of that.

Watching her as I crossed the room with the drinks, I could tell she was doing her level best to keep from staring at Chloe. Not that the bully noticed. She was too busy hamming it up, ensuring that she was the center of attention, laughing her fake laugh and overdramatically tossing her head back. It was like watching a comedic imitation of an overreaction to a joke, and it rang so false that I worried about Marcus.

Maybe all those high school football concussions caused permanent mental damage.

When I passed her cocktail to her, Maggie downed half of it in one go. "Are you drinking yours?"

"I had planned to, but..." I held mine out to her.

"You're a saint." She reached out for it then paused, her hand falling back to her side. "On second thought, I'm going to need my brain fully functioning to figure this out."

As she bit down on her lower lip, I studied her. Maggie

looked great, but no matter how much I reassured her this morning before we left, she still struggled to believe she looked good enough. She was a fantasy come to life, and yet, she stressed over every detail. The right gold bracelet, the best gold and pearl earrings. She asked if her lipstick was too dark, even though it was just a shade darker than her own pink, pouty lips.

The only way she could have been more beautiful was if she were naked.

"Jules?"

I blinked away from my thoughts. "Yes?"

Maggie subtly nodded her head toward my cousin, both wearing expectant smiles. "Can you introduce us?"

"Ah, yes. Sorry, lost in thought. Maggie Bryant, this is Apollo Black."

He laughed, eyes wide. "This is Maggie? The high school crush?"

She giggled and heat filled the tips of my ears.

No one in the world could grind my gears like Apollo, largely because he had been like an older brother to me when I was a boy. I grew up seeking his approval. He was the cool cousin, the one who gave me my first hit on a joint. The one who drove the hot cars and dated models.

Apollo knew about my crush on Maggie from the moment I mentioned her. He encouraged me to make a move on her and gave me advice on how to get her to be my girlfriend. I tried it all and failed. None of it worked because Maggie had little in common with the type of girls he dated. It took hindsight and maturity to realize why his advice hadn't worked.

I gave him a tight smile. "She was my friend, thank you very much."

As he shook her hand, he threw his other arm around

my shoulder, pulling me off-balance. "Julian's a terrible guy. Undateable. Run while you still can. I'll hold him for you."

Maggie laughed as I shoved him back, Apollo laughing as well. She teased, "Nah. I think I'll keep him out of the dating pool to protect the single women out there."

I shook my head, defeated. "Fantastic. Now I get it from both sides?"

They grinned at me. Apollo's smile was a little lopsided, which was his only physical flaw. His jet-black hair had a tight curl, and he let it grow shaggy like a rugby player. Fitting, considering he had a build like one. If it weren't for that crooked smile of his, he would have been close to perfect.

He taunted, "Admit it, Fool-ian, you missed me."

"Fool-ian?" Maggie asked with an amused grin. "He tells me you're an attorney general, Apollo. Surely, you can do better than that."

"Of course, but when I was a kid, Fool-ian was the height of mockery. Thought I'd bring it back. Gotta keep the most successful person in the family in his place." Trademark Apollo, using insults to talk me up to the woman I was dating. He was a good guy, even if he was a dick about it. That way, he could hide in plain sight.

"Speak of the devil," Marcus said behind me. He yanked me into a bear hug that teetered on the border of pain, then held my shoulders at arm's length, grinning. "Long time, no see."

I had a thousand questions I wanted to ask, most of them revolving around Chloe, but she stood next to him, carefully observing every word and expression.

"Indeed, it has been a long time." I introduced him to Maggie, and right after they shook hands, Chloe leaned to his ear and whispered something I couldn't catch over the

Accidental Fiancé

din of the crowd. While she spoke, her eyes darted to Maggie. It was obvious she was talking about her but there was no polite way for me to interrupt so I simply said, "Chloe, dear, why don't you share with the rest of the class?"

Her blue eyes sparkled with feigned innocence. "What do you mean, Julian?"

"What were you whispering about?"

"That's between us," Marcus said. The gloating smile on Chloe's face was enough to turn my stomach. With three words, my cousin confirmed everything I hoped wasn't true.

Not only was he dating Chloe, but he was under her spell.

It hurt me to see that. As a kid, he had been my other role model. Where Apollo was bold and gregarious, Marcus was more measured and reserved. Unlike Apollo, Marcus kept his brown hair cut short, his green eyes wary and watchful. He had the body of a former football player. Muscular, though he was getting a little soft around the middle.

Apollo teased, "It's not nice to keep secrets, especially among friends."

My cousins knew exactly who Chloe Foster had been to me in high school. They were there for me the day after I got into the worst fist fight of my life—Apollo stitched me up himself. Marcus had continuously murmured, "We are in so much trouble," while Apollo worked on my brow and I tried not to squirm. That was why my eyebrow healed so badly. My fault, however, not Apollo's. He was only trying to help.

Just as it was my fault that Maggie was in the line of fire now.

"Well, you kids have fun," I said, sharply avoiding whatever was coming next. "We're going to find Piper and tend to whatever mischief she's up to." I slung my arm around Maggie to get her out of there.

"Oh, but you've only just arrived," Chloe chided.

"That's the funny thing about parenthood, Chloe—you don't always get to decide how you spend your time." I escorted Maggie into the hallway, where we had evidently been keeping all of our air. Filling my lungs greedily, I asked her, "Are you alright?"

Maggie shook her head, a stark expression on her face like she'd seen a ghost. "I-I don't know if I can do this."

Shit. "She's awful, I know. I had no idea Marcus was dating her. I don't know what he's thinking."

"Didn't you say he runs some historical preservation company?"

"A charity, yeah."

She blew out a breath. "Chloe told me at the reunion that she'd been volunteering at a historical society. Maybe that's how they bonded."

A sinking feeling took over deep inside of me. I took her hand and led her down a narrow hallway that the staff used. Near the end of that hall was a storage closet I used to hide in when I was a kid, and sure enough, it was still used for storage now. Shelves lined three walls of the small space, each full of cleaning products. I led her inside and closed the door behind us, shoving a mop handle between the knob and one of the shelving units as a makeshift lock.

"She set him up," I rasped, too angry to think clearly.

"What?"

"She set all of this up," I explained as I paced. "Chloe volunteering? What, out of the goodness of her heart? No way. She went to his charity on purpose."

"You think she hunted Marcus down?"

My throat went dry. "Without a doubt. We live in a major metro area with millions of people, and I don't believe in coincidences. This was a calculated plan on her part."

"But why?" Maggie asked.

I wasn't sure. "Money?"

"He runs a charity. How much money could he have?"

I huffed a laugh. "Charities make more money than you think, but more importantly, he's a Black. He has access to the family funds just as much as any of us do."

"You think it's an embezzlement scam?"

"No, that takes too much work. I think she's a gold-digger."

We fell silent for a beat before Maggie quietly asked, "Do you think she was whispering the truth about us to Marcus?"

"How would she know?"

"I'm not sure. But she's always acted like she knows everything about everyone so it's hard not to believe that." Maggie hugged herself, then turned away, her lower lip trembling.

I brushed her curls from her face, pinning them behind her ear. I let my palm linger on her cheek to savor the soft warmth. But then I felt her shake, and it crushed me. When she peered up to meet my gaze, my breath stuck in my chest. My voice scratched out, "Maggie, I won't let her get away with this. Not here, not now, not ever. Say the word, and we leave."

"It's just..." She lost her voice as she pressed herself against me and wrapped her arms around my waist. She whispered, "Just hold me."

When I closed my arms around her trembling body, I

vowed two things: One, I would destroy Chloe Foster, and two, I would do whatever it took to prevent Maggie from feeling me harden up while we hugged.

We were friends. Nothing more. No matter how much my heart cracked every time, I forced myself to believe it.

Chapter 21

Maggie

I was certain Julian felt my heart drumming in my chest as he held me. It pounded so loud in my own ears that it drowned out the sounds of the kitchen chaos across the hall. Surely, he knew how much this was killing me. Being near him. Smelling him. Feeling his body against mine. I swore I felt his hardness but that could have been just my imagination.

He cleared his throat and took a step back. "You good?"

"I don't know what I am but I think we should go."

Julian took a deep breath then blew it out slowly. I knew that face. It was the same one he had that day after kissing me behind the cafeteria, the yearbook picture. Absolute disappointment. "Are you sure?"

We had come up with a safe word for me to use if I felt overwhelmed and needed a quick exit. Coconut. His mother was allergic to it, so there was little chance of saying it accidentally while we were among the rest of his family because there was zero chance of it being served in any capacity. If I said coconut, this was over. No more Chloe, no more bone-penetrating dread.

And no more being Julian's fiancée.

That thought panicked me worse than the idea of seeing Chloe again. I wasn't ready to give that up. I knew it wasn't real, but I didn't want it to end. "No, I'm not. I just... I can't think straight right now."

Again, he reached out for me, pulling me to him. This time he was the one who needed the comfort, his hand rubbing up and down my back and he rested his chin on the top of my head. "I've got you, Maggie."

The words calmed me, unlocking something deep inside. Julian got me. He made me feel seen. Understood. I nestled my head against his chest and melted into his embrace. Our bodies fit perfectly together. He felt like home.

I should have been unsettled by the thought but I wasn't.

I breathed in his clean, cucumber scent. It gave me a new surge, aiming my face at his mouth. I pressed my lips to his before I knew what I was doing.

He let a moment pass before he pulled back, shock widening his eyes.

Oh God, he's pissed. I broke the contract. I'm so fucked. I stammered, "I'm sorry. I shouldn't have done that. I—"

Julian's mouth crashed into mine with hunger as he framed my face with his hands and staggered me backward against the door. His soft stubble burned my face as his kisses grew more urgent. His hands pawed for access, over my shirt, my pants, any part of me he wished.

And I let him. I wanted it and I would have begged for his touch.

I arched myself against his hand, groaning for more. His teeth on my throat, his fingers shoving into my pants. My kiss ripped away the leash we held on ourselves. I tugged at the hem of his polo shirt, pulling it up and out of his pants. I latched onto his mouth, eagerly feeding on his enthusiastic grunts when I groped him.

He pushed me harder against the door. His chest heaved with every heavy breath as he stared at me in that barely lit supply closet. I didn't know how he was breathing, I wasn't. I couldn't. If he ended this, it might be the end of me.

He whispered my name then spun me around and jerked my pants down, pulling my hips back to him. In a flash, his fingers glided into me. As wet as I was, it was no challenge. I cried out, but his free hand slid over my mouth. His hot breath caressed the shell of my ear.

"Shh. Wouldn't want anyone to hear us, now would we?"

When his fingers plunged deeper, I bit down on his hand, a strangled cry escaping my lips. He hit my spot again and again until I shook for a new reason. His reason.

I licked his hand. I would have licked anything he wanted me to. His teeth clamped onto that tender spot between my shoulders and my neck as he fingered me, and pleasure shot through every part of me, fracturing my mind. Any question of what was happening vanished without a trace.

I worked myself on his fingers, so close to the edge I wanted to cry. Julian's fingers slipped out and he pulled my hips back even further until I was up against his hard cock. That hot steel shoved deep, and I cried out unfettered this time. His groans echoed after my sounds died down.

He covered me with his body while he pumped into me. His fingers encircled my wrists, pulling my arms out to either side of the door frame and pinning me there. It was like he was telling me with his body that he had me. That he would protect me. I had never felt safer. Or more turned on.

Every stroke brought me closer. It continued to build until I couldn't breathe or speak. Breathy moans fell from my lips, pushed out by every pump of his body into mine. I was beyond thought, beyond comprehension. I was enveloped in pure bliss, and when my orgasm hit, I saw sparks. Pleasure ran circles through my body, all that heat and electricity bursting beneath my skin like a flash. I didn't hear him until I started to come down.

"...that's it, dirty girl, come on my cock," he grunted on his thrusts. Thankfully, he had one arm banded around my waist to keep me upright. I'd gone limp at some point.

With a weak breath, I gasped, "Come for me."

"Can't," he growled. "Nowhere good for it to go."

I wriggled from his grasp. "Pull out."

As he did, he uttered, "You okay?"

I turned and attempted to drop to my knees in front of him, but he was too quick and caught me. I said, "I'm okay. Let me do this."

When I swallowed him into my throat, he lost his balance and leaned on the doorframe to stop from falling on me. I loved tasting myself on him. It was as if I'd marked my territory. But there was something else there. A flavor that was entirely him and I loved it.

I stared up at him realizing quickly that watching him from this angle became my second favorite view of him. The first was how he looked when he was on top of me. The feel of his thickness slipping between my lips was addictive. I memorized the veins and the hint of a curve, the shape of the bulbous tip.

"Jesus, Maggie, if you keep this up, I won't be able to stop."

I scraped the underside of his cock with my tongue and took him deeper into my throat to make my point that I had no intention of stopping.

"Fuck," he grunted. He laced his fingers into my hair and guided me at his pace. Bobbing back and forth, I noticed when his grip changed. He smacked the doorframe as though he had too much pent-up energy and had to let it out somehow. He should have been letting it out on me.

I popped off the end of him. "Stop holding back."

His voice was hoarse. "Yeah?"

I nodded once and started again. That was all the permission he needed.

His fingers tightened in my hair, and he thrust into my mouth, gagging me until I moaned on him. He held me in place to take what he needed, twitching against my lips. He fucked my face almost as hard as he fucked my body, and as much as he pulled my hair to guide me, I was right there, meeting him beat for beat. Anxious for it, almost as if his orgasm would make me come, too. I cupped his balls and his curses spewed out as he throbbed in my mouth and came, slapping the doorframe while he shot into me. I looked up at him with a mischievous grin as I swallowed every drop.

Julian pulled me to my feet and kissed me like the answer to all the world's problems was somewhere in my mouth. By the time he let me go, my face was sore from the blowjob as much as the kissing. He pressed his forehead to mine, and for a while, we stayed like that, breathing each other in.

After a few minutes he murmured, "Feeling better about Chloe?"

I laughed sharply. "Who?"

He grinned. "Good."

But after the high came down, her name plunked into

the pit of my stomach like a rock. "You weren't thinking about her while we—"

"No!" he said with too much volume. He chuckled at himself and lowered his voice. "No, of course not. After what you just did... you made my mind go blank and I had to remember why we were in here instead of my bedroom upstairs, and that brought me back to her."

"Your brain moves way too fast after sex."

"No argument there." He sighed as we put ourselves back together. "We should probably rejoin the others." He removed the mop handle from the doorknob, placing it back where it belonged.

"And hang out with Chloe while praying she doesn't fuck all this up for us? I'm in no hurry for that, thanks. I'd rather stay in here and get high off the cleaner fumes."

He chuckled under his breath as he tucked his polo back into place. "I really know how to show a girl a good time, don't I?"

That cut me a little too deep. "Don't do that, Jules."

"Do what?"

"Don't..." It was hard to put the words in the right order, my head was still jumbled from the sex. "Don't make light of yourself, of what happened in here."

He paused, frowning. "We've never had sex in this closet before, so what are you talking about?"

I wasn't sure I should say it. What if our high school kiss meant more to me than it did to him? But I didn't have the wherewithal to shut up. "You joked like that after you kissed me behind the cafeteria. You were trying to make it so it wasn't a big deal."

His lips parted. "You remember that?"

"Of course I do. I was freaked out by it."

Accidental Fiancé

"That's what every guy likes to hear," he said sarcastically.

"Stop it. Stop joking when you're uncomfortable. Stop making light of important things. Just, stop."

He started to say something else but instead closed his mouth and sighed. "You don't know how much it took to kiss you behind the cafeteria, Maggie. How I'd been working up the courage for months. How I'd wished you'd give me a sign. But no sign came so I went for it. And instead of you kissing me back or saying something—*anything*—to encourage me, you made a joke about how it wouldn't improve your grade." His voice turned raw. "What else was I supposed to do?"

That question struck me at my core. He was right. What else was a teenage boy to do? The truth was, he handled it with grace, given the circumstances. But now, things were different.

"You're right about that day. But we're not kids anymore."

"That kiss meant everything to me back then," he countered. "Still does."

"So how much does what just happened in here mean to you?" I couldn't believe I asked the question, but it came out of my mouth of its own volition.

"I—"

The door swung open before he could complete his response, flooding the small space with too much light. For a moment, I couldn't see. However, I didn't need to. I knew all too well who stood in front of me by her cutting voice. "Found them!" Chloe's claw captured my wrist and pulled me out of the closet. She wasn't alone.

Marcus, Apollo, and a few others I had yet to meet stood in the hallway, all with silly smiles on their faces.

They knew what we had been up to, my tussled hair and his shifted clothes said it all for us. My face flushed hot but I tried for a weak smile. "Um, hi."

Chloe draped an arm over my shoulders. "Looks like the two of you got lost on your way to checking on the kids." She winked. "Go change into your swimsuits. We're doing cocktails and games by the pool. You won't want to miss this."

I very much doubted that.

Chapter 22

Julian

The trudge up the stairs seemed longer this time. Every step was heavy bearing too many thoughts. What the hell just happened in the closet? She kissed me, and I lost all control. I almost admitted how I felt, though I wasn't even sure what that meant. Not really. It was the sex. It tainted my brain, making me weak and stupid.

I could not let that happen again.

As we headed upstairs, I heard Chloe cackle. I knew it was at our expense. Not that I cared—Chloe's opinion meant nothing to me—but my family's opinions meant everything. By the end of the week, I had to ensure they liked Maggie and hated Chloe. Maggie could be closed off and reticent, so that was where I had to focus my energy. I needed to get her out of her shell and show them what made her so special.

They'd figure out Chloe was awful all on their own.

Once we were in my room, I closed the door behind us for privacy. Despite her irritation at my tendency to joke during uncomfortable situations, I had to try. I'd do anything to see Maggie smile. "Chloe's a real piece of work, isn't she?"

Maggie hiccupped a laugh. "She's like a dog with a bone, and we're the bone."

I smiled, trying to figure out something to say, but her words hung in the air, and all I could hear was her saying bone. That was the only thing on my mind. Sex. With Maggie. Our unspoken tension felt like air pressing in at all sides and I couldn't think.

I grabbed my trunks. "I'll change in the bathroom."

"Do you mind if I do?" Maggie asked. "I need to fix myself up a little before I face your family again."

"Sure. Of course." The truth was, I wanted a door between us. Just a little space so I could think clearly. She darted into the bathroom and closed the door. The thin border between us allowed me to breathe again.

I changed and laid on the bed, watching the ceiling fan spin above me. I'd had the best blowjob of my life in the supply closet not fifteen minutes ago. Almost confessed I was falling for Maggie ten minutes ago. Mere moments after that, I nearly decked Marcus as I passed him in the hallway for having the audacity to invite a plague into our home.

I checked the clock. How the fuck had it only been an hour since we'd arrived?

Clearly, the contract meant nothing to either of us, Maggie's payment aside. She'd get that money no matter what happened and after getting humiliated by Chloe, I planned on tacking on a hefty bonus. Not that it would make up for things, but it might be a balm to Maggie's nerves. Or it might alleviate my guilt. Either way, she was taking home a lot of money. I'd make sure of it.

But then the question became, which home was she taking that money to?

The thought of her no longer being in my house after this, of her going back to her apartment, of her leaving us behind, cracked something within me, shaking me to my core. I hated the thought. But I didn't know how to change things between us. Furtive fucking in the supply closet was not the way to woo someone.

I didn't know how to woo Maggie or if I even should. When she rejected me in high school with that disinterested confused look in her eyes after I kissed her, it was enough to put me off of dating for a long time. It hurt too much to be rejected by my fantasy. Now, with Piper in the mix, I couldn't risk damaging my relationship with Maggie. My daughter would be crushed if Maggie never came around after this week.

Too much risk. But the reward…

The bathroom door unlatched, calling my attention. When Maggie walked out, time stopped, and my brain stuttered. She wore one of those retro swimsuits that tied around the neck, her breasts threatening to spill at the top. Bright red. A heartstopper. Little sandals and matching red shorts. She was a vision. A fifties fantasy in real life. A—

"You're staring."

"Uh, sorry. Ready to go?"

"Do I look—"

"Yes," I rasped.

"You don't even know what I was going to say."

"Whatever it is, yes. I'm not sure you should be allowed to wear that."

"What, why?"

I scrubbed my hand over my face, trying not to tell her what was on my mind. "If my cousins hit on you, you tell me."

She laughed. "What are you talking about? They know I'm here with you. They wouldn't dare."

I wanted to take her in my arms and kiss her until my face went numb. How could she be this innocent after what we did in the closet? After everything we had done?

I faced her, wishing our circumstances were anything but what they were because I wasn't sure what that was anymore. "You look amazing. This outfit... you might be covered up, but you're also devastatingly indecent."

Her face flushed pink. "It's just an outfit."

"It's *the* outfit. Every woman down there will be jealous of you." I thought for a moment. "Except for Phoebe. She might hit on you."

"Another cousin?"

"My third youngest. Early twenties, septum piercing, purple hair last I saw her. You can't miss her."

She nodded. "Ready?"

"Let's go."

As much as I was irritated by Marcus' choice in girlfriends, I was happy to see my family. We had a love-hate relationship, but this one week out of the year, while tense, was usually a good time. Or at least I tried to convince myself that it was good for Piper. My daughter loved coming here.

She splashed at the shallow end with her cousins and their friends, thirty kids ranging in age from four to fourteen. They played games and slid down the slides, shouting for their parents to watch them. Piper would have, too, but she was too busy hosting a contest to see who could hold their breath the longest under water.

Maggie's eagle eyes were on Piper, watching every movement under the water and breathing a sigh of relief when she popped back up.

"She's fine."

She smiled at me upon realizing I had noticed. "It's just... when her head goes underwater, it's hard not to panic."

"Believe me, I understand. But you see them?" I pointed to the six people in bright orange windbreakers and not much else. They patrol the pool area with a sharp eye. Don't forget she's taking swim lessons, too."

"Who are they?"

"Professional lifeguards. They're here to allow the parents to be able to relax a little bit. It's okay to just let her do her thing, they've got it under control."

Maggie sighed, her eyes still on Pip. "I'm not sure how to turn it off. I have to leave the pool every time her swim coach comes over, or I freak out when she goes under too long."

I took her hand in mind and gave it a squeeze. "That's how I know you'll be a great mom."

She smiled fully at that but it died fast.

Oh right. None of this is real.

A bevy of cater waiters in short shorts with billowing open shirts delivered cocktails and snacks to those on the loungers, causing Maggie to lean in and quietly ask, "Are they models?"

"Can't say. Mom hires from the same company every year, though. She likes good-looking men to gape at." The thought made me a bit less comfortable as we sat on the loungers in the shade near Apollo.

Maggie giggled as one of the cater waiters took our order, her tone dropping into her mischievous register after he left. "Are you sure they aren't hired hands for more than just serving drinks? He was very flirty."

Apollo sat up at that, smirking. "You mean, does Aunt Artemis hire sex workers for her family party?"

"I didn't mean anything by it," she blurted.

"I've been wondering the same thing for years. Anytime I've asked, she swats my shoulder and tells me to mind my own business, so..." He shrugged with a grin.

But I couldn't let my brain go there. Mom having a sex drive? Pass. I said to Maggie, "He was probably flirting with you because you look incredible."

"Aw, look at Fool-ian, scoring brownie points," my cousin teased.

I rolled my eyes beneath my sunglasses but enjoyed the way Maggie's lips turned up at the corners into a sexy smirk. "He might be a fool, but he's my fool," she replied.

If only.

"Sounds like Julian got himself in trouble again," Chloe taunted as she and Marcus joined us. They took the empty loungers to my left, and I was glad to play defense between her and Maggie. Chloe wore a blue bikini that matched her eyes.

After our drinks came, I asked, "So, what game is it that you had to get us out here for, Chloe?"

"Pool volleyball?"

Marcus didn't like that idea. He groaned and dug his head back against the thick pillow on his lounger. His guayabera shirt slid apart, revealing his belly. "Anything but that, babe. I'm here to relax, not to let Apollo spike the ball in my face again."

Apollo snorted a laugh. "Like you ever had a problem with balls in your face."

Marcus flipped his brother off. "Not volleyball."

"Spin the Bottle?" Another collective groan went up

Accidental Fiancé

but Chloe was undeterred. "No wait, I've got it. Truth or Dare."

I blew out a breath as the others complained. I was inclined to agree with them. If we played that game, Chloe would have the upper hand. She knew the most about me and Maggie, and while I wasn't as paranoid as Maggie, Chloe had a gift for ferreting out things you didn't want known.

But maybe I could use it to my advantage. I wasn't the only person here with a secret. I could use the game to show Marcus who she really was. "I think that's a great idea, Chloe." I slowly smiled at her. "You go first."

She looked like the cat who ate the canary. "Love to. Apollo, truth or dare?"

"Dare."

"Recite the alphabet backward."

His jaw clenched, and I couldn't figure out why he suddenly looked so pissed off. But his glare was unmistakable and aimed at Marcus. "Seriously, man?"

Marcus shrugged mildly. "I didn't say shit."

I asked, "What's going on?"

Chloe smiled, eyes wide and innocent. "What's wrong, Apollo? Did I say something out of line?"

"Man, fuck this," he muttered under his breath. He stood and dove into the pool.

"All I did was ask a simple question. It's a game. Why is he taking it so personally?"

Marcus sighed. "Because he thinks I told you about his near DUI. Reciting the alphabet backwards is one of the roadside tests."

"Well, that's hardly my fault, I didn't know."

But none of it sat right with me. "Apollo got a DUI?"

"Almost. Given that he has friends in high places he

was able to get it expunged, removed from his driver history. But he's embarrassed that it happened."

"Why the fuck didn't he call someone for a ride?" I asked. "Hell, a ride share is a better idea than a freaking DUI. He's smarter than that."

"And that's why he's embarrassed," Marcus explained. "He was just slightly over the limit as it was. He didn't realize how hard the beer would still hit him after having a burger and fries at the bar with me."

"We all make mistakes," Maggie said. "Obviously, he's not gonna let that happen again."

My cousin nodded. "Exactly. He had sworn me to secrecy about the whole thing, so I get why he would be mad if he thinks I blabbed. But seeing as he had a hissy fit just now, I figured I should give you guys context." He noted to Chloe, "Especially you, babe. He's not mad at you. I don't think he's even mad at me. He's mad at himself."

"It's fine," she said. "We all go through difficulties. Volunteering has really shown me that."

"And how has volunteering at the historical society shown you that everyone goes through difficulties?" I couldn't keep the question to myself.

"History is filled with people going through difficulties, Julian. Open a textbook sometime. Or does Maggie still do your homework?"

"Maggie never did my homework."

"That's not how it looked."

Maggie sat up. "I didn't realize we were being so closely monitored."

Chloe examined her manicure. "I didn't have to monitor anything closely. You two were so obvious about it."

"Truth or dare, Chloe," Marcus cut into our sniping.

"Truth."

"If you could be invisible for a day, what would you do?"

I chuckled. Marcus was still the nerd I knew with the biggest comic book collection I had ever seen. It did not surprise me to hear him ask a superhero question.

"Invisible for a day? That sounds awful."

He asked, "Awful? You could do anything. Rob a bank. Steal an armed truck full of money. Spy on your sexy neighbors. Anything."

Before she answered, I said, "You know, I thought you were asking a superhero question but I was wrong. You're asking a supervillain question, which is making me second guess everything I thought I knew about your comic book collection."

Marcus laughed. "Maybe when I was younger, I was into the heroes. These days, I'm old enough to know the villains are the interesting ones."

Well, that just made him and Chloe make a lot more sense.

"If I had to be invisible for a day, I would probably go to Tiffany's and try on all the engagement rings," Chloe said, bringing us back to the point. "A girl has to be prepared, right, Maggie? Let me see your ring again."

Maggie raised her hand, flashing the diamond at her. "See?"

"I thought you said it was big enough to be a difficulty when you were baking. I can't imagine that getting in the way." She tipped her head at me. "Thoughtful of you to get her a ring so small, otherwise, she might have lost it in a muffin."

"Looks plenty big to me. Too big, really. She has tiny hands," Marcus chimed in.

"I'm going to the restroom." Maggie left us behind, probably too pissed to speak. It was all over her face.

Apollo waved at his brother from the deep end, beckoning him over. Marcus tensely grumbled, "Great, now I get to explain why I told everybody about Apollo's DUI." He removed his shirt before diving in and swimming to his brother, leaving me alone with Chloe. Goody.

She flattened her lounger and laid back. "Didn't need to ask you truth or dare. I already know your truth."

I feigned boredom while everything inside of me tensed up. "And what's that, Chloe? What do you think you know?"

"You're faking your engagement."

An incredulous laugh chirped out of me. How the fuck did she know that? "Is that right? Someone should have told my jeweler he could have used cubic zirconia instead of the diamond."

"Oh, the ring is real enough. But you two? No. And you're going to pay me a million dollars a day for me to keep this quiet during Yaya's birthday week, or I'll tell everyone the truth."

Chapter 23

Maggie

Bedtime had been uncomfortable, to say the least. I went into our shared bedroom and waited for Julian to show up but I dozed off before he arrived. I woke up when he finally came in. "Oh hey."

"Sorry, I didn't mean to wake you."

"It's fine. Coming to bed?"

"I can sleep in the chair if that's what you'd prefer."

My brain was foggy. "Why wouldn't you sleep in the bed?"

"I just figured you wouldn't want me to. It's up to you."

"Don't be silly." I pulled the blanket down a little for him by way of invitation.

"I'll get washed up." He left for the bathroom, and I was left with questions.

Why wouldn't he sleep in our bed? Did we have a fight? But then Chloe's face came to mind, and reality cracked through my haze.

We're not a couple. Why do I keep forgetting that?

When Julian came to bed it took all the strength I had not to cuddle him. What happened earlier in the closet was an unexpected one-time thing. Neither of us acknowledged it and I wasn't sure what I would say anyway.

I had no idea what had been about to come out of his mouth when Chloe threw open the door. I had my suspicions, of course. But none of them tracked with reality. None of them made any sense. Julian Black did not love me. He wasn't in love with me. The sex? That was just two horny people wrapped up in a moment. He was trying to comfort me. Or distract me. But it wasn't about how he felt.

We have a contract in place that clearly defines how he feels.

I was just another tool to him. Another person to buy and sell. A way to keep his family off of his back. It was one thing when we were just friends doing each other a favor. But the moment money entered into the situation, it changed everything.

I had to do my best to remember that. But I didn't want to. I wanted to put that damn contract out of my mind. I wanted to pretend that this was real, that I could somehow fit into this life.

Chloe made it plain by the pool that I never would. That was why I had to leave. She and I both knew that the rock on my finger was enormous. Her taunts were not about the size of my ring. She was trying to point out that *I* didn't matter. That I was unimportant. And when Julian didn't stand up for me against her, I didn't know what to do. In that split second, he proved her right. I looked to him for some sort of clarity but he was watching Chloe, and then Marcus spoke up, closing out the conversation.

We had to talk about it. In the dark, I whispered, "Julian?"

But all I got was a snore in return.

***

The woman of the hour finally arrived at breakfast the next day. According to Julian, she liked to show up late to her own party to make a grand entrance, and to guarantee that everyone was already there waiting for her. Hera Galanis—Yaya—was a striking woman. Petite and thin with short gray curls, only a fool would think she wasn't a powerhouse. Energy, authority, and positivity radiated from her. Clearly, the family's green eyes came from her genes; she had the same gray slash in her iris as Julian did.

When she moved in to hug him, she spied me over his shoulder. With a thick Greek accent, she asked, "And who is this lovely one?"

"Yaya, this is Maggie Bryant."

She released Julian then took both of my hands in hers before hugging me tightly. "Welcome to the family, Maggie."

I felt the words as she said them. Immediate acceptance. No hoops to jump through, no games to play. This woman loved with her whole heart. It made me want to be worthy of that love. And it made me feel guilty to be lying to her. Still, I kept my smile firmly in place. "It's a pleasure to meet you, Mrs. Galanis."

"No, no. You call me Yaya. You're family."

I beamed up at Julian, then back to her. "Thank you, Yaya."

"Is everyone ready?" she asked Artemis.

"Ladies, to the cars," Artemis announced.

"Um, what?" I asked in confusion.

"Did my son not tell you?" she asked. "It's Ladies Day at the spa."

My head instantly whipped around to question Julian. "What?"

His expression crumpled and he knew he was in trouble. "I must have forgotten to mention it."

Before I could even speak, Artemis looped her arm in mine. "Not to worry, Maggie dear, the spa will take care of all of us. Come along."

I did, not that I had much choice. We piled into a series of large black SUVs. I was grateful I didn't end up in the same one with Chloe. When we entered the spa, I immediately noticed there were no other patrons in sight.

"Welcome, welcome." A woman wearing sage-colored scrubs came forward. She had a soft, kind appearance and a warm smile. "Mrs. Black, it's so good to see you."

"Thank you, Olivia. If I'm not mistaken, Maggie, this is your first time ever being at a spa, correct?"

Spas were not exactly a high priority for me in my life because frankly, I couldn't afford them. I had only been once before today. It was nice, but nothing like this place.

The lobby was decorated in sage and silver, the air scented with peppermint, vanilla, and lavender. A decorative wood and stone waterfall wall was situated behind the lobby desk. Instead of typical bamboo, delicate live orchids were placed throughout. Relaxing flute music played on the surround sound.

I explained, "I've been to a spa before but I've never been to *this* spa."

"Splendid," Olivia said, quickly corralling me from the group. "Mrs. Black, while Douglas takes care of the rest of you, I will attend to Maggie."

A young man wearing the same uniform as Olivia emerged from the back and escorted the rest of them from the lobby. Olivia helped me select services from a digital menu. "Pick as many as you would like for as long as you'd like. You'll be here all day."

"We're going to be actively relaxing all day? I don't know if I can do that."

She laughed. "We'll do our best to help you out."

I made my selections though I was sure I was going to need several breaks from other people touching me. I didn't know how anyone could stand to do this for a whole day.

The thought of taking a break went out the window as soon as the massage therapist put his hands on my shoulders. Moans of intense pleasure came out of me and I simply didn't care. As he worked his magic, I wasn't sure where I was anymore.

Afterward, I soaked in a eucalyptus bath and sipped cucumber water. There were three heated pools in a room lined with salted walls. I was so stoned from my massage that I wasn't sure what the attendant had said to me about the details of the salt room but I know it was something cleansing. Once I hit the warm water and the bubbles cascaded over me, I was done.

"Maggie, so glad we could catch up in here." Chloe invaded my pool and my eyes popped open in horror. But not even she could damage my massage high.

"I'm pretty sure we are caught up, Chloe. Feel free to leave."

"Nonsense." Chloe plucked my left hand from the water. "No ring today?"

"Julian's got it for safekeeping. This seems like the kind of place I could lose it."

"Hmm. I really am happy for you two. We always wondered about you in high school."

I had no urge to indulge her today. "Oh?"

"Well, you know, there was the lesbian rumor, which

made Julian look like a hopeless little puppy dog, always following you around. How humiliating for him, right?"

"Seriously, Chloe, do you ever think before you speak?"

She laughed it off. "Then there was the way you dressed. You were so ample up top—it was almost cruel how you taunted the boys with those lowcut shirts then get upset when they talked about you. Why did you tease them like that?"

I shook my head at her. "I didn't wear lowcut shirts, Chloe, I just wore shirts. Not my fault I have what I have. Those boys' parents should have raised them better than to comment on other people's bodies."

She shrugged, still smirking. "I was always your biggest defender, of course, but then there was Julian."

She was trying to get me to ask for more information. As long as I did that, she was the center of attention, and as long as she was the center of attention, she felt important.

I blew her off. "That's nice."

Her blue eyes came alive, excited to tell me something against my will. "Come now, don't play coy. You know exactly what I'm talking about. Julian is your knight in shining armor. It's really quite romantic. He finally got the girl of his dreams."

Maybe if I just keep agreeing, she'll get bored. "Julian's always been a romantic."

"Especially when he faced down Grant Worthington. You remember him, right?"

The football quarterback who took up the slack whenever Chloe wasn't around to annoy me. He was the first boy to start shaving and had a five o'clock shadow in the sixth grade. He developed faster than the others, shooting up six inches during the summer in between freshman and sophomore year. An awkward boy who grew into a handsome young man. As Rosewood High School's favorite son, I worried Julian would be arrested for breaking Grant's throwing arm.

"I remember him. But why are you rehashing the old days? Don't you have new accomplishments to talk about? Or did you peak in high school?"

Chloe bit her bottom lip, her crow's feet pinching ever so slightly. I'd struck a nerve. Knowing her, she wouldn't let that stand. "If I were you, I probably wouldn't want to relive old times, either. Especially considering what Julian did for you."

"Out with it."

"Didn't he tell you the details about the fight with Grant?" But before I could respond, she answered her own question. "He didn't, did he? He didn't want you to know what happened."

"But clearly you do."

"I'm trying to do you a favor. You should know who you're marrying."

If this were a real engagement, she'd be right about that. So I played along. "Fine, tell me."

"Well..." She shifted in the water to get closer to me. "Grant and I had been dating for a few months, and he was such a devoted boyfriend. Handsome, student body president, captain of the—"

"I remember, Chloe. Go on."

"We were smoking behind the cafeteria and minding our own business when Julian showed up out of nowhere and picked a fight."

"You just said he was being a knight in shining armor, so how is that picking a fight?"

She shrugged. "I misspoke. He walked right up to Grant and started attacking him, beating him and shouting, 'It's not true!' It was horrifying. Thought you should know he has a temper."

"You made it sound like he did it to help me. What—"

"I have a treatment." She stood, water cascading down her skin. I'd better go, or I'll be late."

I snatched her hand and kept her in the pool. "Tell me what else happened."

"Grant was trying to protect the student body from a predator," she hissed. "Julian acted like an animal."

"I don't understand what you're talking about."

"Mr. Poundstone."

The name whooshed through me like a ghost. My beloved chorus teacher, the one who believed in me. The one who gave me the solo for the state competition. The one who picked me over Chloe. I lost a breath and loosened my grip. "What about him?"

"After your affair came to light—"

"We never had an affair!" I barked. "I don't know why anyone thought that!"

She clicked her tongue at me, watching my every move. "Mm-hmm. Well, Grant felt it was his duty to protect the student body after he heard those things, so he went to the principal with the information."

I gripped the edge of the pool to steady myself. The words came out slowly. "Nothing happened between me and Mr. Poundstone, Chloe."

"Right. You *earned* the state competition solo."

"You think I'd sleep with an old man, a teacher, for a solo?"

"I think Julian was angry you were sleeping with Mr. Poundstone, and by the time he heard about it, Mr. Poundstone had already been fired, so he took out his anger on the man who exposed you."

Absentmindedly, I shook my head. "He'd never do that."

"Believe what you want, Maggie. But Julian Black, wonderful as he is now, had a real anger problem in high school. He must have thought he was defending your honor or something." She rolled her eyes and stepped out of the pool. "See you later."

It made no sense. As senior year wound down, the state competition had been the only thing on my mind—that and keeping my grades up for scholarships. The solo had been decided a few weeks before Mr. Poundstone was fired. Just enough time for a rumor like that to destroy a career teacher. With Grant's word being gold, no one would doubt him.

Julian attacking Grant out of nowhere sounded like total bullshit. He knew that Grant made up a lie and got a good man fired to avenge his girlfriend's disappointment. Julian was angry, sure. But it was justified. He wanted to clear Mr. Poundstone's name.

And mine.

A shiver of realization bolted through me. He had attacked Grant for me despite the odds. Grant was huge, and he had a knack for fighting. We'd seen it on the football field and in the halls. Julian should not have been able to walk away from that fight with just a busted eyebrow. By all rights, he was the one who should have ended up in the hospital, not Grant. Julian risked everything for me, and a primitive part of me loved him for it.

Chapter 24

Julian

Marcus laid back in the leather recliner, a puff of smoke rising from his cherry cigar. It flared as he breathed it in. "Do you think the girls know this is what we do while they're at the spa all day?"

"Does it matter?" Apollo asked, readjusting in his recliner as he sat up and looked down. "Harriet, nice work."

His nail tech smiled, nodded, and kept filing at what he called his foot, but what we called evidence there was a hobbit in our bloodline somewhere.

My pedicure ended half an hour ago, but I was relaxed as hell and not ready to get off the lounge recliner yet. Other family members were hanging out in various spots in the house, but when the ladies left for their spa day, a few of us had one of our own. We were happy that they were having a relaxing day together, and it was nice to be able to hang out with the guys without distractions and get our own services.

"Maggie didn't ask what we'd be doing, but it wasn't like Mom gave her time to. I think she wanted to get her out of here as fast as possible to stop me from objecting."

Accidental Fiancé

"Why would you object to her joining spa day?" Apollo asked.

I sipped my cognac. "I wouldn't exactly object as much as try to warn her about everyone."

"She's a big girl," Marcus said. "I'm sure she can handle herself."

Now was as good a time as any. "So, what's up with you and Chloe Foster? You know how much of a pain in the ass she is. You were there after that fight I had with her boyfriend."

"That was high school stuff, Julian. I'd like to think we're all past that. You holding a grudge?"

"I wouldn't be if I believed she's changed. She hasn't." *Except she didn't blackmail me in high school like she's doing now.*

It wasn't about the money. I wasn't thrilled about it, but a million dollars a day for seven days wasn't going to dent my bank account. What pissed me off was that she knew about us somehow and she had no shame using it against us. I was glad today was spa day; I welcomed the break from having to look at her smug face for a while.

"You gotta learn to get over shit," he said matter-of-factly. "It's not healthy to carry all that baggage."

I bit the inside of my cheek to stop from shouting, "Your girlfriend is blackmailing me!" Instead, I mildly shrugged. "I don't know about that, Marcus. I think when someone is part of the reason your face is scarred for life, you get to hold a grudge of some sort."

Apollo sighed exaggeratedly. "I did the best I could with what I had at the time. I'm much better at stitches these days."

Marcus laughed. "Yeah, well, being Chloe's new

boyfriend, I don't plan on hitting Julian anytime soon, so we won't have to test that theory."

"Do I smell cigar smoke in my house?" Mom's question carried down the hall.

I never saw Marcus move so fast as when he jumped out of his chair and bolted for the backdoor to the lounge, lit cigar in hand. She had done the same thing since we were kids whenever she knew we'd been misbehaving. She'd shout the accusation like she was angry, but then gave us enough time to cover it up. I wasn't sure if she did it so she wouldn't have to punish us or if it was because Mom liked being the fun parent.

The nail techs, estheticians, and massage therapists who had descended upon the lounge knew it was time to clean up when Mom returned. We paid them extra to be ghosts and slip out of the house unnoticed. They were packed up and gone before Mom poked her head through the doorway.

"Smells like a brothel in here. What have you boys been doing?"

"Nothing, Mom. How was the spa?"

"Wonderful, as always."

Maggie walked in next, making a beeline straight to me. She took my face in her hands and kissed me within an inch of my life in front of everyone. My mind blanked out completely. She whispered, "Take me upstairs. We need to talk."

I swallowed, realizing everyone's eyes were on us. "Excuse us." I grabbed Maggie's hand and led her upstairs while my younger cousins chuckled behind us. What the hell had happened at the spa to make Maggie demand a private talk? And why the kiss?

When the door was closed behind us, I started to ask, "What did Chloe—"

But before I could get the words out, Maggie pounced on me, her mouth on mine, her hands pulling at the waist of my shirt. I could have gotten lost in her so easily.

As much as I liked where this was headed, I needed clarity. We'd gone down this road in the closet, and things got weird after that. I didn't want that to happen again so I took her hands in mine and broke the kiss. "Maggie, tell me what happened at the spa."

Her eyes were glazed, and her breaths came out in puffs as her chest heaved. "Later, I promise."

Good enough for now. I pulled her to me, relishing the soft warmth of her body on mine. When I reached around for her ass, she let out the sexiest moan as I squeezed. I backed her to the bed. We lost half our clothes between kisses on the way there.

I gave her a playful shove, and she tumbled back onto the mattress, where I peeled away the remaining layers until I was rewarded with every inch of her silken skin. Whatever they'd done to her at the spa, her skin glowed. She had never been so beautiful as when she laid there, splayed out like my own personal feast.

Every part of her was deliciously sweet. I licked her from her ankles up while I tore away at what was left of my clothes. But it wasn't enough. I needed to be inside of her more than I needed to breathe. My cock ached for it, and when I pulled her to the edge of the bed, her lips parted in shock and anticipation. "Please, baby, don't make me wait."

I didn't. We moaned together as I began to enter her. Just a few inches at first, I hadn't done as much as I liked to normally get her ready so she wasn't as prepared for it. Her tight heat doubled my vision. I worked my way into her slowly, back and forth, until I buried myself deep inside. When I was as far as I could go, I scooped her up and carried her to the head of the bed to lay her on the pillows.

Things took a turn from there.

I couldn't explain what had changed from one second to the next. Maybe it was me. But moving her higher up onto the bed shifted things. This wasn't some frantic fuck in a closet or a lust-filled loss of control. I stared into her warm brown eyes, and in that breath, I couldn't deny it anymore.

I rubbed my thumb over her bottom lip and she pulled me down for a kiss. It wasn't long before our bodies started up again. I went deeper into her with every thrust. Slowly, methodically, with every stroke to draw out our pleasure. As I gazed into her eyes, I swore our hearts synced up along with our breaths.

Maggie met me on every thrust, her hands on my face, my neck, my back. She grabbed my ass and pulled me deeper still as she belted my waist with her legs. When she clenched on me, and her body went rigid, I kept pace for her. "That's it, baby. Be my good girl and come on my cock."

Her gasps made me crazy, and as she came, she cried out my name. I refused to stop, even as my own orgasm begged for release. I throbbed so hard it took my breath away. She whimpered beneath me, "Now you." That's all I needed to hear, my climax coursing through me as I spilled into her, the pleasure almost too great to bear.

I spooned her tightly afterwards. Although I didn't understand what was happening between us or what any of it meant, I was going to enjoy it while it lasted. Still, I wondered what brought this on. I whispered in her ear, "I think you owe me an explanation."

She took a nervous breath. "I know what happened with Grant Worthington."

It was like a record scratch ripped through my head.

Fucking Chloe. I didn't know how she knew everything, but she always seemed to. Of course, she knew about my crush. Eighteen-year-old me wasn't exactly subtle.

"I never meant for you to find out. That was private and not your problem."

Maggie rolled over to face me. "I think it's sweet."

"Sweet?" I asked as I sat up. I was naked, but this was a different kind of exposure. The kind I tried to avoid like the plague. "Maggie, what happened that day—"

"What *did* happen that day? According to you, I mean."

I rubbed my temples to stall. Lying to Maggie wasn't an option. "I found out Grant had been the one to go to the principal with that bullshit about you and Mr. Poundstone."

"So you knew it wasn't true?"

"Of course."

"Go on."

I hated telling her. I'd thought for sure none of it would ever come out, considering how much my mother paid Grant's family back then. But the NDA only covered him—not Chloe—and after he moved across the country, I thought that would be that.

"It was right after Dad's funeral, a couple of days out from it. I wasn't in the best frame of mind. When I found Chloe and Grant smoking behind the cafeteria, I snapped at him, told him to take back what he had said about you and Mr. Poundstone, told him to make it right."

"What did he say?"

I'd never forget it. "He said, 'You're just mad your girlfriend's a slut.' Then Chloe handed him one of those loose bricks from the cafeteria expansion project and he swung on me with it." I pointed to my eyebrow. "After that, all I saw was red. Either from anger or the blood pouring down my face, probably both. Whatever it was, I pounded on

Grant until I heard something break, and he screamed. That brought me back to myself." I felt sick saying the words out loud. "I need you to know, I am not that guy."

"Jules, I know that," she said as she cupped my cheek in her hand. "He hit you. He hurt me. He got a man fired. A broken arm is fair payback."

"When I thought of you suffering because that asshole told a lie, I lost my shit. I was a stupid kid with an unrequited crush, and—"

"Wait, a *what*?" she breathed.

No, no, no, fuck. All these years, all this time, and now *is when it slips out?*

I had to get out of there. I grabbed my clothes. "Forget it. I shouldn't have said anything."

"Talk to me, Jules. Please."

I yanked my shirt over my head. "The fight was not your fault, Maggie. Let me be clear about that. It was my crush, which made it my problem to deal with, and I behaved badly. That's all on me. Don't beat yourself up over my stupid decision."

"I'm not." But her hollow voice said otherwise. Maggie's guilt bloomed in front of my eyes.

My heart raced and I felt sick. "This was why I never told you about any of it. I knew you'd blame yourself. Please don't."

"I—"

"I'm going for a walk. I'll be back in a while." I shut the door behind me and ran outside, desperate for some space.

Chapter 25

Maggie

What the fuck was that?

He had a crush on me back then and I didn't realize it. Too many thoughts flooded my head before washing out with the tide minutes later, and then they were back, over and over again, like the rhythm of the ocean. I felt like I was going down a spiral staircase in my mind at the same time. My body flashed hot and cold. I called the only person I could think of.

When she answered, she said the last thing I expected. "Quiet down, you filthy pig boy. Hello?"

"Did I interrupt something?"

Nora laughed. "Yes. But when has that ever stopped me?"

"Can you put the filthy pig boy on hold so we can talk? I'm kind of in the middle of a crisis right now."

"Of course." She didn't bother to put the phone on mute. Her voice went dark. "You will lay there and think about what you've done. I'll be back when I'm back." Then I heard the sound of a door closing. "Alright, doll, what can I help you with?"

"Before we get to me, what the hell are you up to?"

"Date night."

"You're dating men again?"

She sighed. "I'm trying one out. You know they never last. So what is going on? What is this crisis you're going through?"

"Julian admitted that he had a crush on me in high school, and that's part of why he attacked Grant Worthington."

"How is this news?"

"You *knew*?"

I could practically hear her eyes roll. "My dear, sweet Maggie. What did I say? I told you he had a crush on you. I told you that you had a crush on him. If people would just listen to me."

"I thought you were just saying that! You make blanket declarations all the time, Nora!"

"And when have I been wrong?"

I hated to admit she had a point. "Okay, if you know everything, then what the hell am I supposed to do with this information?"

"Tell me what he said. How did all of this come out about Grant?"

I explained what Chloe had told me at the spa then what happened after I got back to the mansion. "I'm still not sure what to think. But apparently, he didn't tell me any of this because he thought I would feel guilty. He admitted he attacked him in part because of the crush he had on me."

"Do you?"

"Do I feel guilty that Grant Worthington finally got his ass kicked and for a good reason? No. Not even a little bit." Maybe I should have. We were just teenagers back then.

Accidental Fiancé

But Grant was the one who lied about me and got a man fired because of it.

"What about Chloe? What does she have to say about any of this?"

"Only what I told you. I haven't redressed or gone downstairs yet."

"Hmm," she muttered, more to herself than to me. "You mentioned that at the spa, you realized Julian had defended you back then, and then your voice went all soft before you continued. Why?"

My breath got locked in my chest for a blink. "Because when I realized that he did it for me, I... it uncorked something deep. And now I don't know what to do about it."

"He fought for you and it turned you on," she replied.

"No. I mean, yes, but no, that's not what got me. It was that he did something to protect me, and he didn't even try to take credit for it. He didn't do it to show off or brag about it later."

"Most teenage boys would do anything for that kind of street cred, to fluff their feathers to the girl they were trying to defend."

"Exactly! He did it because it felt like the right thing to do."

"And because he was overwhelmed by his crush on you."

I snorted a bitter laugh. "Yeah, that's in there too. He can have more than one reason for it."

"I'd say most people have more than one reason for anything they do. I suppose the more important question at this point is, where do you go from here? He uncorked something deep, as you put it. You two have been banging your brains out and—"

"Not that much."

"Twice since you got there. You've been there twenty-four hours. That's a lot, even for me."

"Is it?"

"Not really," she admitted with a laugh. "I was just trying to make you feel better. My point is, obviously things are escalating between the two of you. With your history coming to light, it seems as if things are pointing you down a certain path. But only you can choose to walk down that path."

Hearing that, I decided to admit it. "I feel like I'm falling in love with him."

"No. You're not."

I frowned at my phone. "Pretty sure *I'm* the one who gets to decide that."

"Precisely. What I mean is we do not fall in love. We *choose* to love."

I had heard Nora talk poetically about the topic for years. She did not believe in falling in love. It wasn't some head-over-heels helpless thing to her. Love was a decision to be made according to her rules.

"I know you have your own rules about love, Nora, but if it is a choice, then why do I feel like I'm falling whenever I see him? Why do I feel less solid and shaky every time he walks into the room? I feel too weak to breathe around him, and my heart pounds like a drum every time I look into his eyes. Tell me that's not falling in love."

"That's not falling in love, doll, that's a cardiac condition. Have you been checked out?"

I couldn't help but smile. "You're an idiot."

"The smartest idiot you know."

That was probably true. "So what do I do about all of this?"

"You have to figure out what it is you want. Once you

figure that out, go to Julian with it. But don't go to him unless you know exactly what it is you want, be honest with yourself and him. Men are not good at helping us figure that out nor are they good at realizing our needs and wants."

"I know that, that's why I'm talking to you."

"You think I can help you figure out what you want? Doll, I've got a male senator strapped to my bed with a gag ball in his mouth and a pig mask over his eyes who I had crawling around on all fours an hour ago. I barely enjoyed myself. I don't know what I want. How am I supposed to tell you what you want?"

"Well, crap, that's not much help. By the way, I did not need that visual."

"Oh, come on. Sure you did."

"A senator?"

"What can I say? I like to stay politically active."

"That tracks. You've always been an avid voter."

She laughed. "The things he did to my ballot box—"

"Don't. Just need advice."

"Oh, come on, he's a senator. You're not at least a little curious?"

"Okay, fine, give me one good detail, and then get back to me, because I really need some help here."

"Alright, but it's gonna be the filthiest one that we've done so far, and it involves a butt plug with a coiled pigtail on the end of it." She dove into the details, and even though it wasn't my scene, I sort of understood the appeal. Kind of.

"...oinking as he finished. Honestly, it's some of my finest work."

"I didn't realize you had a thing for barns."

"Variety is the spice of life. Now, back to your problem. Tell Chloe to fuck off and go get your man."

"He's not mine to get. He took off after we finished. What am I supposed to think about that?"

I heard her fingers snapping for attention. "He's held on to this secret for fifteen years, and he's terrified that he's going to make you feel bad about what he did. Considering what he's said about the fight, I imagine he's filled with his own guilt about it. Regarding both Grant and you. Since he took off after sex, it's obviously eating away at him. Don't overthink it. No thinking, just doing. Go get your man. And if Chloe acts up again, I will drive up there, and kick her ass."

"Shouldn't I be the one doing that?"

"Well, yes, in an ideal world. But Doll, you've never stood up to her, not really. So if you need to tag me, please do so. I am feeling froggy, and I'd like to jump."

"Sounds like you need to deal with Senator Filthy Pig Boy more than Chloe right now."

She laughed heartily and said, "Whatever it takes to get my stress out. Now, can you handle this, or do I need to come up there?"

I wasn't sure if I *could* handle it, but I didn't want her to stop what she was doing and come up, even though I knew she would. "You stay put. I'll sort this out. Thanks for letting me interrupt your night."

"Anytime. You know I've got you."

"So, which senator is it? The young one or the old one?"

Another laugh. "You know I don't divulge such things. When it comes to celebrities, anyway."

I knew what that meant. "Bodyguard standing right there?"

"Giving me the evil eye as we speak."

"Good luck with that."

"Yeah, you too."

We hung up and I felt lost, untethered. What the hell was I going to do?

Chapter 26

Julian

Our estate wasn't the biggest around. Twenty-five acres wasn't that much compared to some of our neighbors. But it gave us enough room to weave some trails between the trees, the road, and the driveway. Plenty of mileage for me to run my feelings out.

The problem was, I wore the wrong shoes.

By the time I headed back to the house, I'd slowed down considerably on account of the blisters on my heels. I'd wound around the mansion I don't know how many times, but I ended up walking up to the pool area. There, on the loungers, were Mom and Yaya, each with a bottle of ouzo, a pitcher of water on the table between them.

Yaya smiled up at me, patting the empty lounger beside her. I've always thought that Yaya was one of the prettiest women I'd ever known. She had smiling eyes, the kind that looked as if she was about to break into laughter at all times. Her hair was always done perfectly, her outfits always pressed. She took a lot of pride in her appearance, telling us often how no one believed her age. "Sit. Drink with us. I've hardly seen you since I've been here."

How could I say no to that? She poured me a glass of ouzo splashed with water, and I took it. I raised the glass. "Yamas." Ouzo always tasted like licorice gone bad, and tonight was no exception. "Happy birthday, Yaya."

She folded her small hands over herself. "Thank you, Julian. Now, tell me, what of this girl you brought with you? Piper likes her."

It wasn't news to me, but I had to ask, "What makes you say that?"

"She can't stop talking about her."

Mom smiled and nodded. "She's smitten. You've done well."

"Thanks," I said stiffly. "I am having a little bit of a crisis right now, however, so if you two don't mind, I'm going to head back inside."

"You will stay here," Yaya emphasized each word. "You tell us your troubles."

That was not going to happen. "It will pass. Nothing to worry about."

"That's for us to decide," Yaya said.

Mom added, "You know you can tell us anything, honey."

But there were too many layers, and I didn't want to get into it. "I've known Maggie since high school, which means there's years of stuff to deal with, you know? Sometimes, some of it comes out of nowhere, and I'm unprepared to deal with it right away."

"Does this have anything to do with that Chloe girl?" Yaya asked.

Why does she have to be so damn insightful? "It's honestly just stupid kid stuff. It'll pass."

"Whatever it is, Maggie is a lucky girl to have you," Mom said.

"Thanks, Mom."

"Whatever it is, he better get it under control before my official party in two days," Yaya teased. "There will be cake and no fighting. A real American birthday party, not a Greek one."

I chuckled despite myself. "No worries, Yaya. I've got it all under control."

Only I didn't have it under control. Not when I tucked Piper in and almost cried when she asked where Maggie was. Not when I found Maggie in our room, and I sent her to tuck Piper in. She looked up at me with so much *something* in her eyes. "She wants me to come and say goodnight, too?"

I gulped. "Yeah. I think she was a little disappointed that you hadn't come to tuck her in."

Maggie scurried to get dressed and left without another word. By the time she returned for bed, I was half asleep. "Sorry, did I wake you?"

"What time is it?"

"Just after eleven."

"Piper kept you this long?"

She smiled and shook her head, taking off her robe. Her satin and lace pajamas accentuated her curves, the sight stirring me awake. "No. After I tucked her in and got her to sleep, I ran into Yaya in the hallway. She started telling me about Greece, and we ended up talking for a long time. That woman has lived a life."

I smiled as she crawled into bed next to me and turned out the light. "Yes, she has."

"Was she really a lion tamer?"

"She worked for a circus, believe it or not. Whether she was actually a lion tamer is up for debate. But she does have an extensive picture collection showing her in a variety of circus jobs, including one where she's standing next to a lion with a whip in her hand. Mom swears she never did any of that. That she went to one of those photo shops where they can superimpose you into already existing photos. But she looks very active and involved in the pictures, so I don't argue with either of them on it."

Maggie yawned. "I prefer to believe she actually did it."

"Same here."

She cradled onto my shoulder, and it felt right. "Okay if I sleep here?"

My voice went hoarse. "Yeah." I laid an arm on her back, and neither of us spoke for a long time. I knew I shouldn't have left so abruptly. I should have stayed to make sure she was okay, that she wasn't blaming herself for what I'd done to defend her. Yet another mistake. I laid there beating myself up over it most of the night. But at least I got to listen to her breathe as she slept. She was so peaceful in my arms.

I must have dozed off because when my stupid ass cousins banged on my bedroom door and threw it open, I jerked awake. "The fuck?"

"You know the drill, lover boy. Time for the hunt," Marcus said.

"Get the fuck out."

"You've got two minutes," Apollo chimed in, shutting the door while they waited in the hallway.

A groggy Maggie asked, "The hunt?"

"It's the counter to the lady's spa day. Guys only," I explained as I dressed. "We don't ever actually kill anything. It's more like a hike with guns."

"You're not even fully awake, and you're going to be handling firearms?"

"Family tradition." I pulled on a pair of jeans and a tee

with a flannel and boots. "I'll be back in a few hours. This usually takes us to about noon."

"I'll keep an eye on Piper."

"Sleep. Please." Loudly, I said, "I'm sorry my *asshole* cousins woke you up."

"We can hear you through the door, you know," Apollo responded.

It made me smile. Maggie too.

"When you get back, can we talk about everything?"

"I promise. We'll talk about everything."

She motioned for me to come close, then pulled me in for a kiss with a gleam in her eyes. "I'll hold you to that promise."

That was all it took for me to hurry out the door. The sooner we finished the hunt, the sooner she and I could talk, and the sooner we might actually make this into a real thing.

I found myself at the front of the group, with Marcus and Apollo trailing closely behind. The rest of the men in our family were walking more leisurely, each carrying a flask of ouzo with them if they were old enough, and for our family, that meant at least fifteen. "Why are you guys so slow today?"

"Why aren't you slower?" Marcus asked. "Didn't Maggie wear you out?"

"Don't talk about Maggie like that."

Apparently, that was the wrong thing to say because he responded with, "Oh, it's like that, huh?"

"I don't talk about you and Chloe's sex life. You don't need to talk about mine. That's all."

Apollo grinned. "He's protective of her. I think that's sweet."

"You're serious about this girl, aren't you?" Marcus asked.

Accidental Fiancé

"I wouldn't have put a ring on her finger if I wasn't."

"You know, Chloe has a lot to say about her."

"She always has. In fact, Chloe has a lot to say about a lot of things."

His eyes narrowed on me. "What's that supposed to mean?"

"I'm not going to rehash mine or Maggie's history with Chloe. You're well aware of what the situation is. I don't know how you could choose to associate with someone like her, but that's your business, not mine."

"I'm not the one engaged to the girl who cheated on me in high school."

That stopped me in my tracks and I spun on him. "What did you just say?"

"Guys." Apollo stepped between us. "We're not doing this."

"The fuck we're not," Marcus said, scooting past him. He sneered in disgust. "I'm glad you've been able to put the past in the past with Maggie, but I haven't. The fact of the matter is, she cheated on you in high school with that music teacher, and now you wanna marry her. What the hell is that?"

Anger surged through me. "Watch your fucking mouth."

"Guys!" Apollo snapped.

"You see how defensive he is over this chick?" he growled at his brother. "I'm your cousin, Julian. This is embarrassing for all of us. For the whole family."

I stepped up to him. "You don't know what you're talking about."

"I know plenty. Chloe told me everything."

"That would be the problem, wouldn't it? Getting your information from that... person."

He clenched his jaw, and Apollo snapped his fingers between us. "Hey, hey. Eyes on me." "You, up the trail." He pointed at me. "Marcus, back to the house. Now."

"We're not kids anymore, Apollo. You're not the boss of us," Marcus said. For once, I was inclined to agree with him. "This is between me and Julian."

"Fine, but hand me your pieces."

We both turned over our shotguns. "Chloe's been lying to you, and if you want to play the family card, remember it goes both ways."

"And I'm sure Maggie's been so perfect."

"She didn't fuck the teacher! And we never dated in high school, so even if she had, she still wouldn't have been cheating on me!"

"You seem to just roll over for whoever cheats on you, including Britney."

Without much of a thought, my fist collided with his face, and time slowed down. Next thing I knew Apollo's hands were on my chest, shoving me against a tree. "What the fuck is wrong with you? We're fucking family, Julian!"

Uncle Dino caught up to us, eyeing me, then his son. He crouched over Marcus to study his face. I couldn't look away as blood poured from his nose. Uncle Dino had been a boxer, I assumed he was assessing the damage.

My uncle grunted, "I warned you."

"Papa, I—"

"I tell you not to speak of his lady friend. And what do you do?"

Marcus huffed out a breath. "But Papa—"

"What did you do?"

His son didn't answer. He pinched his nose instead.

"Apollo."

"Yes, Papa?"

"Take Marcus back. Get him cleaned up. And Julian?" he said my name as he stood and faced me.

I felt so small when I looked at him. It was worse when the rest of the guys caught up to us, all spouting questions at the same time. But Uncle Dino held me in his cold gaze, and I couldn't look away. Hitting his son was one thing. Looking away would be an unforgivable insult. "Yes, Uncle Dino?"

"Never pull your punches."

I didn't hear that right. "What?"

"You had good form. But you pulled it at the last second. Never pull your punches. It's disrespectful."

I was aghast. "He's your son—"

"And my son can take a hit. Don't disrespect him like that again." He nodded curtly, then continued on the trail as his sons went the other way back to the house. I followed Uncle Dino into the hills.

Chapter 27

Maggie

I lazed in bed as long as I could stand it before I got up. I was too excited. Julian and I were finally going to talk about things and clear the air. Nora was right. I had to make a choice to pick a path. I wanted Julian on that path.

I wasn't sure when it happened, but I was a woman in love.

I cleaned up and dressed for the day then hunted Piper down in the kitchen having breakfast. She was humming along, singing a waffle song to her pancakes with her other cousins. What one had to do with the other, I didn't know. But she was happy, and she grinned with a mouthful of pancake when she saw me.

The breakfast kitchen was bright and sunny, painted in yellow with white daisies everywhere. The friendly staff tended to the children's needs, while the caterers kept a large breakfast buffet full with a vast variety of choices.

"We're gonna swim after breakfast," she said between bites. "Will you come swimming, too?"

"Of course." I was just happy to be invited. I made myself a plate of pancakes and sat next to Piper. Apparently, she had saved me a seat.

I knew the situation with Julian was complicated. We had some things to work through. But Piper was not one of them. I had never seriously dated a dad before. In fact, it was something I usually tried to avoid. Sitting with Piper, however, made me wonder if I had just been waiting for the right dad with the right kid to come along. We simply clicked.

After breakfast, we changed into our swimsuits and jumped in the pool for a little while. The lifeguards were already at their posts. I assumed they stayed in the pool house to be close by during the week of the party. As we began another round of Marco Polo, Piper's cousin Sophia and the other kids joined us, their mothers close behind.

And Chloe.

But she was easy to ignore because she didn't get in the pool, which made it feel like a safe zone. After an hour or so, though, the illusion of safety was shattered.

"What the hell?" Chloe barked as she stood and ran to meet Marcus. As he and Apollo approached, I noticed Marcus had an icepack on his face.

I couldn't hear anything they were saying from where I stood in the pool, so I excused myself. "Piper, Sophia, I'll catch up later." They continued to play as I climbed out and quickly walked over to the trio.

I could see that Marcus had a black eye forming where the icepack didn't cover. Apollo looked fine. "What happened? Is Julian okay?"

"He's fine," Apollo quickly replied. "Marcus had a little accident."

"How?" Chloe demanded.

Marcus rolled his eyes at himself. "Talking shit."

"Talk shit, get hit," Apollo teased.

"It was Julian, wasn't it?" she accused.

"Yeah, but—"

She whipped around to face me, pointing against my chest. "I told you, Maggie. I fucking told you. Julian is a menace! He was in high school, and he still is now!"

"Lower your voice. His daughter is right over there." I jerked my chin toward Piper subtly.

"You think I care? He savaged one of my boyfriends, and now, he's going after his own cousin! She deserves to know her daddy is a monster!"

The mothers on the pool terrace had been watching our drama with rapt attention, and now the kids were too. I was not about to allow that.

I snatched a towel from a nearby lounger and wrapped it over Chloe's back as I forced an unnatural smile onto my face and firmly gripped her shoulders. I forcibly guided her into the house, keeping my tone jovial. The guys followed us inside the lounge. "Here we go, dear, you wouldn't want me to get all mama bear on you now, would you?"

Chloe tried to shake my grip and failed. "Let go of me!"

I waited until the door closed before I released her. My fingers nearly became cramped in the process. "Now, you're welcome to say whatever filth you want, but you will not talk shit about Julian in front of Piper, do you understand me, Chloe?" I came in close, intentionally invading her space. "Because I want to make sure you understand exactly what I mean by that, so there isn't any confusion."

"Your fiancé has attacked two of my boyfriends, Maggie. I will say whatever I want—"

I held a finger up to silence her. "Not in front of Piper,

you won't. You can either keep your mouth shut around her and swallow your pride, or you can swallow your teeth. Which will it be?"

The three of them stood there in stunned silence before Chloe scoffed a laugh, trying to deflate me like a souffle pulled from the oven too soon. "You've always been such a kidder, Maggie."

"I'm not kidding." I stepped even closer. This was one fight with Chloe I was not going to back down from.

"Okay, ladies," Apollo said, cutting in. "I've already failed at breaking up one fight today. Don't make it two."

Marcus laughed, then whined, "Fuck, dude, don't make me laugh. It hurts."

That stole her attention and she turned to him. "Let me see."

He lifted the icepack, and while I couldn't tell if his nose was broken, it was certainly swollen. He'd wake up with a healthy shiner in the morning. "I've had worse."

"From me," his brother teased.

Marcus slugged his shoulder but didn't disagree. "It's no big deal, Chloe."

"Like hell it isn't!" She faced off with me again. "Is Julian obsessed with me or something?"

"Huh?"

"Maybe that's why he's attacked two of my boyfriends."

"Can't speak for the other guy," Marcus said, "but I kind of earned this."

"Shut up, Marcus," she ordered. "No one was talking to you."

Apollo's eyes widened at that, and he smirked but said nothing. He didn't have to, his face did it for him.

Marcus tried again, "Uh, Chloe, listen—"

With her eyes on me, she put her hand in his face to

shut him up. "Julian is obsessed with me, isn't he, Maggie? That's why you put on this little show, right?"

I blinked at her. "What show?"

"The mama bear comment? That thing in the closet, as if he can't keep his hands off of you? Showing up here to make me jealous?"

"We didn't even know you'd be here!" Though, with the way life had been screwing with me lately, I should have expected it.

The others returned and crowded the lounge. Julian walked in next to an older man who had to be Marcus and Apollo's father. When Julian saw me standing with the three of them, his face sank.

But as Chloe smiled wide and evil, every scrap of heat left my body. She loudly proclaimed, "Your so-called fiancé *is* obsessed with me. That's why he tried to make me jealous at the reunion by using you. Have some self-respect, Maggie."

"You are out of your mind."

"I'm not the one pretending here," she said confidently as she folded her arms under her breasts.

"Julian doesn't give a shit about you!" I shouted at her.

She kept her evil grin trained on him as he joined us. "I think he might disagree."

"Chloe." He stood tall, glaring down at her. "I think you need to back off."

"Why? What will you do? Hit me too?"

"Hardly. But I still think it's in your best interest to go to Marcus' room and cool off. Maybe you could tend to your boyfriend's wounds."

"The ones you gave him, you mean?" she said snidely.

Marcus flatly interjected, "I'm fine, Chloe, thanks for asking."

She barely rolled her eyes at him as if that was more effort than he was worth. "We're not done here."

"I think you are." Julian subtly stepped between me and her. He lowered his voice. "No one wants more of a scene than what has already happened. Especially you."

Why especially her?

"Is that a fact?" she asked, smirking up at him. "I'm pretty sure you're the one who doesn't want a scene, and besides, I've already made enough money from this deal anyway."

"Chloe," he growled.

"Money?" I directed my question at Julian.

But he didn't look at me. He only glowered at Chloe. "Don't."

The sneer on her face sealed his fate. She became animated as she spoke. "Don't what? Tell the truth?"

I knew it. I knew she knew the truth. Fuck. I said carefully, "Chloe, I think we'd both do well to go and cool off, don't you?"

"No, I don't. I think you'd feel better if we got some things off our chests. Why don't you start?"

All eyes were on me. No matter what happened, I wasn't about to say a peep. "I don't know what you're talking about."

The lounge door that led to the pool area opened, and some of the moms joined the group which only made things worse.

"Well, if you don't want to start, I guess I will," Chloe began. "These—"

"Chloe, can I talk to you in private?" Marcus interrupted.

"No." She returned her attention to the rest of the group. "I've been sitting on this for far too long, and I respect your family too much to keep it inside any longer."

"Then get on with it," Marcus' father said. "We haven't got all day."

"I had planned on something a little longer, but for you, Daddy Dino, I'll keep it short," she said flirtatiously. Then she pointed at me and Julian. "Their engagement is a lie."

Chapter 28

Julian

My heart stuttered to a stop the same way time had done when I punched Marcus. I huffed out a thin breath. Chloe was clever in her own way—I still had no idea how she knew the truth—but there were other ways to deal with her. Like making her seem incompetent.

With all the simulated concern I could muster, I asked, "Chloe, are you feeling well? Did you hit your head or something? You're looking a little green."

"I'm fine," she said, a big gloating smile on her face. "You two are the ones who probably aren't feeling well right about now."

As much as I wanted to point out how wrong she was, I kept up the faux concern and looked at her boyfriend. "Eh, Marcus, does Chloe take any meds that you know of? Mood stabilizers or something similar? Did she miss a dose? Does booze interact with them? I noticed she's been hitting the bar a little hard."

He smirked a little at that. "Can't say."

"Hey!" She snapped her fingers at me for attention. "I am not crazy!"

"No, of course you're not." I smiled and patted her head, which made her jerk away. "We don't use that term anymore. Undermedicated, mentally unstable, I'm not sure what the current acceptable word is."

"It's neither of those," Apollo said.

I lifted a shoulder. "Whatever. I'm not feeling politically correct at the moment given what she just said about us."

"Julian! Stop talking about me like I'm not here!" she demanded like a child.

"You can always leave and make that a reality. The door is right over there," I said, pointing to it. "Pretty sure no one here would miss you."

"Your engagement isn't real! Everyone here should know the truth. How you can lie to your own flesh and blood like this is beyond me," she rambled, trying to retain the spotlight. "It's truly awful. But then again, what should I expect from the man who attacked two of my boyfriends like an animal?"

"Chloe," Marcus started. "I know you're upset for me, hon, but I'm fine. You don't need to make a big deal out of this. Guys fight sometimes. We're cousins, that's just how we are."

"No," I cut in. "That's not how we are. We're not kids anymore, and mere words should not be enough to provoke me. I'm sorry I hit you. It won't happen again."

He shrugged it off. "I was out of line. I'm sorry I talked shit about... I'm sorry for what I said."

I nodded once, accepting his apology. "We good?"

"You owe me a beer."

"Deal."

Chloe snipped out, "Oh, my God. Is no one here upset with these two liars?"

"I'd like to hear more about this so-called fake engagement," Yaya said as she parted the crowd to come closer.

Shit. With that statement, Chloe's bullshit had legs. I couldn't ignore a request from Yaya. She was the matriarch of the family, the one everyone—including me—respected. If I lost her support on this, I was cooked.

I firmly told her, "Chloe's a known liar, Yaya. She always has been. Don't pay her any attention."

"*I'm* the liar?" Chloe laughed. "You two said you've been living together for months."

"We have been," I replied. "What of it?"

"Then why didn't your daughter's teacher meet Maggie until about three or four weeks ago?"

How the hell does Chloe know Etta? And why would Etta tell Chloe about me and Maggie? She is so fucking fired. Piper will hate going to a new teacher, but she is four, and she'll get over it.

Maggie's shoulders caved in at that, her resolve cracking. But she tried to play it off. "Etta doesn't like me, so if she gossiped about me, I'm not surprised."

"How I raise my daughter is none of your concern," I snapped at Chloe.

"You rented a car for Maggie around the same time she first met Etta Pence, didn't you?" she continued. "Why not just buy her one? It's not like you don't have the money."

How does she know all of this?

Maggie's chin went up, even as her voice wavered. "Have you been stalking us? Why are you inserting yourself into our lives, Chloe? Don't you have one of your own?"

Chloe's head swiveled like a bird of prey spotting a target. "Well, Maggie, that's the thing. I hadn't heard a word about you two being a couple before the reunion, and yet both of you were acting a little suspicious and cagey while you were there, so I did a little digging. After your bakery's fire, you were about to be evicted from your apartment until you suddenly found yourself living with Julian almost a month ago, that is. But that doesn't make sense with your engagement timeline, does it?"

At least I wasn't being blackmailed anymore. Now that she had spilled the tea, she had nothing. I growled, "I'm done explaining myself to you, Chloe. So is Maggie. Whatever game you're playing, it's over. You should leave. Now."

"I think Yaya and everyone else here deserves the truth."

And maybe one day, I'd tell them. But this was not the day. "The truth is, you're very tired and undermedicated and probably drunk, and I think you should stop embarrassing yourself and Marcus with this nonsense." I turned to my family. "Everybody, let's get this party back on track, shall we? Who's up for shots?"

Half my family chanted, "Shots! Shots! Shots!" in response but Yaya's eyes sharpened on me, causing my pulse to quicken. We'd be talking about this sooner than I had hoped.

"I have proof!" Chloe shouted over everyone in one last ditch effort.

Maggie squeezed my hand. I didn't remember her taking it.

Chloe held her phone over her head but the screen was turned away from me. I could have easily grabbed it from her as close as I was, but if I did that, everyone would know

I had something to hide. I had to wait and see what came next.

She handed it over to Marcus. "See that? Two million dollars deposited into my bank account over the past two days."

"Where did you get that kind of money? I thought you were broke."

She swallowed, irritated. "I told Julian I'd expose him if he didn't pay me a million dollars a day during the week of this party. An innocent person wouldn't pay if they had nothing to hide, nothing to be blackmailed with."

Maggie looked up at me, shock and disappointment on her pretty face. "You didn't tell me."

"It's two million dollars. Not a big deal."

"Not a big deal?" she whispered as her cheeks flushed pink.

I couldn't tell if she was hurt or angry. I hadn't told her about Chloe's blackmail and now I was acting as if that kind of money was nothing. Considering Maggie's financial woes, it could have been either one. Whatever the case, I had upset her, and I fucking hated that.

Just as I was about to apologize, Apollo asked Chloe, "Did I hear you right? You just admitted to blackmail?"

She huffed at him. "It's barely blackmail. It's two million dollars. That's practically petty cash to him, and besides, that's not the point. Julian only paid up because he knew I could blow his lie apart."

"Why didn't you tell me?" Maggie asked me directly.

We couldn't talk this out now in front of everyone. Not when I wasn't ready to tell them the truth. I had to word this as carefully as possible.

"It was easier to pay her than to stonewall her. I wanted things to go as smoothly as possible this week, so paying her and not making a big deal of it seemed like the better idea." I scowled at Chloe. "You could have held out for more. I would have paid it just to shut you up, not that your accusations hold any merit. Instead, you couldn't hold your wad, and now, all you're getting is two million. Happy?"

Her smug smile was hard to take. "I'm not *un*happy."

"You should have told me," Maggie said, her voice cracking. "I deserved to know."

Chloe taunted me. "She's right about that, you know."

"I should have," I admitted to Maggie. "That was my mistake, and I will spend the rest of my life making it up to you." Was I proposing for real this time? I checked in with myself. There was no part of me that didn't mean exactly what I said. I wanted to spend the rest of my life with Maggie Bryant, come hell or high water. I added, "If you'll let me make it up to you forever, I mean. If that's what you want." A messy proposal, if ever there was one.

Maggie took a quick breath, her eyes lining with tears. "I don't know about that."

"Maggie—"

She pulled her hand from mine and stepped back, her eyes never leaving me. Then she turned and ran, my family clearing a path for her, concern on all of their faces.

I started to follow but Yaya's iron grip caught me. "Let her have a minute, Julian."

"I have to go talk to her."

"That woman needs to be able to think, to breathe. You'll do her no favors by crowding her."

"If I don't go to her now, I will lose her forever."

Her cheeks lifted with her smile, lining her face with decades of past joy. She let go of my wrist. "Very well. Go on."

I nearly ran ahead, but Yaya's knowing smile unnerved me, stopping me in my tracks. "What was that about?"

"She needed a minute, and you would not have argued with me if you did not love her. By holding you back, she gets her time, and I learn whether this drama was worth it."

"Yaya—"

"Now go."

Chapter 29

Maggie

Everybody knows.

While I dressed, that was all I could think about. Everyone knew what I had done, what *we* had done. I had never been a liar. Not really. Not before the reunion. But I was backed into a corner.

No. I made a choice. I could have taken Chloe's bullshit for a night and been done with it. Instead, I blew up an entire family's yearly reunion. I ruined everything. For Julian, for Piper. For fifty or so members of his family downstairs. It was all my fault.

Except for the things that were Julian's fault.

Why in the hell didn't he tell me about Chloe blackmailing him?

The door handle jiggled but I had locked it. Two knocks came before Julian's voice asked, "Can I come in?"

"No."

"Maggie, we need to talk."

"You need to talk. I don't." That wasn't exactly true but it was close enough. When it came to Julian Black, every time I went with my gut, I bombed horribly. My instincts sucked around him, so I had to do the opposite of what my gut was telling me. Talking was out. Opening the door was out. As long as he stayed in the hallway, I couldn't fuck this up.

Not exactly a long-term solution but it was all I had for now.

Metal clinked against metal, and the next thing I knew, the door opened. Julian walked in, key in hand. "I'm sorry to barge into my own room, but we have to talk."

"No, we don't." I couldn't look at him. If I looked, I'd say something stupid like telling him I loved him and we could work through this. Clearly, the universe didn't want us to be together. Otherwise, this would be easier.

That was how love was supposed to go, right?

"Fine. You don't have to talk. Just listen."

I shook my head and snatched my luggage from the closet. I laid it out on the bed and got to work. "I'm not listening."

His brow furrowed. "Then I will talk to hear myself speak."

I shrugged. My clothes had been carefully hung in the closet or folded into drawers by the invisible staff that made things happen in this place. It would have unnerved me if it wasn't so convenient. I gathered my things and started laying them carefully into the suitcase.

"Maggie, what are you doing?"

"I told you. I'm not talking."

He groaned in frustration. "Fine but I don't want you going anywhere. We need to work this out."

"There's nothing to work out."

"That's not true."

I didn't speak. Packing was the only way out of this conversation so I kept at it.

"You want to know why I didn't tell you about Chloe blackmailing me?"

I glanced up at him.

"Because of this. Because I knew you would overreact. You were already worried she would rat us out, and if you knew she knew, you would have freaked.

"So, you kept it from me for my own good?"

"Yes!"

My nostrils flared, and I could not keep my thoughts inside, no matter how hard I bit my tongue. "It's a good thing we're not actually engaged then, Jules, because you don't want a partner. You want another servant."

"What?"

"Hot tip—if you ever want a woman to be a real partner to you, then you tell her when someone is blackmailing you! You do not keep it inside to protect her. You let her help you get through it and you come up with a plan together so neither of you is blindsided in front of your entire family!"

I had never seen a man shrink before. Not the way Jules did right then. He stuttered, "You-you're right. About the blackmail thing. Not the servant thing."

"Bullshit." I resumed packing. "Why else have the contract written up?"

"Because..." He growled under his breath. "Because I was trying to do right by you. I explained this."

"Treating me like another servant was doing right by me?" *I have to stop engaging. Stop talking.*

"I have never treated you like a servant, Maggie."

"Paying me for my companionship sounds like a servant to me. Or is escort the right word?" I couldn't shut up.

He pressed his palms to his temples, groaning again. "Maggitha Eileen Bryant, I swear to God—"

"What did you just call me?" I interrupted him.

He chuckled. "You always told me Maggie wasn't short for anything, so I made up names for you in my head."

"Maggitha?"

He shrugged. "It's better than Margaret."

I took a breath and shook my head, trying not to laugh when I really wanted to bark at him for making a joke during another serious discussion, and went back to packing. This time, I shoved things into my luggage. I had to speed this along. "Whatever you say, boss."

Julian pulled my luggage across the bed out of my reach. "We are not having this conversation again. You know why I did it. I did it to protect you."

"That's all you've ever done, isn't it? Protect me." *Not love me.*

Worry etched across his face. "Why are you saying that like it's a bad thing?"

I didn't know how to answer that. If he didn't understand it instinctually, how could I explain it to him? Did I even owe him an explanation? Not technically. But I wanted to tell him.

And where did following your instincts get you with Jules so far? Fucked.

"It doesn't matter why I said it like that. Just give me my luggage."

"Tell me why protecting you is a bad thing, and I will."

A hard knot formed in my throat. I couldn't look him in the eyes so I just stared at my clothes. My voice came out in a whisper. "Jules, don't do this to me."

He slid the suitcase next to my pile of clothes. His voice went cold. "Fine. Take it."

Despair dug its way through me. I couldn't keep my thoughts inside, no matter what lines they crossed. Tears trickled down my face. "You always protected me, Jules.

When the football team picked on me, you were there. When Chloe and her idiot friends talked shit about me, you were there. Always defending me. Didn't you think I could defend myself?"

He blinked at me, confused. "But you never did."

"No, I didn't." I wiped my face, willing my tears to stop. But they didn't listen and continued to spill down my cheeks. "But maybe I would have learned to stand up for myself if I didn't always have you and Nora to do it for me. Maybe I wouldn't have made up this huge lie about us when we were at the reunion and told Chloe to go fuck herself instead. I lied, and now... now your family hates me."

He rushed around the end of the bed and took me in his arms. I let him. "It's not your fault."

His words choked me, and I shoved him off. "It is my fault, Julian! Don't you get that? I fucked up. *Me*. I chose to lie about things to Chloe and I pulled you into it. I made that choice. Now I have to live with the consequences, and you have to stop protecting me from them. I will never be able to stand on my own against people like Chloe if I have people like you always there to swoop in and save me. That's why protecting me all the time is a bad thing."

He cleared his throat. "I won't apologize for protecting you, Maggie."

"I'm not asking for an apology. You thought you were doing the right thing. That's all you've ever done. That's all this ever was." I finished packing and closed the suitcase. "You're a good man, Jules. That's why this hurts so much."

"What do you mean that's all this ever was?"

A sickening feeling struck my heart. More ugly words came rushing out. "I think you and Nora have it wrong. Our history, I mean."

"What's Nora got to do with us?"

"She said she thought you had a crush on me back then."

"I did. I told you that."

"I know." The pancakes in my stomach turned to lead. "I know you think you had a crush on me. But—"

"Don't. Don't you dare."

I closed my eyes, noticing my tears had dried up. I felt empty inside. "Julian, you didn't have a crush. You never saw me as an equal, so how could you have a real crush on me?"

He muttered, "What are you saying?"

"I was little more than a project to you. Someone to protect. Someone weaker, not an equal."

"You've never been more wrong, Maggie."

"I think you liked me well enough, but I also think you confused that with love, probably because of teenage hormones and the fact your dad just died." I took a deep breath before I lied to him. "It's fine, Jules. It's in the past. And whatever this was, it's in the past, too." When I stepped to move around him he blocked me. "Don't."

He took my face in his hands and slanted his mouth over mine. His fingertips turned my head toward him. I wanted this so badly to be real. My toes curled in my ballet flats, and a thrill wound through me hard enough to get me wet.

But not hard enough to shake me from reality.

His green eyes peered into my soul. "This isn't in the past. *We* are not the past, Maggie. We are not over before we begin. We are just getting started."

I wanted all of it—everything that his eyes and his kiss and his touch promised. But it was tinged with something awful. Something I couldn't live with in a thousand lifetimes. "Julian, do you realize that every time you helped me or protected me, you did it out of pity?"

His face twisted like I had punched him in the gut. "What?"

I sighed, trying to fill my lungs with enough air to allow my broken heart room to breathe. "When you think about it—really think about it—you'll understand." I wheeled my bag toward the door. "I deserve more than pity from a partner. We both deserve to be loved the way we need to be. Goodbye, Julian."

Chapter 30

Julian

The midday sun spilled through the half-open windows, casting a warm glow on the walls, but it did little to ease the tension crackling in the air. I stepped between her and the door. I couldn't just let her walk out of my life. After all we had been through, we were worth more than this. Fighting for her, for us, was the only thing that made any sense.

But as I stood there, she refused to look me in the eye. Her voice wavered when she glanced toward the door behind me. "Julian, I really should go."

"Please, Maggie, just hear me out." My heart raced. I hadn't expected the truth to come out. Chloe had millions of dollars on the line, but I guess that was a small price to pay compared to making us suffer. I would get my revenge on Chloe. I just didn't know how yet.

Right now, the only thing that mattered was Maggie. I needed her to stay. I needed her to be my rock. And more than anything, I needed to make her understand.

The words flowed out of me like a river. "I never pitied you. I loved you back then, and I love you now. I have always loved you. Pity has nothing to do with how I feel about you. It's not like that for me. I have and will always love you, don't you see that?"

Her eyes widened, and for a moment, I thought I saw a flicker of hope in them. But it quickly faded, and she shook her head as if to clear away the thoughts swirling in her mind. "Julian, you don't understand," she said, her voice breaking. "Everybody knows the truth now, and that changes things."

"It changes nothing. You're still you, and I'm still me. I've never had this kind of connection with anyone before, and I know you feel the same. Tell me different, and I'll walk away." A pure bluff. How could I ever walk away from this woman again after truly knowing her, her kiss, her touch, the way she tasted? I could never walk away from her now. It would be like walking away from my own heart.

She swallowed. "Feelings don't matter. Reality matters, and in the real world, we would never work. We both know it. Besides sex, what do we have in common?"

"Shared history, mutual admiration, chemistry, the drive to succeed... do I need to go on?"

"Don't make this harder on both of us."

"I'm not! You're the one making this hard!"

"Then let me make it easy and let me walk out of this room."

But I couldn't do that so I changed tactics. I knew it might only gain me a few more seconds with her but I needed them. "Why do you think I pity you, Maggie? I don't understand."

"I just explained it to you."

"How could I pity you?" I went on, irrespective of her thin explanation. "You're strong, you're resilient. You make me feel like I can take on the world. None of that says pity. I don't care about anybody downstairs judging us for what we did. We lied. They'll get over it. We'll be embarrassed for the week, and then we'll leave and it won't matter because we'll have a life together. The rest doesn't matter. Only us."

She crossed her arms as if trying to shield herself from my words. I could see the struggle in her eyes while fear, confusion, and a deep sadness twisted my heart. I could only assume she felt the same way.

Maggie cleared her throat, shaking her head. "I can't be the person you need me to be. If you've ever pitied me, even just once, I can't handle that."

"Why do you keep thinking that I pity you? I've *never* pitied you." I tried for earnestness in my tone, but it verged on a desperate growl because I was, in fact, desperate and frustrated. I needed her to understand how I felt, and I wasn't getting anywhere in showing her the truth that was in my heart. Her words hit me like a punch to the gut.

Silence stretched between us, demanding, suffocating. Tears welled in her eyes, little stars on the verge of falling. I'd make a wish on every one of them if that meant she stayed.

My heart ached for her, for the terrible memories she carried. I thought she might respond. Say anything at all. But she didn't. The silence threatened to ruin everything.

I couldn't take it anymore. I needed to bridge the gap between us.

"Don't go," I pleaded, my voice barely above a whisper. "Let's get through this together. Let's be here for each other. We did something stupid, but we did it together. There's no reason to break that streak."

She didn't say a word, but she also didn't move. It gave me a tiny flicker of hope.

As she continued to refuse to make eye contact and bite

her lip, I knew this wasn't going to go how I needed it to. The space between us widened, even though neither of us moved. Every muscle in my body tensed like I was under attack. But there was nothing. Nothing to say, nothing to be done.

It felt over. We both knew it.

But I was stubborn and not used to not getting my way.

"Maggie..." I reached out, brushing my thumb against her cheek. The softness of her skin sent a jolt through me. How could this be over? It made no sense. I stumbled over my words. "All of this, it'll fade away. Let's watch it fade away together."

And then she broke. A single tear escaped and slid down her cheek. It ruined what little pride I had left.

I couldn't help but lean in, pressing my lips against the trail of her sorrow. It was a gentle kiss, an unspoken promise that I would be there for her. No matter what came of today, I would be there. She had me wrapped around her little finger, and she didn't even know it.

She trembled at my touch, and as I kissed her tears away, the world outside faded to black. It was just us, our past, our present, and the electric connection that pulsed between us. I kissed my way to her lips.

But before I got there, she whispered, "Jules, I can't."

I pressed my forehead against hers, breathing in her scent, her heat. I needed all of it, all of her. Even if only one more breath. One more hit of this drug I'd so willingly given myself over to. "Just stay with me a little while longer." I was sure she could hear my heart drumming in my chest. "Please, Maggie."

That was the encouragement she needed. She surged forward, and our lips met again, more fervently this time. It was

Accidental Fiancé

as if the walls that had kept us apart crumbled, leaving nothing but the raw, unfiltered passion we'd held back for so long. Her hands wove into my hair as I pulled her closer, deepening the kiss, pouring everything I felt into that moment. I lost myself in the taste of her, the sweetness, the hint of salt from her tears.

But just as quickly as it had begun, the moment seemed to dissolve.

Maggie pulled back, her breath shaky as she looked into my eyes, searching for something she couldn't seem to find. I felt a chill sweep through me, a sense of impending loss. I knew it was done. Coldness washed over me, leaving a trail of agony in its wake.

"I can't do this," she said. "I don't want to hurt you."

"You're not hurting me if you stay," I replied, pathetically needy. I had run out of things to say and ways to convince her. If that kiss couldn't do it, and if my words couldn't do it, then I didn't know what could. I tried one more time. "We made some bad choices, but we can figure this out together. My family will get over it."

But she shook her head, tears spilling down her cheeks now. "And what about me, Jules? Do you think this is something I can just get over? Once again, Chloe beat me. Humiliated me. She came out on top like always. I'm just a joke to her and to your family. To you, I'm simply a weak and helpless—"

"Don't put those words in my mouth. Not ever."

She began to say something else but stopped herself. She stepped to the side to move around me. A struggle bared down on her face—some inner war I wasn't privy to. After a shuddering breath, she said, "I'm sorry."

I grabbed her wrist gently. "Don't go. Please."

She looked down at my hand on her wrist, and for a

heartbeat, I thought she might stay. But then she pulled away, breaking free of my grasp. "No."

A single word that brought my whole world crashing down.

But I wasn't completely without pride. Close to it, but I was still a man, dammit. I swallowed against the knot in my throat, determined to force my needs down for her. "Do you want me to go downstairs with you? Play defense against Chloe? I'll stop her from bothering you on the way out."

Something about what I had said sharpened her resolve. If looks could kill, I would have been dead on the spot. Maggie uttered, "You just have to play the big strong hero one more time, huh?"

"God, Maggie, it's not like that, and you know it."

Her voice went flat. "I don't know anything anymore."

I knew there was nothing else I could say or do. Preventing her from leaving felt cruel to both of us, and it wasn't what she wanted. I didn't want to keep her if she didn't want to be kept.

So, I stepped aside. It was the hardest thing I had ever done. But if she wanted to do this without me, then I wasn't going to stop her.

She opened the door and slipped through it, leaving me hollow and heartbroken. I leaned against the wall, the silence of my childhood room pressing in on me like a weight. I had poured my entire heart out yet I still lost her.

This wasn't how it was supposed to go. Not when I could still feel the taste of her on my lips, the salt of her tears lingering in my mouth, and the ache in my chest where hope had once lived. Her scent lingered in the air like a ghost.

I had fought for her, for us. But sometimes love wasn't enough to hold on to someone when they were determined to leave. I learned that in my first marriage. Britney had made it clear that what I wanted didn't matter when she had an affair with an old business partner. After she left me for him, it hurt, but it was nothing like this, nothing like what I felt for Maggie.

It wasn't real love.

I sank down on the edge of my bed, the world outside continuing to turn without me as I grappled with the realization that it was over.

Chapter 31

Maggie

My heart pounded louder than the thud of my suitcase against the polished wood floor. Ornate chandeliers above flickered in the midday light, casting pale shadows that danced across the walls of the mansion. It felt surreal, the opulence surrounding me now. A strange reminder of the chaos that had unfolded.

As if I needed to be reminded that this was not my world.

This was the world of people like Chloe. People like Julian. The ones who never had to struggle for a damn thing in their lives.

With one last deep breath, I tightened my grip and lifted the luggage, feeling the handle dig into my palm. I began my descent, each step feeling like another farewell. A final goodbye to the life I had wanted to cling to.

I couldn't believe I was leaving, but after everything with Julian, I knew it was time. It was beyond time. No more playing pretend. No more lies. Bryant's lived in reality.

Accidental Fiancé

As I reached the foyer, alert faces lingered near the grand entrance. Chloe stood at the center, her arms crossed, an imperious smirk plastered across her face. Eager to brag about her triumph, no doubt. Marcus leaned casually against the wall, his expression unreadable. Apollo fiddled with his phone, pretending not to notice the tension brewing in the air.

The dead would have noticed it.

"Look who's finally leaving," Chloe said, her voice dripping with mockery. "I was starting to think you'd never get the hint."

I was done backing down from her. I set my luggage on the floor and raised an eyebrow. "Always full of nice things to say, Chloe."

"Always good to see the trash taking itself out."

"Oh, are you leaving, too?"

She looked me up and down. "That's a nice outfit. What's that old saying about putting lipstick on a pig?"

"Unsure, but I remember the word for women like you thought it's impolite to use outside of a kennel."

Marcus and Apollo snorted and smirked but said nothing.

Chloe snapped, "You never belonged here, you know. You can dress up and pretend to be one of them, but we all know the truth."

I took a steadying breath, feeling the weight of her words but refusing to let them crush me. "I *might* not belong here, but you *definitely* don't."

Her smirk faltered for a moment but she quickly regained her composure. "Oh? And what makes you say that?"

"You're as much of an outsider here as I am." I stepped forward, a fire igniting within me. "You hide behind your designer clothes and your snide remarks, but we all see you for what you are. You think you're better than everyone else, but you have nothing but cruelty to back that up, and cruelty is the weapon of the weak. I only wish I had realized that sooner."

"Now you listen here—"

"No, Chloe, I'm done listening to you. You're pathetic, and you're small, and when you get what's coming to you, I'll be there to make sure it sticks."

The space between us crackled with friction, my declaration clinging to the air itself. I glanced at Marcus, who looked as if he were about to step in, but I held up a hand to stop him. This was between me and Chloe.

"And by the way," I continued, my voice steady. "I finally figured it out. *You* started that rumor about me and Mr. Poundstone."

Chloe's eyes widened for a split second before the mask slipped back into place. "What are you talking about?"

"I believed all this time that it was Grant who started it. But he had nothing to gain from creating such a specific rumor. You, on the other hand, had everything to gain. You wanted the solo that I got. You were angry with Mr. Poundstone that he didn't give it to you, just like you'd been given everything else. So, you created that rumor for your petty revenge. Did Grant know that it was a lie? Did he get Mr. Poundstone fired on accident? Or was he in on it too?"

Chloe's heart-shaped mouth opened and closed like a guppy a few times before she spoke again. "What if I did? What does it matter now? Mr. Poundstone moved on. Why won't you?"

As far as I was concerned, that was as good as an admission. But I pressed on. "Why would you do that? Why would you try to ruin me? What did I have that you didn't already have, Chloe? I had next to nothing back then, and you knew it. My mom and I were practically homeless. I wasn't cheer captain, that was you. I wasn't a popular girl like you. That solo was the only thing that I had going for me and you tried to take that away, too. Why?"

Chloe sneered, glaring. Her face flushed red with anger as her jaw worked. She growled, "You brought it on yourself."

"How? By being your punching bag for twelve years?"

"You thought you could just walk in there, sing marginally well, and take what was mine. You're selfish, Maggie."

I laughed in disbelief. "You're joking, right? Have you any self-awareness?"

"If you thought I'd just roll over and let you do it, then you had another thing coming," she spat. "You're a nobody. A nobody trying to be a somebody. There's nothing sadder. You'll never be one of us."

"I don't want to be you!" I shot back. "You don't get to decide who I am or what I'm worth. That upsets you, doesn't it?"

Chloe's expression darkened, and for a moment, I thought she might lash out again. But instead, I saw a flicker of something else. Fear, perhaps? The realization that she had lost her hold on me? She remained silent, scanning me as if she were hunting for a new crack to pry open.

But I had filled my cracks with the truth. Funny how being ripped apart was the thing that fixed me.

I took a step back, my heart racing. "You keep trying to break me, Chloe Foster, yet I'm still standing. I never deserved your hate, but I realize now it was never about me. It was about you. What you say about me says more about you than it does me, and that eats you alive, doesn't it?"

"You don't know what you're talking about," she hissed.

I shrugged. I was done with Chloe, with feeling like an asshole for lying to Julian's family, with all of it. There was nothing here for me. Not anymore. Time to start a new chapter of my life story.

I'd rebuild myself from the ground up.

As I stood there, staring Chloe down, I saw it in my head. I'd move back in with Mom and Dad, get a job, and save up my money until I could open another bakery. Maybe I could even write a cookbook while I worked toward my new bakery. It would take years of work, but the time would pass anyway, so I might as well work toward something good.

A life I could be proud of. The world was my hard-earned oyster. I just had to seize it.

Chloe's shoulders heaved with her angry breaths, charging up like a weak battery. "If I were you, I'd—"

"I'm not interested in your advice. Save your breath. It's just hot air, anyway." With that, I grabbed my suitcase and pushed past her, knocking against her bony shoulder and not bothering to look back.

Marcus' expression was a fresh appraisal of me like he was seeing me for the first time. Apollo gave a nod of respect as I passed him. But then he glanced down at his phone, once again acting like he wasn't paying attention to anything else.

I wondered how many times he'd done exactly that. Play pretend. I understood the urge. It was easier to pretend than to acknowledge anything uncomfortable. It was the one reality that a Bryant never liked to face. But I faced it today.

Maybe I wasn't like the others in my family, after all. Or maybe it was a new day for the Bryant's. Hard to say. As of today, though, I was done eating my words or swallowing my feelings. No more biting my tongue. That chapter was closed.

I told Julian the ugly truth—he didn't love me. He was confused, and pity was not a foundation to build anything on. Even though I thought I might choke on the words, I got them out. I said my piece and left it at that. To my surprise, I was still breathing, and better than that, I was proud of myself.

Walking away, I felt lighter. The burden of Chloe's cruelty and the remnants of my past were finally behind me. The path ahead was uncertain, but it was mine to shape. No more playing someone else's game or by someone else's rules. I was ready to find my own way, free from the shackles of a life I never truly belonged in.

Chapter 32

Julian

I watched from the second-floor balcony as Maggie carried her luggage through the foyer, shoulders back, her steps steady, and her head held high. A pang of pride shot through me, even as she marched away. Seeing her spar with Chloe was incredible. I couldn't believe she stood up to her like that.

If she wasn't leaving me right now, I might have been aroused by seeing her so thoroughly trounce Chloe. But she was walking away, away from what we had built together, even if it was a lie at first. The ache was suffocating, and even though I hated it, I couldn't deny the strength she carried. She'd been through hell—betrayal, rumors, her bakery burning down—and yet she still moved through the world with grace. That was Maggie. Human resilience.

As she neared the door, Chloe hovered nearby. Marcus was with her, along with a few others who gravitated to the foyer. Somehow, no matter how awful she was, people fell in line with Chloe, even if only to see what she'd do next. She was a venomous snake, eyeing her prey, and still, people always wanted to watch.

I clenched my fists as I watched her lips curl into that signature sneer, the one she saved for when she was about to strike.

Here we go again.

Before I could run down the stairs to tell her to shut up, she sniped, "Before you leave, Maggie, there is one more thing I'd like to say."

"I've no interest in anything else that comes out of your mouth."

"Such a shame about your little bakery. I guess some dreams aren't meant to last."

Maggie stopped cold, and I swallowed. How dare Chloe say that? But I had to let Maggie handle this. If I stepped in to rescue her now, she'd hate me forever.

Her hand dropped to her side and her back stiffened, but she didn't respond immediately. She was calm and calculated. The woman I had fallen in love with—again.

Chloe, emboldened by the silence, took another step closer, her voice lowering into a sarcastic taunt. "You must be so devastated with that insurance money tied up. I mean, how are you going to rebuild when the fire marshal's report is taking so long? You know those things can drag out for months, maybe even years."

I froze. How did Chloe know about the fire marshal and the insurance? To my understanding, that wasn't public knowledge. My chest tightened as I leaned closer, trying to hear Maggie's response.

Her voice was soft but steady when she finally spoke. "Are you close personal friends with the fire marshal? Because there's really no other way you would know that."

"I have my ways." Chloe's grin widened. "You don't deserve that insurance payout, and I will make sure you never see a single penny from it."

Maggie stood there for a moment, the meaning of Chloe's words settling in. Then, in a voice sharp enough to cut glass, she asked, "Did you have anything to do with the fire?"

I held my breath. The whole room seemed to join me.

Chloe's eyes gleamed. She crossed her arms over her chest, tilted her head slightly, and said, "Of course I did."

Maggie gasped. "Why?"

"I had put our little rivalry behind me until I started getting involved with the reunion committee. That's when I learned how you and your family were doing. How your dad came back to his senses, how you had turned your life around from a nearly homeless existence with your mom into a successful baker, looking to expand. How your bakery had become your whole world." She shrugged and smirked. "So, I took it away."

A wave of nausea rolled through me. Chloe destroyed everything that Maggie had worked so hard for. I wanted to run down there and scream at her. But I forced myself to listen while getting my phone out to record her words.

Maggie's voice broke through the shock. "Why? Why do you hate me so much?"

Chloe's face twisted as her anger became uncontained. A brow raised as she glared. "I go through all this trouble, and you don't even know why I'm doing it?"

"What did I ever do to you?"

"Do you remember the parent-teacher night in elementary school? It was fifth grade. Mrs. Harrington put out lemonade and cookies and—"

"Yeah, I remember," Maggie said roughly. "What does this have to do with anything?"

"My dad was there, and your mom was flirting with him the whole night. She broke up my family!"

Accidental Fiancé

"What are you even talking about?" Maggie shifted her stance like she was ready for a fight, but she clearly hadn't expected that.

"My parent's marriage was never the same after that night," Chloe continued melodramatically. "They got divorced, and I had to watch my family fall apart. That's *your* fault, Maggie. If you hadn't brought your mother that night, my parents would still be married."

All of us stared at Chloe, utterly baffled as Maggie managed to find her words. "You've hated me this whole time, tormented me all these years, because ten-year-old you thought my mom flirted with your dad, ultimately leading to your parent's divorce? Are you being serious right now?"

"Your mother destroyed my family."

Maggie blinked, taken aback. "Chloe, that's insane. My mother never—"

"She did! I saw her!" Chloe snapped, her voice rising. "Your mother ruined my life, and I've been paying for it ever since!"

Apollo stepped into the fray, ever the prosecutor. "What did you see her do exactly, Chloe?"

"Her mother groped my father right in front of everyone!"

"Groped him?" Maggie was aghast until she searched her memory for a beat. "Didn't he spill lemonade on his suit or something along those lines?"

"Yes, and she insisted he take the jacket off so she could run it under the tap. She helped him undress right in front of the whole class! I had never been so humiliated in my life!" Chloe snarled, "If you hadn't brought her that night my parents would still be together!"

"*That's* what you call flirting?" Maggie ran her fingers through her hair. "My mom innocently helped your dad because he was freaked out over his suit, and you took it upon yourself to light my bakery on fire because of how you interpreted her kindness *when we were in fifth grade*? Is that what you're telling me?"

Chloe's jaw locked tight. "She was flirting with him."

"She was helping him, you psycho!" Maggie shook her head in disbelief.

It was like the air had been sucked out of the room. No one dared to speak.

Even Marcus paled. His eyes shifted from Chloe to Maggie and then to the floor, trying to make sense of nonsense. The silence continued for a few more heartbeats before Marcus straightened, finally breaking the tension. His voice was low and filled with disgust. "You set fire to Maggie's bakery because of something you *think* happened between your parents? That's fucked up, Chloe."

Her eyes flickered to him, confusion flashing across her face. "Marcus, this has nothing to do with you. Back off."

He shook his head, stepping away from her. "We are done. I'm not going to stand by and support whatever this is. You've gone too far." His voice was cold, final. "It's over between us."

Chloe's face crumpled with shock then anger, but Marcus didn't give her a chance to speak. He turned and walked away without looking back, his footsteps echoing through the foyer.

But Apollo had plenty to say. He looked Chloe up and down, his gaze as icy as his tone. "I'm filing charges against you on Monday, Chloe. You'll be lucky if this stays a local case, but I can't promise that it will. I suggest you don't leave the city."

Chloe's face bleached, the reality of Apollo's words

sinking in. "You can't be serious. It wasn't a big deal. No one was hurt."

"You're lucky nobody was hurt. Arson is a serious crime," Apollo replied smoothly. "And you just confessed in front of several witnesses." He gestured around the room.

I couldn't help but admire Apollo's stoicism. The way he dismantled Chloe's arrogance with just a few sentences was impressive. But what really mattered was Maggie. She just stood there in the middle of the chaos, unbroken. I'd never been prouder of her.

As Chloe turned and stormed off, humiliated, I jogged down the stairs, trying to find the right words to say to Maggie. But before I could reach her, she turned and met my eyes.

"Julian," she said quietly. Her voice held both finality and a deep sadness.

What could I say? That I was sorry? That I had made a mistake by letting this happen? That I loved her? She thought she knew how I felt about her better than I did, so there was no convincing her otherwise. There was nothing I could do to stop her from walking out of my life. "I'm sorry. About Chloe, about what she did to you."

"This isn't on you. What happened, it's done. Don't give me those sad puppy eyes." A hint of a smile on her plump lips gave me hope for her. Chloe may have burned down her bakery, but she didn't destroy the thing that mattered most—Maggie's heart and grit.

I swallowed hard. "I know that it's not my place, but I'm proud of you for standing up to her. For everything."

She gave me a small smile. "Thanks for that."

Apollo ushered the others toward the lounge and away from the foyer. As I reached for the door to open it for

Maggie a moment later, we heard Chloe scream out, "I am not going to prison! Do you understand me? I will not go!"

We both snorted a laugh, trying not to crack up. I wondered if a last-ditch effort would even matter at this point. But I had to say what was on my mind. "Do you think Chloe will look good in prison orange?"

Maggie's stiff upper lip attitude shattered.

Chapter 33

Maggie

Chloe's incessant screams echoed through the house. Marble floors and hardwood surfaces bounced sound quite well, evidently. She had stormed off, humiliated and defeated.

I'd be lying if I said I didn't enjoy it. The memory of her face twisted in anger and degradation kept me smiling. I knew I was supposed to be better than that. She was the petty one, not me. But there was poetic justice there.

As I stood there, I couldn't help but revel in the fall of Chloe, at least a little bit. Chloe deserved what was coming to her. After everything she had done to me, the feeling of seeing her brought to her knees was one I wouldn't forget anytime soon.

The moment I confronted Chloe, the way she had crumbled, it felt like part of my past had been set free. The weight I had been carrying all of these years because of Chloe had finally been lifted.

The mystery was over, a lifetime of unasked questions answered. I had always wondered what I'd done so wrong to make Chloe Foster hate me so much. But I'd done nothing wrong. She was a nut job.

I had seen the way Julian had looked at me during the confrontation, the admiration in his eyes as I stood my ground. That wasn't pity.

It was love.

He reached his hand out for me and I took it willingly, abandoning my luggage by the front door, and followed him upstairs.

Once inside his room, I stood there for a moment, watching him. I felt as though I was seeing him for the first time. All those furtive glances. His protective nature. He wasn't worried that I couldn't handle myself. He simply wanted to be there for me. Because he loved me.

I felt like a fool.

"Julian," I said softly, breaking the silence.

For a moment, neither of us said a word. We just stared at each other, the air thick with something unspoken that had been building for far too long.

He swallowed once. Twice. As if trying to find the words or the nerve to say them. "You're staying?"

I nodded, stepping closer to him. "If I'm still welcome. Here. With you."

He closed the distance between us in a few long strides until he was standing right in front of me. I loved having him close. His presence was comforting. "Maggie, I—"

But before he could finish, I reached out and placed a hand on his chest. He fell silent. His heartbeat was strong beneath my palm, and I could feel the steady rise and fall of his breaths. He looked down at my hand, then back up at me, his expression unreadable.

I whispered, "What now?"

"That depends on you. Why did you come up here with me?"

I squirmed against the depth of that question. There were so many reasons, but only one that mattered. "I had to. Needed to."

"But what about everything you said before?"

It was hard to admit that I was wrong. That I had let my high school insecurities interfere with who I'd become and what I wanted now. It made me feel childish and pathetic, but I had to own it.

I cleared my throat. "I was stupid. I let Chloe get in my head and convince me that I was the pathetic thing she accused me of being. That I was just someone to be pitied instead of someone to be loved. And I thought that you saw me the same way she did. I—"

"Are you saying," his words came out slowly and quietly, "that's the way you saw yourself?"

The question struck hard. I watched his Adam's apple bob as he waited for an answer. I didn't want to give it. But I owed him that. "Yes."

"Why?"

"Because I was poor and unpopular, and those things don't usually make a girl feel all that confident. It took me a while to come to embrace who I am despite how I grew up, and teenage me was not there yet. I suppose there were residual echoes of things inside my head, that is, until I saw Chloe have a meltdown over absolutely nothing." A nervous laugh escaped me. "But I can't say those issues won't come up again. I'm human. Insecurities are real, and when things started to fall apart, they crept up again. I might be poor but I'm proud and receiving anyone's pity doesn't sit well with me."

He exhaled out his nose, a little frustrated. "Maggie, you

have never been someone to pity. When we met, and I asked for your help with algebra, did you think I did it because I felt sorry for you? Or because I admired you and knew you could help?"

I chuckled a little at that. "You definitely needed my help. You couldn't solve x for shit."

He grinned. "Damn straight. And when I asked you to go to the movies with me, was that out of pity or because we shared an interest in those movies?"

"I get it now."

"What about when we went for long walks downtown at all hours, just hanging out and talking about nothing?" He raised a hand to my cheek, touching me softly. "Did I feel sorry for you then, or did I want to spend time with the prettiest girl I had ever seen?"

My heart swelled in my chest. My words tripped over my lips, quiet and unsure. "I don't know."

"I don't feel sorry for you, Maggie. I never could. You're not less-than, you're not a thing to be pitied. You're a woman to be loved and adored, cherished and worshipped every day."

It was impossible not to fall into his sparkling gaze. "I made a mistake, Jules. Can you forgive me?"

His gaze intensified, and I could see emotion flickering in his eyes. He paused as if overwhelmed but then he steadied himself, and his voice became clearer as he spoke slowly. "I can forgive you if you tell me precisely what you want. Chloe aside, high school bullshit aside, tell me what you want. Why you came up here with me."

I took a deep breath, feeling the truth rise up in my heart, unable to stop myself from saying it. "I want you. I never stopped wanting you."

Accidental Fiancé

The words gave texture to the air between us. Heartache, longing, love. For a moment, Julian didn't move. He just stared at me as if he couldn't quite believe what I had said.

Then, in a rush of movement, he closed in, his mouth crashing into mine in a searing kiss that stole my breath.

The world seemed to fall away. The only thing that mattered at that moment was him. His lips against mine, his body so close. The way his hands trembled slightly as he held me. It was a homecoming, like all the pieces that had been scattered were finally falling back into place.

I kissed him back with everything I had, pouring years of frustration, love, and desire into that single moment. His hand slid from my face down to my waist, pulling me closer, tighter, and I could feel the desperation in his touch. We had both been holding back for so long and I knew that it was finally our time.

"Stay," he whispered against my lips, his voice husky, pleading. "Stay with me, Maggie. Don't leave again."

I pulled back slightly, just enough to look him in the eyes. "Yes," I whispered. "I'll stay."

His lips were on mine again, more urgent this time, ravenous. His hands roamed my body as he backed me toward the bed. My heart raced as I felt the mattress against the backs of my legs, and before I knew it, I was lying on my back with Julian on top of me.

This time, things would be different. There were no more lies or pretenses between us. This time, we could actually discover each other. Discover the love that had never been able to properly be explored until now.

Julian's hands slid under my shirt, sending shivers down my spine as he explored every inch of me. I gasped as he kissed my throat, his lips hot against my skin. Heat, so much heat. Inside of me, between us, pouring from his body.

He leaned back just long enough to pull my shirt over my head. His eyes dark with desire as he took me in. "God, Maggie," he murmured, his voice full of reverence. "You're so fucking beautiful."

I blushed under his gaze but I didn't look away. I wanted him to see me. All of me, just as I saw him.

I reached for him, tugging at his shirt until he pulled it off, revealing the thick muscles of his chest and arms. My fingers traced the lines of his body, marveling at the way his skin felt beneath my touch. It was like discovering him all over again, and it made my heart ache with how much I had missed him. Even though I hadn't actually left him behind, it felt like a lifetime since we last touched, and this time, there was so much more at stake.

This time, we were an us. Not him and me. But *us*. This wasn't a hookup built on a lie. It wasn't a fly-by-night lapse in judgment. This meant something. It meant everything.

Julian leaned down, his lips finding mine again as his hands slid down my body, unbuttoning my pants and pulling them off with one swift motion. His touch was electric, every brush of his fingers sending waves of heat through me, and I couldn't stop the soft moans that escaped my lips as he kissed his way down my neck to my collarbone. The curve of my breast. When he sucked my nipple into his mouth, I let out an ungodly sound from my very soul. I tugged at his belt, desperate to feel him closer, and he let out a low growl as he helped me free him of the constraints of his clothes.

When he finally pressed his naked body against mine, skin to skin, it was like everything else in the world ceased to exist. There was only us, only the burning and the need and the overwhelming desire to be together. "Are you sure?" Julian asked, his voice husky as he looked down at me, his breath coming in ragged gasps.

I nodded, my heart pounding in my chest. I had never been surer of anything in my life. With that, he kissed me again and reached between my thighs. He cupped my pussy, and my back arched off the bed. His touch was a live wire of pleasure. He stroked my clit, finding my rhythm almost by instinct.

I rode his fingers, grinding up to meet his hand like it was my own. He slipped a finger inside. I rocked against it, and when he brushed against my spot I saw stars. I clenched tight around him as my climax built.

He teased, a whisper in my ear. "That's it, right? That's the spot? I want to get this right—"

"Yes!" I hissed.

"Are you sure?" Another finger probed me. "I think we'll have to keep at this so we can be absolutely sure."

I whimpered his name and felt him smile against my cheek. I was so close.

"If you're not sure, I might have to stop."

"Don't you dare!" I gasped.

He let out a low chuckle. "I love it when you tremble like that. Like you're helpless to what I'm doing."

"I am, don't stop!"

His stubbled jaw grazed against my ear. "Never." With that, he worked me double-time, sending me screaming into the stratosphere. I came so hard that I was sure everyone in the house heard me. There was no holding back, no keeping it in. My orgasm ripped through me, ecstasy wiping my brain clear.

My body pulsed as he rubbed the head of his cock against my wetness. He watched me writhe, still gasping from the intensity of the orgasm. His shoulders heaved with his breaths. Hoarsely, he said, "I need to be inside you."

All I could do was weakly nod.

He thrust himself in up to the hilt, sending us both groaning. The feel of him took my breath away as he filled me up. He drove us up the bed until we were in the middle —I hadn't realized we had been half on and half off. Once in place, Julian was in charge.

He rolled himself into me like a dancer, hitting my tempo again. He cocked his hips exactly right to keep me on edge. With every thrust, inches of him glided against my spot, with every withdrawal, I got it again. I was too lit up, too sensitive. I didn't know what was different but as good as he had been before, this was something else. Something devastating in the best way possible.

I rode him from underneath, unable to hold still. He wrapped his arms under me to make us as close as two people could be. His hard body pressed against mine, his lips and teeth and tongue meeting my mouth, jaw, and neck. We were like a pair of wild animals, hungry for only each other.

But then he pulled out and for the briefest moment, I was confused. What had I done wrong? Then, without a word, he picked me up, flipped me onto my stomach, and reentered me.

The new angle allowed him to bare down on my spot with every stroke. Our bodies slapped together, the sound echoing through the room. Just as I crested over another orgasm, he reached around my hip for my clit, and I came apart. I screamed into the pillow until my throat hurt.

"That's it, baby," he growled as he guided me through

my climax. "Come all over me." He didn't let up. He triggered another orgasm off that one, and I could barely breathe, but I didn't care. I needed this. Needed to lose myself in him. In us.

After my third, he grabbed my hips with both hands and pounded me for a minute. I thought he was about to come too as he throbbed inside of my body—his usual giveaway.

But nothing about today was usual.

He laid on my back, nearly slowing to a stop. There, buried deep inside of me, he bit my earlobe and said, "Do you know how much I have missed you, baby?"

"I missed you, too."

Julian pressed deeper into me before pulling out again. He turned over and pulled me onto his lap as he sat up against the headboard. He cocked his hips up as he pulled me down his length, and I held his shoulders for balance. Face to face, body to body.

I loved this. Watching his expressions as I rode him, or rather, as he drove me on himself. His fingers dug into my ass while he maneuvered me up and down his cock. I felt like I was getting close to the edge again and staring into his eyes made it all the more delicious.

The intensity there had become so much more. Connection. Submission. Love.

Now that my strength was back, I wanted in on this. I looped my arms around his neck, and just before I kissed him, I murmured, "Let me."

He slowed down to let me take over as I kissed him, and before I knew it, I was in full control of this ride. The addictive slide of our bodies drove me on, and orgasms were almost pointless now. A little one hit, and I moaned in his mouth. A bigger one took over, and he ate my scream. He wrapped his muscled arms around me, unwilling to allow an inch between us.

We were one creature with no beginning or end, sustained by orgasms and love. Nothing else existed but this.

When his body tensed, I knew it was coming to an end, and I was overjoyed at his impending pleasure. I shuddered as I whispered against his jaw, "That's it, baby. Come for me. Fill me up."

His head tipped back as he grunted, and we came together, trembling in pure bliss. I nipped at his exposed throat, hungry to sink my teeth into the meat of him. His grip tightened, pulling me closer still as he poured into me. He ground his hips up, sealing us, sealing our love.

Afterward, we lay tangled together on the bed, our bodies still humming from the intensity of it all. Julian's hand rested on my hip, his fingers drawing lazy circles on my skin while I rested my head on his chest, listening to the steady rhythm of his heartbeat.

For a long time, neither of us said anything. We didn't need to. The silence between us was comfortable, filled with a sense of peace that I hadn't felt in a long time. Peace, but also power. There was a strength between us now, a connection no one could sever. Maybe it had always been there.

Eventually, Julian broke the quiet. His voice was soft and filled with wonder. "I can't believe you stayed."

I smiled, my fingers trailing down the length of his arm. "I never wanted to leave. Not really."

He kissed the top of my head. "I'm glad."

I tilted my head up to look at him, my heart swelling with love for this man who had fought for me time after time. Not because of pity but because he loved me. There was no more doubt in my mind or my heart. He let me stand on my own two feet when things went to hell, standing by and supporting me but allowing me to find my voice. He wasn't my protector, he was my rock. And if I was lucky, he would walk by my side for the rest of my life.

Chapter 34

Julian

The evening air was cool, the California winter breeze wafting through the open window in my bedroom, mixing with the warmth of Maggie curled up beside me. The sheets tangled around us, and her head rested softly against my chest. Her breaths were slow and rhythmic as she drifted off to a peaceful sleep. I lay there, staring up at the ceiling, unable to wipe the goofy grin from my face.

Maggie and I had been pretending for so long, caught in this elaborate dance of fake smiles, staged kisses, and carefully crafted lies. But now it was real. More real than I ever let myself imagine it could be. I had fallen for her long ago, but now she was mine. Not for the sake of appearances but because she wanted to be.

It was more than a high school crush or some idiot teenager's idea of love. I was in love with her. Madly, stupidly, deeply head over heels in love with her. The kind of love you don't recover from. She was a part of me, down to my bones.

I had known it before, but when she stood up to Chloe

Accidental Fiancé

earlier, strong, unyielding, and brave, I knew there was no turning back. There never really had been.

I looked down at her, her long curls splayed across my chest, her lips slightly parted. My heart ached from the fullness of everything I felt for her. Was there a word for something deeper than love? Whatever it was, I felt it so sharply that it stole my breath and my thoughts. I was hers in a way I didn't know existed before she returned to my life. Maggie Bryant was essential to my very existence.

I stifled a laugh. I sounded like a stupid kid in my head, all fluff and no brains. Flowers and smiles, nothing but cocksure instinct on the matter. But I couldn't deny how I felt, either. I belonged to this woman, heart and soul.

I brushed a lock of hair from her face gently so as not to wake her. She stirred but settled back into the crook of my arm, her fingers tightening briefly on my side as if, even in sleep, she didn't want to let go. If I hadn't been hooked on her before, I was now.

I chuckled softly to myself, savoring the moment. I had never felt this way before, not with my ex-wife, not with anyone. The kind of peace that came from being with someone who just fit. Maggie fit in every way. And now that the dust had settled with Chloe and the lies were behind us, it felt like the future was something we could build together. It felt real. Or that it could be real.

All I had to do was reach out and grab it.

Carefully, I slid out from beneath her, making sure to tuck the blanket around her before slipping on a pair of jeans and a t-shirt. The mansion was quiet. Most of the chaos from earlier had dissipated, thankfully. I imagined Chloe left by now. That would explain the quiet. I needed it to clear my head and let the reality of what was happening sink in.

I padded softly down the hall, the hardwood cool beneath my bare feet. The farther I got from my bedroom, the more the familiar scent of cigar smoke teased my senses. The smell grew stronger as I approached the lounge, and I couldn't help but smile.

Yaya.

Sure enough, there she was, sitting in one of the oversized leather chairs, a cigar delicately held between her long fingers. There was something oddly comforting about the scent of cigars and the way it reminded me of my childhood.

As a family, we never spoke of Yaya's affinity for cigars. My cousins procured her favorites for her, though. It was an unspoken rule. If you brought cigars to the house, you had to bring her favorite— Opus X Robusto—from the Dominican Republic. We'd hide them in her room for her so when she came to visit, she could sneak a few away from her daughter's watchful eye.

Mom was in total denial about her habit. She thought cigars were trashy and she refused to associate her mother with anything unbecoming of a woman, so she pretended Yaya didn't smoke them. Instead of blaming Yaya for the cigar smell in the lounge, Mom hassled me and my cousins as the cause for the scent. Even though I didn't smoke them myself anymore, I'd always take the heat for Yaya to make Mom happy so she could go on pretending her mother wouldn't do anything so unladylike. Maybe that was where I got my gift to pretend from. *Thanks, Mom.*

Marcus sat across from Yaya, staring into the fireplace with a glass of bourbon in his hand, a look of contemplation on his face.

"Ah, Julian!" Yaya called out as I entered. She waved her cigar around, a trail of smoke curling up toward the ceiling. "Couldn't sleep after all the excitement? You were in your room for an awfully long, *loud* nap." She winked. "The halls echo, you know."

Hot embarrassment rose in my chest. I took the chair next to her and brushed past the teasing. No point in denying what happened when they heard... whatever they heard. I swallowed against a dry throat. "Mom's not around?"

Yaya chuckled, taking a long drag from her cigar. "She went for a swim with Piper and the other kids. She'll be in the pool for hours. We practically have the house to ourselves."

I glanced at Marcus. His brow was furrowed, his eyes still fixed on the fire. Tension ridged his shoulders the same way he gripped his glass. White-knuckled. Steaming.

I leaned forward in my chair. "You doing okay, Marcus?"

He looked up as if only now noticing my presence. The tension transformed into something else, but I couldn't read it. His voice was gruff. "I'll be fine."

"You sure about that? You're not looking too good."

"Gee, thanks."

I rolled my eyes. "You know what I mean. Are you going to be okay about you and..." I didn't want to say her name, it felt like breathing life into a corpse at this point. "Everything?"

"I always knew Chloe and I had an expiration date. I just didn't think it would be today, or that arson would be part of the reason, for fuck's sake—"

"Language," Yaya chided.

"Sorry, Yaya," he said before returning his focus to me. "It was coming one way or another. At least some good can come of it, right? Apollo says he's got a solid case against her already, with the confession and witnesses. Hopefully,

Maggie will be able to get some closure on the whole thing..." He trailed off, sadness in his eyes, but also relief. Marcus had never been the type to hold onto something that didn't serve him. Even still, I knew this stung. I saw it on his face. Staring into the fire again, he uttered, "She had never been good to me. I think I knew that for a long time, but love, or whatever it was, makes you stupid, you know?"

I tried to sound supportive. "Better now than later. She was a poison. You deserve better."

"I should have listened to you. Thanks for not pointing that out." He took a sip of his drink. I let him sit with his thoughts and didn't drag out the topic. It was the only way he would find his way through it.

I turned back to Yaya, watching as she puffed her cigar, her sharp eyes glinting in the firelight. She had been the matriarch of this family for longer than I had been alive, the glue that held us together. And in many ways, she knew more about each of us than we knew ourselves.

"Yaya," I started, leaning back in my chair, "there's something I need to ask you."

Her eyes flickered over me as one eyebrow raised out of curiosity. "Oh, and what's that, dear?"

I hesitated for a moment, but then I took a deep breath and said it. "I know you have a ring for each of us from the old country. The one you've been holding onto for my next bride. I want to give it to Maggie."

She exhaled a long stream of smoke like a dragon. Her eyes narrowed in the way they always did when she was assessing something. "You never asked for it for your first wife, Julian. So why now? Why Maggie? What's different about her?"

I smiled, the answer easily coming to me. "Because

Maggie is the only woman I've ever wanted to give that ring to."

Yaya tilted her head, studying me. Her lips quirked into a smile. "You swore off marriage after your divorce if I recall correctly. Said it wasn't worth the trouble."

I let out a small laugh. "I'm allowed to change my mind, right?"

"Hmm." She mused, taking another drag from her cigar. "That's why your mother and I have been pestering you about finding a new mother for Piper rather than a wife for yourself. You were so adamant about it, saying you'd never give your heart away again."

I glanced down, the memory of those dark days after my divorce tugging at the edges of my mind. I had never been so sure. I never wanted to find love again, never wanted to open myself up to that kind of vulnerability.

But Maggie changed me. She changed everything.

"I was wrong," I admitted, meeting her gaze. "Maggie will take care of my heart. I'm not scared to give it to her. I want to. No. I *need* to."

Yaya watched me for a long moment, her expression unreadable, but then she smiled. A real smile, not the mischievous one she often used when she was teasing me. She slowly nodded as if coming to a decision. "Alright, Julian, if you're sure about this, then I'll give you the ring."

My heart leaped in my chest, but I kept my composure, nodding in gratitude. "I'm sure, Yaya. I've never been surer about anything."

She reached into the pocket of her cardigan, pulling out a small velvet box. I couldn't help but laugh at the fact that she'd been carrying it around this whole time. "You have it on you?"

"Once I met the girl, I had a feeling you'd be needing it

sooner or later this week. Thought I should keep it handy. Here," she said, handing it to me. "It's yours. Take care of it and take care of her."

I took the box, my fingers brushing over the soft velvet, my heart swelling with a mixture of excitement and nerves. I had thought about this moment for years, ever since I had met Maggie. But now that the ring was in my hand, it felt real in a way that nothing else ever had. "Thank you."

"You didn't keep mine on you, did you, Yaya?" Marcus asked.

She sighed, setting her cigar onto the ashtray and taking his hand in hers. "No, baby. I didn't."

"You knew Chloe wasn't the one for me."

She gently shook her head. "That girl could never deserve you."

Her words gave weight to the air between them. He took a breath of that truth and let it out slowly before a wry smile split his face. "Next time you see me with a girl, can you tell me ahead of time, so I don't get my hopes up?"

"Like a warning system? You think I'm an alarm for you to use with girls?" she teased.

"Well, yeah." He chuckled. "You're smarter than all of us on this sh—"

She arched a brow.

"Stuff."

She grinned at him. "You're right, I am, and if you bring any more bitches around, I'll let you know."

"Yaya! Language!" he teased.

She laughed and waved her hand dismissively, but there was a softness in her eyes as she turned to me. "Just make sure you do it right, Julian. Don't rush. Maggie is a special woman."

"That's why I want to give her the ring," I said, tucking

Accidental Fiancé

the box into my pocket. As I left the lounge and made my way back upstairs, a sense of peace settled over me. This was it, the future I had dreamed of for over a decade. It was within my grasp. All I had to do was get her to say yes.

When I returned to the room, Maggie was still asleep. She had curled up under the blankets, her breathing steady and soft. I stood at the foot of the bed for a moment, just watching her. My heart swelled with so much love that it hurt, and I never wanted that kind of pain to stop.

Carefully, I slipped back under the covers, wrapping my arm around her waist and pulling her close. She stirred slightly, murmuring something unintelligible in her sleep, before settling back into me.

I closed my eyes, the feeling of her warmth grounding me in a way I'd never felt before. Tomorrow, I'd figure out the perfect way to ask her to marry me, but for tonight, I just wanted to hold her, to soak in the quiet moments that made me fall in love with her all over again. Maggie had always been more than I deserved, and now she was everything I wanted. Soon, she would be mine forever.

Chapter 35

Maggie

When I woke up in Julian's arms, a sense of relief broadened my smile. It was over—the drama, the secrets, the lies, everything that had felt so suffocating over the last few days had been lifted.

We were finally free.

We spent the morning dawdling with his family. A breakfast buffet with Greek pastries and Cuban coffee filled the air with a heavenly scent. Banter-littered chatter rolled through the lounge, and good-natured jokes gave way to raucous laughter. All day long, Julian wore a secretive smirk, and when I asked him about it, he said, "It's nothing. I'm just happy you're here."

Liar.

But he was happy, so I wasn't mad about the lie. In fact, I'd never been happier in my life. We spent the day playing in the pool with Piper and the other kids. Even Marcus and Apollo joined us despite Marcus' recent breakup. I had thought he might go home after the drama with Chloe, but with her gone, he relaxed and enjoyed his family. A few rounds of *Marcus* Polo later, and he was laughing along with the rest of us. It had been a wonderful day.

My family consisted of me, Mom, and Dad. They had cousins and siblings, but we weren't close with them the way Julian's family was, and I loved being surrounded by such warm, welcoming people. None of them even mentioned the lie we told. They accepted me with open arms, no backbiting or sniping about any of it.

I could almost imagine a future like this. Happy and surrounded by love. I was no longer pretending, and when I saw that knowing smile on Julian's lips, I didn't know what it meant exactly, but I wasn't scared by it, either. He'd tell me when the time was right. I trusted him completely.

After a late nap, Julian, Piper, and I joined the others for supper. The dining room was bathed in the warm glow of the chandeliers, the soft flicker of candlelight dancing off the polished mahogany table. Outside, the winter evening was fading into twilight, but inside, the mansion was alive with the hum of conversation and laughter.

I sat next to Julian at the long dining table, Piper on the other side of him. His family was scattered around, everyone dressed in their finest for Yaya's birthday. It was a grand affair. Yaya never did things halfway, apparently, and tonight was no exception.

The table was set with fine dinnerware, crystal glasses, and a centerpiece of fresh flowers that perfumed the air. Laughter echoed around us as plates were passed and conversations overlapped. Even Marcus seemed more relaxed, sipping his wine and engaging in small talk. He smiled more easily without Chloe around, and it was nice to see him that way instead of the grouch he had been when we first met.

Julian's hand was warm on my thigh beneath the table, a

silent reminder of the support he gave me. His touch sent a shiver up my spine, not because it was new or surprising, but because it felt like home. We had made a choice to convince the world we were in love when, in truth, somewhere along the way, the fake feelings we were trying to convey had turned real.

Given he had a crush on me in high school, I'm thinking they came more naturally to him as an adult. Though, I wondered if his feelings had ever been fake. It was hard to dig into that for myself—my feelings for him in high school were never a crush, or so I thought. I wasn't sure if that was true anymore.

Had Nora been right? Had I used Julian as a boyfriend substitute back then? I wasn't sure. But having him around made not having a high school boyfriend easier. She had said he was my boyfriend in all but title, and I couldn't argue against that.

I squeezed his hand and smiled when he looked at me, but a twinge of guilt pulled at my heartstrings for the boy I had romantically ignored. We could have had so many years of happiness if only I had realized the truth back then. There was nothing to be done about it now, obviously, but it was impossible not to wonder about how things could have been if I had understood my own feelings instead of being wrapped up in worrying what others thought about me.

If I had been more self-aware in high school, Piper might have been my daughter. A startling thought.

But life had other plans for me, for Julian. Regrets didn't accomplish anything. Acknowledging and learning from my mistakes was the only way to move forward to a brighter future. I screwed things up before and I refused to do that again. It felt good sitting in front of his entire family as a couple.

Accidental Fiancé

I made conversation with Apollo about his job, both of us dodging the subject of Chloe. Part of me wanted to attend her trial, but another part of me just wanted to be done with all of that. Unfortunately, he said, "You realize as the business owner and victim of the arson, you'll likely be called to the stand, right?"

A weight sat on my chest hearing that. "I had hoped to stay out of it, actually."

"I'll do my best to keep your involvement to a minimum, but there will be questions. We will keep the sensitivities of the case in mind and—"

A clinking sound rang out, and we looked to the head of the table to see Yaya, spoon and crystal goblet in hand. She was as regal as ever, her silver hair swept into an elegant updo, her eyes twinkling with mischievous energy that belied her eighty years. "No more business talk at the table, you two."

I smiled and nodded as Apollo said, "Apologies, Yaya. Fun only."

She nodded curtly and returned to her chat with Artemis. Ears like a hawk, that one.

I glanced at Julian, catching his eye as he leaned back in his chair, sipping his wine. He gave me a wink, and I couldn't help but smile, my heart skipping a beat. Leaning in so only I could hear him, he whispered, "You look beautiful tonight."

Heat rose in my cheeks, and I nudged him playfully. "You're not so bad yourself."

Julian looked effortlessly handsome in his suit, the dark fabric tailored perfectly to his lean frame, his dark hair slightly tousled in a way that made him look like he just walked off the pages of a magazine. It was all I could do not to demand we go to his room and find out how good that suit looked on the floor, but after some gentle teasing at the pool earlier, I learned just how much voices carried in the mansion. My voice, in particular, apparently.

That same spoon clinked against the crystal again, pulling my attention away from him. Yaya stood at the head of the table, this time, a glass of champagne in her hand. "Alright, everyone," she said, her voice commanding attention with ease. "Before we get started on dessert, I think it's time for a little toast."

The room fell quiet as everyone lifted their glasses, their attention turning to Yaya. I couldn't help but smile as I watched her. Tonight, was in her honor, her official birthday dinner. The weight of the past few days seemed to disappear. It was a celebration not just of Yaya's birthday, but also about the fact that we had come out on the other side of everything stronger.

"To family," Yaya began, her voice clear and strong. "To the ones who drive us mad, the ones who make us laugh, and the ones who never let us forget who we are, I am grateful for all of you. Thank you for being here tonight."

There were murmurs of agreement around the table, and I raised my glass alongside everyone else, feeling a swell of warmth in my chest but also an ache. I didn't have a family like this, and her toast was a reminder of that. But sitting there, surrounded by Julian's family, I felt like I belonged with them. I wasn't technically family, but they didn't make me feel that way.

Yaya took a sip of her champagne and then set the glass down with a satisfied smile. Her eyes twinkled as she looked directly at Julian. "I believe there's something else to celebrate tonight, isn't there?"

I blinked in surprise, turning to Julian as he shifted in

Accidental Fiancé

his seat. There was that look again, mischievous but also… nervous?

What is he up to? Some kind of business merger or something? I didn't understand how their family dynamic worked along financial lines, especially after he mentioned how they pooled some of their money together as a family. I could only imagine that any one person's success was everybody's success and a cause for celebration. Maybe he wanted to wait until tonight to announce something big for all of them.

Julian stood up slowly, placing his glass on the table before reaching into his pocket. He pulled out a small velvet box, the kind I had seen in a thousand movies. A ring box: I never thought I'd see one in real life intended for me. Why would he have… oh.

I was confused. *He can't be… no.* My breath caught in my throat as the realization hit me like a tidal wave.

Oh. My. God.

The entire table seemed to hold its collective breath as Julian turned to me, his shining green eyes locking onto mine. I knew what was happening, but it was also like I was watching it happen from outside myself. I couldn't breathe, but I didn't need to. I wasn't in my body anymore.

He stepped away from the table and kneeled beside my chair, holding the box in his hands. He cleared his throat a few times before stealing Phoebe's champagne to wet his whistle. "Maggie," he began, his voice steady but filled with emotion. "You and I started this as a lie. A lie we told to everyone, including ourselves. We said this wasn't real, that it was just a favor two friends were doing for each other. But somewhere along the line, pretending with you became the best thing that ever happened to me. *You* are the best thing that ever happened to me."

My heart was pounding so hard I was sure everyone could hear it. I couldn't speak. I couldn't even think straight. All I could do was stare at him, tears already pricking at the corners of my eyes.

"I don't want to pretend ever again," Julian continued, his voice softening. "I don't want to pretend you're not the love of my life. I don't want to pretend I could ever be happy without you. Maggie Bryant, will you marry me?" He opened the box, revealing a stunning ring, a vintage piece that sparkled in the soft light of the room. It took my breath away.

For a moment, everything around us disappeared. It was just me and Julian, his eyes filled with hope and love, his heart laid bare in front of me. The magnitude of what he was asking hit me full force, and tears slipped down my cheeks.

"Yes," I whispered, my voice trembling. "Yes, Julian, I will marry you."

The room erupted into applause but I barely heard it. All I could focus on was Julian, the relief and joy on his face as he slipped the ring onto my finger. He stood up, pulled me into his arms, and kissed me. The world tilted on its axis, the moment spinning around us as if we were the only thing that mattered.

Julian Black was mine. Forever.

When we finally pulled apart, I could feel the warmth of his family's eyes on us. Piper was grinning ear to ear, clapping and cheering enthusiastically. Everyone else was, too, but it was her opinion that mattered the most to me. Yaya looked utterly pleased with herself as if she had orchestrated the whole thing.

I looked over at Julian's mother, who looked completely baffled. Artemis said, "I'm sorry to interrupt this happy moment but I thought you two broke up. What on earth is going on here?"

Yaya waved her hand dismissively, an amused smile on her lips. "Oh, try to keep up, dear," her voice dripping with playful, sardonic humor. "They were never really broken up. It was a simple misunderstanding."

Julian's mother blinked, clearly still lost, but she slowly nodded, accepting Yaya's explanation without further question. She leaned back into her chair, casting one more curious glance at me before taking a big sip of her wine.

I couldn't help but laugh. The entire evening had been a whirlwind of emotions, but in that moment, surrounded by Julian's family and the love we had just declared for each other, everything felt right. It felt solid. This was really happening.

Julian pulled me close again, his lips brushing against my ear as he whispered, "I love you, Maggie."

"I love you too," I whispered back, my heart full to bursting.

The rest of the night was a blur of toasts and congratulations. Yaya told stories about her own engagement to Julian's grandfather, regaling us with the tales of her wild youth in the circus. According to her, she also set fire to the Vatican (due to a Papal situation I didn't quite follow, but was assured the Pope deserved it), shared an ice cream with a certain president in the eighties (she had chocolate, he had the time of his life), skydived with a world-famous rock star (without divulging his identity, she specified he had sympathy for the Devil), and got a matching tattoo with a famous actor. "What? You don't believe me?"

She started to lift her skirt to show it off, but Artemis jerked her hem back down. "Mom, don't embarrass Maggie. We want her to *join* the family, not run screaming from it."

Through it all, I kept watching Julian, marveling at how much he had changed in such a short time. The worry lines around his eyes and on his forehead had disappeared. His shoulders relaxed and he was breathing deeply for the first time. I leaned against him, relishing the warmth of his body as his family told stories and laughed with each other. I was happy, truly happy.

Strange that we had started this whole thing as a lie, an arrangement meant to serve both our interests. But now, as I looked down at the ring on my finger, I realized that it had become the truest thing in my life. And I couldn't wait to spend the rest of it with him.

Later that night, when his family had finally retired to their rooms and the mansion was quiet again, Julian and I sat together on the balcony overlooking the moonlit gardens. He held my hand, his thumb tracing circles over the back of it, the cool breeze tugging at the loose strands of my hair.

"I can't believe you actually proposed in front of everyone," I said with a laugh, leaning my head on his shoulder. "That was bold."

Julian chuckled, pressing a kiss to the top of my head. "I had to make sure everyone knew. No more pretending, Maggie. Not ever again."

"Never again."

Now, I just had to figure out how to tell my parents.

Chapter 36

Julian

We left a few days later, eager to begin our new life together. The drive home was quiet, but not in a way that felt heavy or uncomfortable. It was the kind of silence that settled between people who knew each other inside and out, where words weren't necessary.

Piper snored softly in the backseat, head drooping. I glanced over at Maggie; her profile softened by the moonlight streaming through the car windows. She had her hair up in a loose ponytail, her fingers playing absently with the ring that I had slipped on her finger just days ago.

My fiancée.

I couldn't stop myself from looking at the ring every few minutes. *The* ring, the one that Yaya had held onto for safekeeping for our brides. The one I never felt right giving to Britney. Our grandfather had decided our brides should get something special, so he had them commissioned as presents for all the boys. A symbol of hope for the future.

Since Phoebe liked women as much as men and told Yaya as much, our matriarch decided to hang onto one for her, too. I remembered the day she told her, how nervous Phoebe had been. But we all encouraged her to do it, and when the time came, Yaya didn't let her down. She simply said, "Whoever you choose, dear, choose wisely."

I knew I had.

It felt surreal. I had proposed to her in front of my entire family, and she had said yes. No doubt, no hesitation in her voice. She said it with her whole self. There was something about her saying yes that made every high, every victory in my life, pale in comparison.

My heart still raced at the thought of that moment and all the moments to come. I would finally get to have a life with Maggie. My inner teenager was as ecstatic as I was. It was everything I had dreamed of for so many years. I loved her with a fierceness that both exhilarated and terrified me, and I couldn't imagine anything better in the world.

She caught me looking and smiled softly, her eyes warm and tired. "You keep staring," she teased, her voice barely above a whisper.

I chuckled, reaching over to take her hand and bringing it to my lips for a quick kiss. "Can you blame me?" I murmured against her skin. "I just want to make sure I didn't imagine the whole thing."

Her smile widened, and she squeezed my hand. "Well, it's real, I promise. I'm over here worrying about how to tell my parents."

"You think they won't be happy you're getting married?" I blurted before my throat threatened to close.

"No, no, nothing like that. It's just... I'm not sure how we'll integrate our lives, not to mention finances, and I know they'll bombard me with all those questions." She yawned, cutting herself off. "They can be a lot, but don't let that scare you. They'll be thrilled once they know I've got my head on straight about all of this."

"They worry about finances a lot, don't they?"

She nodded. "Number one concern for most people, actually."

I hoped they wouldn't object too much when I paid off their mortgage and fattened their 401(k)s and bank accounts. But I wasn't going to tell Maggie that before I did it. Better to ask for forgiveness than permission on gifts, and I wasn't about to let my future in-laws suffer for pride.

I kept her hand in mine for the rest of the drive, tracing absent patterns on her palm, content just to feel her silken skin beneath my fingertips. There had been so much chaos over the past week with Chloe but tonight was different, tonight was ours.

By the time we pulled up to the house, the exhaustion of it all had started to settle in. It was late, well past midnight, and our home was dark, the streetlights casting long shadows across the lawn. I killed the engine and looked over at Maggie, catching the slight hesitation in her eyes as she stared at the house.

"You okay?" I asked, my voice low so as not to wake Piper.

She nodded slowly, but her gaze lingered on the house a moment longer before turning to me. "I'm tired. It's been a long week."

I knew what she meant. It wasn't just the physical exhaustion. It was the mental toll that had come with everything. Still, there was something about the way she said it that made me wonder if there was more on her mind.

"We're home now," I said, squeezing her hand once more before I let go and stepped out of the car. I came around to her side and opened the door, offering her a hand to help her out.

She smiled again, shyly this time, as if still unsure. "Are we?"

"Are we what?" I asked as I pulled a sleeping Piper from the backseat.

"Are we home?"

"This is the home we own."

"No," she said, shaking her head. "This is the home you own."

"Ah." I kicked the door shut and resettled Piper in my arms to carry her inside. Maggie followed along as I made the trip. "We will put your name on the deed tomorrow morning if that's what you want. And on my accounts. What's mine is yours, Maggie. We're a family now, married or not."

Her footsteps died next to me just before I reached the front door.

I turned to face her and found the strangest look on her face. "What is it?"

"I'm not... I didn't... you know this isn't about your money, right? I didn't say yes because you're loaded."

I laughed, then worried for nothing I'd wake Piper. She didn't even stir. "Baby, I know that."

"If you want, I'll sign a prenup."

"Absolutely not. Not unless you want one." I strode to her, watching her pretty face in the moonlight shift from apprehension to something unreadable. "Any lawyer would probably yell at me for what I'm about to say, but I want us bound in every way possible. If that means you could take me to the cleaners in a divorce so be it. But that's how much faith I have in you. It's a non-issue for me. What about you?"

Her lips moved for a moment like she was torn between crying and laughing. She went with laughing. "I have a great ceramic cactus collection I've been working on for years. If things somehow don't work out, I'm taking it with me when I go."

I snorted a laugh and she kissed me. "Deal."

We walked inside, the familiar creak of the front door welcoming us back. The quiet house enveloped us like a warm blanket. Such a difference from the constant hum of Mom's full house. There were plenty of insomniacs in my family, so there was always someone buzzing around that place at all hours during Yaya's week. Here, it was just us.

I kicked off my shoes, tossing the keys on the entry table. I tucked Piper into bed as Maggie stood in the doorway, watching. When I closed the door, she asked, "She'll sleep through the night?"

"She might, she might not, given her night terrors and the crazy week she just had. What makes you ask? You've seen her—"

"I've never seen her this tired before."

I smiled and nodded, leading the way back to the kitchen. "Seeing family and playing with her cousins wears her out. Me too, as a matter of fact. You want a drink?"

She stretched as she spoke. "No, I think I just need to shower and get into bed."

There was something else in her voice, something beneath the surface, but I didn't push. Instead, I watched her walk upstairs, the sway of her hips doing things to me that I was too tired to fight. My mind might have been weary, but my body still thrummed with desire whenever she was near.

I followed her up the stairs, my eyes on the curve of her back, the way her fingers absent-mindedly played with the ends of her hair as she walked. She disappeared into the bedroom, and by the time I caught up, she was already slipping out of her clothes, her back to me as she headed toward the bathroom.

I leaned on the doorframe, watching her in the soft glow of the bathroom light. Her bare skin gleamed, the muscles in her back flexing as she turned on the shower. The sight of her, so natural, so familiar, stirred something deep inside of me. I had memorized her shape years ago, but she was no longer that teenage girl. Her body was curvier, her face, prettier... she mesmerized me.

"Maggie," I called softly, stepping into the bathroom.

She turned to look at me, her expression soft but tired. "Yes?"

I crossed the small distance between us and pulled her into my arms, my hands sliding over the warm skin on her back, her waist, as I pressed a kiss to her temple. Her body melted against mine, her arms hanging around my neck as she sighed into the embrace.

"I love you," I whispered, my lips brushing against the shell of her ear. The words came easier now as if they'd been waiting fifteen years to be said out loud.

She pulled back just enough to look into my eyes, her own shimmering with that same mixture of exhaustion and something deeper, more vulnerable. She whispered back, "I love you too."

I kissed her then, soft and slow, the kind of kiss that reverberated through time. My hands roamed down her sides, feeling the soft curve of her waist, the sweet warmth of her body pressed against mine. She moaned against my lips, her fingers tangling in my hair, as I deepened the kiss, pulling her tighter against me.

There was no such thing as being close enough. I didn't

Accidental Fiancé

know if it was the relief of the past week being over or the euphoria of knowing she was mine for real this time, but everything in that moment felt heightened. My hands couldn't move fast enough, my lips couldn't cover enough of her. I kissed down her throat and collarbone, trailing down to her tits.

She pulled me into the shower, the warm water cascading over our skin as we moved together. Exploring her wet skin was a new delight. I loved how the water made her shine like she was a present just for me. Every touch, every kiss, felt like a promise, a reminder of what we had fought for, what we had won.

I licked my way down her body, savoring every echoing gasp when I found a new spot she liked. Her nipples hardened as I plucked them, and when I kneeled before her, she stopped breathing entirely.

She latched onto the shower bar when I lifted her thigh over my shoulder and dove in, face first. The way Maggie tasted was almost enough to make me come on the spot. I loved it, craved it. Especially when she grinded against me and cried out. No bigger ego stroke than that.

I worked her clit with my tongue, my lips, anything to get her there. My fingers crept along her inner thigh until they reached their target. All that wetness, all for me. I dipped a finger in, then a second one. Her core gripped me in pulses as she closed around them. Slowly, I fingerfucked her while I sucked and kissed and nibbled her clit. She had no choice but to come for me, and when she did, her sounds were amplified by the tiles.

A sound I memorized to replay when I was alone.

By the time we made it to the bed, our bodies were slick with water, our breaths coming in short, ragged bursts. We fell onto the mattress, the cool sheets a contrast to the heat between us. I moved over her, our bodies sliding together, her skin soft and smooth beneath my fingertips. The way she looked up at me, her eyes heavy with desire, made my heart race even faster.

I kissed her, slow and deliberate. I savored the way she moaned into my mouth, how her fingers gripped my shoulders. I wanted her like this forever, underneath me, beside me, with me. She made time stand still. The magic this woman possessed left me breathless.

Every movement, every breath was in sync, as if we were made for each other. She cried out my name, her body writhing beneath mine. I loved the way she jutted her hips up to take me deeper. When she cried out this time, I couldn't hold back. I followed her over the edge, my heart pounding in my chest as I whispered her name in turn. Afterward, we lay tangled in the sheets, the room filled with the sounds of our breathing.

Maggie's head rested on my chest, her fingers tracing lazy circles on my skin. I was tired, and my body was heavy with satisfaction. But there was something about the way she was touching me that told me she couldn't sleep just yet.

"What's on your mind? I asked softly, my fingers playing with the ends of her damp hair.

She was quiet for a moment, her fingers stilling on my abs. "I've been thinking about the bakery."

I stiffened slightly, my mind immediately going back to everything with Chloe, the fire, all the pain that had come from that nightmare. Truthfully, I had hoped the sex would send us both to sleep. I knew she was exhausted—I certainly was.

But if she wanted to have a conversation through the night, I was down for that. I just hoped her concern wasn't

Accidental Fiancé

Chloe-related. I had enough of her in my life. I didn't want to think about her in bed, naked and relaxed.

I asked, "What about the bakery?"

She shifted slightly, propping herself up on one elbow so she could look at me. Her eyes were filled with the kind of sadness I hadn't seen in a long time. She whispered, "I miss it. I miss baking. I miss the smell of bread, the feel of my hands in dough. I miss creating something that was mine."

My heart clenched at the vulnerability in her voice. I reached up and cupped her cheek, brushing my thumb over the smooth skin. God, she was pretty. How could I be so lucky that she had agreed to marry me?

I put the thought out of my mind. Otherwise, I'd get stuck on that, and the conversation would go south. "Do you want another one?"

She blinked, clearly caught off guard by the question. "Another what?"

"Another bakery," I clarified in a steady tone. "Do you want to open another one?"

She looked at me as if she weren't sure if I was serious. But I was dead serious. "Maggie, if that's what you want, then let's do it. Let's get you another bakery."

Her eyes searched mine, her expression a mixture of disbelief and something resembling hope. "It's not that simple, Julian. It took everything I had to get that one off the ground. And now..."

I shook my head, silencing her with a kiss. When I pulled back, I looked her straight in the eyes. "We'll get it figured out. You've been through hell, and you deserve to get back what was taken from you. If opening another bakery is what you want, then we'll make it happen."

Tears filled her eyes, and she smiled, a genuine smile

that made my heart swell and break at the same time. As if kindness was something she never saw coming because she never had it before now. "You really mean that?"

"Of course, I do," I said, brushing a stray hair away from her face. "You've got me now, remember? And I'm not going anywhere. Whatever you want, we'll figure it out together."

She kissed me then, slow and sweet, and I could taste the love that flowed between us.

Chapter 37

Maggie

After that kiss, we settled down. The house was quiet, the kind of quiet that pressed deep into your bones and made you feel like the world outside didn't exist. I lay against him, my head on his chest, listening to the steady beat of his heart as his fingers moved slowly along my back.

Other than the bakery conversation, we hadn't said much after we left his family's estate, and honestly, we didn't need to. After the week we'd just survived, silence felt like a gift. My mind had been spinning for days, overwhelmed by everything that had happened. Chloe's hateful, psycho confession. The proposal. The endless chatter from Julian's family. Not all bad, but it had been a lot.

Here in his bed, *our* bed, all of that felt far away. A distant memory. The warmth of his skin beneath my cheek and the feel of the diamond ring on my finger was what was real.

I shifted slightly so I could look at his face. His eyes were closed, his chest rising and falling in a steady rhythm, but I knew he wasn't asleep. His body hadn't yet fully relaxed and that told me he was waiting for me to say something.

"I've been thinking," I murmured, running my fingers through his hair.

"Oh?" he teased, his eyes opening, a lazy smile on his lips. "Should I be worried?"

I giggled softly, shaking my head. "No, it's nothing bad." I hesitated, biting my lip as I tried to find the right words. "I don't think I want another bakery."

Julian raised an eyebrow, surprised. I could see the wheels turning in his head as he processed what I said. "Really? You sounded like you missed it."

"I do," I said quickly, not wanting him to think I didn't. "I miss the baking, the creativity, the satisfaction of running something that was mine. But I think I miss the idea of it more than the reality. I don't know if I want to dive back into that world."

Julian frowned slightly, the line in his brow deepening. "Then what do you want?"

That was the question, wasn't it? I had spent so much time defining myself by the bakery, by the work and the struggle of building something from nothing that I hadn't allowed myself to think of what I wanted beyond that. I had wanted to expand the bakery, sure, but that was going to take eight years or longer, according to my projections.

I couldn't deny that my life had drastically changed. Over the last few days, especially after everything that had happened with Chloe's confession about the fire, I had been forced to think about just how much. Re-opening the bakery, building the clientele, and becoming successful enough to expand, all of that felt daunting in a way that didn't make me happy. Not anymore.

"I want to be here," I said finally, my voice soft but

Accidental Fiancé

certain. "I want to be home, with you and Piper, and if we have any other kids someday, I want to be home with them, too. I want to be a housewife, a stay-at-home mom." My thoughts ran away with my mouth. "I'm rambling, please stop me, or tell me I'm crazy, or... anything. Just please make me stop talking"

Julian's expression melted as he looked at me, his eyes wide and warm. "Kids? You're thinking about kids?" he asked, wonderment in his voice.

My heart did a funny little flip at the way he said it, like the idea was new to him but also something he'd been wanting to hear. I smiled as I traced my fingers along the curve of his jaw. "Yeah, I am. I think I want that."

For a second, he just stared at me, his eyes locked on mine as if he were trying to memorize my face. Then he grinned that boyish, charming smile that always gave me goosebumps. "Does this mean you want kids with me?"

I rolled my eyes, laughing at the surprise in his voice. "Of course, I do, you idiot. Who else would I want them with?"

He pulled me closer, his arms wrapping around me as he kissed me slow and deep, as if the idea of starting a family had made him fall for me even more. "I love you," he murmured against my lips, his breath hot and sweet.

"I love you too," I whispered back, feeling the warmth of his words settle into my chest. Each time I said it, I wanted to say it again. Wanted to scream it from the rooftops. I loved Julian Black in a way that was overwhelming. There was nothing I wouldn't do for this man. He gave me peace and relaxation, and I wasn't sure if I ever really had that before him.

Growing up in a struggling household, relaxing wasn't something we did. Relaxation was as much a luxury as any brand-name purse, so it didn't come easy. Life was hard work, and achieving success was even harder. If I wanted something, I had to push for it.

But now, I had Julian, someone who made me feel like I could breathe fully for the first time in my life. Even if he lost all of his money tomorrow, I knew we'd get through it because we had each other.

The truth was, I hadn't been sure about kids for a long time. Not until I reunited with Julian. I had been so focused on my career, on making something of myself, that the idea of slowing down and settling into a family life hadn't seemed possible. Another luxury for rich people, not for people like me.

Lying there in his arms, it felt like the only thing that made sense.

"But," I added, pulling back slightly to look him in the eye. "I'm not saying I'm done with baking. I just don't want to run a bakery again, not right now anyway."

Julian tilted his head, curious. "So, what's the plan then?"

"I've been thinking about writing a cookbook," I replied, the words coming out slowly. I was still getting used to the idea, but the idea compelled me to say it out loud. "Something that combines the recipes I've learned over the years, maybe with a focus on simple, accessible baking. Something for people who want to bake at home but don't have a ton of time or money. Then maybe I'll write another about baking up single servings, or baking for two. Not everyone wants to bake enough for a large family—I'm still mastering that skill myself, to be honest. It'll be a lot of work, and you and Piper will have to eat a lot of mistakes, I hope that's okay."

His eyes lit up as he listened, and I could see him processing the idea, his mind already working on how to support me. I had never seen that look in a partner's eyes before and it was refreshing. "That's brilliant," he said, his voice full of excitement. "You'd be amazing at that."

I smiled, feeling a surge of relief at his understanding. "It's something I can do from home," I added. "So, I can be here for you, for Pip, for any other little ones we might have running around someday."

Julian laughed, the sound deep and rich as it rumbled through his chest. "So, we're really doing this, huh? Kids, cookbooks, the whole deal?"

I nodded. "Yeah, I think we are."

He grinned, pulling me closer until our faces were just inches apart. "I can't wait."

Before I could respond, he kissed me again, this time with slow, deliberate intensity that sent a shiver down my spine. I moaned, my hands sliding up his chest as I kissed him back, letting everything else fall away. All I could think about was him, his lips, his hands, the way he made me feel like I was the only thing that mattered. Everywhere he touched me, I came alive.

Especially in my heart.

His hand slid down my back, his fingers brushing over my skin. I loved the way he touched me. Part ownership, part worship. I pulled him closer, my body arching into his, craving the closeness, the intimacy. Every touch, every kiss was electric, like we were rediscovering each other all over again.

"I thought we were supposed to be talking about cookbooks and kids," I teased, pulling back just enough to look into his eyes.

He smirked, his hands still exploring the curve of my waist. "We are," he murmured, his lips brushing against my neck. "But I can't help myself when you're this close."

I laughed, the sound turning into a soft moan as his lips found that sensitive spot just below my ear. I shivered against him. "You're impossible."

"I know," he whispered, his voice low and full of desire. "But you love me anyway."

He was right. I did love him. I loved him so much that it overwhelmed me, like it was too big to fit inside my chest. How could anything be this good?

But when he reached between my legs, I stopped overthinking it. He knew my body as if we had been together for years, not just under two months. The craziest two months of my life, to be sure, but still. I didn't understand how he knew exactly how to play my body but it didn't matter.

I loved the way he made me feel like I could do anything, the way he looked at me like I was the only woman in the world. I loved the way he loved Pip and the way that he cared for his family. The way he was always there, steady and strong no matter what. Even when I was at my worst, he stood by me. I couldn't ask for more than that.

I kissed him again, harder this time, losing myself in the moment and the heat that was building between us. His hands were everywhere, my pussy, my hips, my thighs, pulling me closer, making me feel like I was going to come apart at the seams.

I breathed his name. My voice was barely audible as he rolled us over, his body pressing into mine. He rocked into me, an inch at a time, until we were joined in that perfect way. His lips brushed against my jaw. "I'm never letting you go."

"You better not," I murmured. Electricity flowed through my core, branching out and lighting me up from the inside.

We got tangled up in each other again, and before I knew it, he had me on his face, working his tongue against me, his arms banded around me. I bent forward to take him in my mouth. I loved the taste of him and the way he groaned as he thrust up into me. I purred on his length as his tongue worked my clit. An unbroken circle of pleasure.

My climax soared, and I came on his face until I shuddered and nearly collapsed. He slipped away, mounting me from behind before he slowed things down and rolled us onto our sides.

Julian clasped my hip with one hand to pull me backward on his cock as he thrust forward, all the while planting lazy kisses on my neck. "I love you so much, baby."

I was too far gone to speak, too wrapped up in the pleasure he gave me. After a deep breath, I managed to murmur, "I love—oh, fuck!"

"That's it, let me feel you come on me."

I erupted on him. Sparks burst in my mind while my body followed suit. My head pressed back against his shoulder, but he held firm and grounded me to my body until I returned to it.

Julian gently bit my shoulder and declared, "My turn." Then he went at me with a ferocity that made me want more. He gripped my hip and thrust inside of me, shocking my body into another orgasm that matched his own.

It was all so damn good. Every ounce of it. The sex, the love, the family, the messy, beautiful chaos of it all. I couldn't wait to see what came next.

Chapter 38

Julian

There was something about the way Maggie laughed that made everything feel lighter, like my responsibilities weren't as heavy, the day not as long, and the world a little more manageable. I heard that laugh ringing through the open meadow as Piper chased after a butterfly, her little arms waving wildly in the air.

"Careful, Pip," Maggie called out, shielding her eyes from the sun as my daughter zigzagged through the tall grass and wildflowers. California winters weren't much of a burden just north of Malibu, and we were determined to enjoy it. Happiness had etched a permanent shape on her face over the past few weeks. Warmth and contentment had settled there since the chaos and excitement had died down. Her smile lines had intensified as though permanent now.

I hoped so.

We were free today, so she planned a picnic. The three of us were in the middle of nowhere—a field tucked away from the rest of the world with nothing but wildflowers, the scent of freshly baked cupcakes, and the occasional chirp of a bird to remind us that life existed beyond this moment.

I had never been this content. Not in years. Not since before my first marriage fell apart. After that, I was convinced romantic love was something I would ever have.

But here I was, sitting on a blanket next to the woman who had changed my life. I was the luckiest man alive, and I vowed to never forget that or take it for granted. I would show Maggie how much I loved and appreciated her every day for the rest of our lives.

My daughter, laughing and singing in the distance, caught our attention with a silly dance. When she stepped to the side, I realized she was mimicking a butterfly caught in the breeze. Piper's tiny giggles blended with the sweet hum of the meadow.

"Look at her," Maggie said. Her voice was soft as she leaned into me, resting her head against my shoulder. "She's so free."

"She is," I agreed, watching Piper twirl in circles, her dress billowing around her like a miniature flower blooming. She was happiness personified, all innocent energy and pure joy. I noticed she was like this more often ever since Maggie joined our little family. Happy, cheery. She was even sleeping better. Far fewer night terrors, down to one a week.

Piper's doctor asked if anything had changed at home, and we explained our situation. After emphasizing that it wasn't my fault, she added that sometimes kids can sense trouble with their parents, and that can cause night terrors. She reemphasized it wasn't my fault and I assured her I understood, but part of me felt guilty anyway. The toils of fatherhood, I supposed.

"Dancing, carefree..." I felt Maggie smile against my arm. "She's like you."

I raised an eyebrow, amused. "Like me? I don't know about that."

"No, really. She's playful, always full of wonder. You give her that, Julian."

I had always hoped that she would have those qualities. Whimsy. A wild imagination. I was always reading silly books and watching mindless movies with her. I had wanted to instill that sense of joy in her. I wasn't sure if I had done my job, but it was nice to hear that from Maggie. Still, it was hard to take all of the credit. Piper was definitely her own person.

I chuckled, shaking my head. "I think you give me too much recognition. She's her own little whirlwind."

Maggie gave me a knowing smile, one that told me that she saw far more than I ever gave myself credit for. She always did. She had a way of seeing the best in me, in Piper. In everything. It was one of the many reasons I loved her.

I reached out and took her hand, brushing my thumb across her knuckles. "It's you, you know. You make us better, Maggie."

She laughed shyly, but there was something in the way that she did it, like she wasn't used to compliments yet, even though I gave them freely. One day she'd get used to them. I would make sure of that.

She teased, "You're just saying that because I brought cupcakes."

"Well, that certainly helps." I watched as she unwrapped one and handed it to me. The icing was a swirl of pastel colors, soft pinks and purples that reminded me of the wildflowers blooming around us.

"My trainer already loves you. You don't have to keep feeding me."

She rolled her eyes and passed me the treat. "Just eat it."

"You're spoiling me, you know."

"It's only fair," she replied, handing another cupcake to Piper, who had come running by. Her cheeks were flushed, and her hair was wild from the butterfly chase. Maggie continued, "You've done plenty of spoiling yourself, sir."

Piper plopped down on the blanket beside us, her face lighting up as she took a bite of her cupcake, crumbs falling onto her lap. She said the same thing that she said every time Maggie made something for her. "These are the best. Better than last time."

Maggie smiled, brushing a stray curl behind Pip's ear. "I'm glad you like them, sweetheart."

As I watched the two of them interact, something inside of me swelled, something warm and solid and so full of love that it almost scared me.

Maggie had come into our lives like a quiet storm, turning everything upside down in the best possible way. She wasn't just someone I loved; she was someone who had become a part of us, a part of our family. The missing piece to the puzzle.

I couldn't imagine life without her, without everything she brought into our lives, the way she loved Pip like she was her own. Maggie was more than I ever expected or deserved. As I looked at her, sitting there with Piper, her face lit up by the afternoon sun, I knew without a doubt I wanted to be with her for the rest of my life.

I had proposed on the surest whim I had ever felt, and every day, she proved me right.

"Maggie. I said quietly, my voice barely a whisper.

She gave me a questioning look. "Hmm?"

"I love you."

She blinked, surprised at the suddenness of my words,

and then smiled, her cheeks flushing just slightly. "I love you too, Julian."

They were simple, those three little words, but they felt bigger than the sky above us. And yet, saying them was so easy. Because loving Maggie was easy. Being with her was easy.

I knew we'd have more trials and tribulations ahead; we had an actual trial coming up. Chloe Foster had been arrested, and since she gave the arresting officer hell, Apollo added assaulting a police officer and blackmail charges, which made it impossible for her to post bail with the money she'd blackmailed out of me. As much as I didn't want to deal with the pandemonium of a trial, it would be good to have Chloe Foster's evil shadow out of sight for a while when all was said and done.

Life was never going to be perfect. I wasn't naïve enough to think that. Marriage, no matter how privileged you were, was still work. But there was nothing I couldn't face with Maggie at my side. We could do anything as long as we were together.

"Can we do this every day?" Piper asked, knocking me out of my reverie, her face smeared with icing as she reached for another cupcake. "The picnic, I mean. And the cupcakes. Lots of cupcakes."

I laughed, reaching out to wipe a smudge of frosting from her nose. "Maybe not every day, Pip. We'll run out of cupcakes."

"No, we won't," she insisted. Her eyes were wide with determination. Maggie makes the best cupcakes, and we'll never run out."

Maggie chuckled beside me. "I do need to practice for my cookbook."

I glanced at her, my heart swelling again at the way she

Accidental Fiancé

sweetly looked at Pip. The way she stepped up into a mother figure role without hesitation or question. It surprised me every day. I wrapped my arm around Maggie's shoulders. "I think we can manage a few more picnics. But next time, the cupcakes will be for the two of you only, or Dixon will make me do burpees until I puke, again."

Piper, satisfied with my answer, turned her attention back to her cupcake, happily munching away, oblivious to the universe shifting around us.

The three of us sat there, enjoying the cool breeze as it swept in over the Pacific. The late afternoon sun cast a warm glow over the meadow, natural beauty taking over my senses. It was one of those rare moments where time seemed to stand still, and nothing mattered except the people you were with and the love you felt for them.

"I can't believe how happy I am," Maggie murmured after a while. Her voice was quiet as she leaned against me, her head resting on my chest. "It feels like a dream."

"It's real," I promised, pressing a kiss to the top of her head. "And it's only going to get better."

She tilted her head up to look at me, her eyes searching mine for a moment before she took a breath and let it out slowly. Her lips curved into that beautiful, easy smile that always made my heart skip a beat. "You really think so?"

"I know so," I said, feeling the weight of the words settle into my chest. It felt like a foundational truth, something undeniable. "We're just getting started, Maggie. There's so much more ahead for us."

Her eyes went bright with happiness, and she leaned up to kiss me, an unspoken promise behind it. I kissed her back, savoring the moment, the lingering frosting on her lips, the way her lips fit so perfectly against mine.

"Eww, gross," Piper exclaimed, covering her eyes with her hands as she giggled. "No kissing! Boys have cooties!"

Maggie pulled away, laughing as she looked over at Pip. "Sorry, sweetheart, no more kissing."

"Thank you," my daughter said deliberately in two hard syllables as though she had pronounced a new decree. She giggled as she grabbed another cupcake and took a big bite, clearly more interested in the dessert than our little display of affection.

I couldn't help but laugh, too, shaking my head as I looked at Maggie. "Guess we'll have to save that for later."

She winked at me, her smile mischievous. "I'll hold you to that."

We stayed in the meadow for a while longer, watching as Piper chased butterflies, listening to the soft rustle of the wind through the grass. The day was perfect, a snapshot of happiness that I knew I'd hold onto for the rest of my life.

As I sat there with Maggie by my side and Piper's laughter filling the air, I realized that this quiet, simple, beautiful life was all I had ever wanted.

And it was only the beginning.

Unintentionally Yours Series

Get ready to fire up your kindle with these cinnamon-roll billionaires! When spicy, sugarcoated accidental engagements, marriages, and babies bring opposites together.

Each book follows the story of their own couple and are standalones with a very satisfying HEA.

Read the Unintentionally Yours series on Amazon:

Unintentionally Yours series page

Accidentally Engaged: A Fertility Doctor Next Door Romance (Hudson and Sophie)

Accidental Vegas Vows: A Silver Fox Boss Romance (Damien and Olivia)

Accidental Twins: A Silver Fox Dad's Best Friend Romance (Adrian and Ava)

Accidental Baby Daddy: A Single Dad Runaway Bride Romance (Oliver and Lexie)

Accidental Fiancé: A Single Dad Fake Engagement Romance (Julian and Maggie)

Happy reading!

xx

Mia

Boulder Billionaires Series

Fire up your kindle with these four bossy billionaires from Colorado! These swoon-boats will impress, grovel and pleasure their way to a delicious HEA with their sassy woman. And they won't take no for an answer - not in the office and certainly not in the bedroom.

Each book follows the story of their own couple and are standalones with a very satisfying HEA. You'll also enjoy cameo appearances from your favorite characters throughout the series.

Read the Boulder Billionaires series on Amazon:

Boulder Billionaire series page

Big & Bossy: A Fake Engagement Second Chance Romance
(Jackson and Mandy)

Brute & Bossy: A Fake Relationship Opposites Attract Romance
(Wade and Raylene)

Beast & Bossy: A Fake Relationship Enemies to Lovers Romance
(Hunter and Lottie)

Bad & Bossy: A One Night Stand Secret Baby Romance
(Cole and Dana)

Happy reading!

xx

Mia

Printed in Dunstable, United Kingdom